Nothing But Trouble

Allegra Gray

Interior design by THE KILLION GROUP
www.thekilliongroupinc.com

ISBN: 0692332502

ISBN-13: 9780692332504

DEDICATION

For my husband, Bryan, whom I met, fell madly in love with, and married during the writing of this book.

Chapter 1:

In which desperate times call for desperate measures...

March 1816, London

The initial flood of suitors had all but dried up. Only a trickle of men interested in marrying Charity Medford remained, and *they* had to face her brother in law, the Duke of Beaufort. So far, he'd deemed each and every one of them eminently unsuitable. Not the most auspicious way to begin one's second Season.

"Fortune hunters, curiosity seekers, and philandering old men," he'd remarked with disgust after the departure of the last one.

Since the duke had paid for both Charity's dowry and the home where she lived with her widowed mother, his opinion was rarely challenged.

Not that Charity had any desire to challenge him. She simply lowered her eyes and responded, "I shall endeavor to do better, Your Grace." In truth, she agreed with the duke. He'd done her a favor in rejecting these suitors. None of the men who'd come calling interested her. No man did.

She trudged up to her room, reflecting. That wasn't entirely true…men did interest her. Some of them interested her quite a lot. *Marriage,* however, was what she objected to.

Last summer, she'd made her bow to Society and basked in the praise that came with being born a natural beauty. "Charming," they said. "Lovely." "A diamond of the first water." She could have married then, and married well. Instead, she'd had the audacity to poke her nose where it didn't belong—into an intrigue between the Ministry of Defense and a group of French conspirators. Undeniably, the worst decision of her life. She'd gotten herself kidnapped, and even though she'd been rescued, nothing—nothing at all—had been the same since.

She'd tried so very, very hard to rid herself of the nightmares that plagued her. Nightmares that sent her back to the dark abyss where she might have died. Had it not been for the bravery and determination of her brother in law and his friend, who'd traced the French spies to their hideout, she would never have been found.

Charity knew she'd been fortunate to escape with her life— and even more fortunate to escape with her reputation, since her role in the whole fiasco had been kept quiet. Still, when the nightmares came, reason left her. They were no ordinary dreams. She'd walked, talked, shrieked, and stuck out at those who tried to calm her. At least, that's what she'd been told afterward, when she awoke—if waking was even the right word for it.

That was why she couldn't marry. A husband would expect her to sleep in his bed. What would he do when she woke shrieking, or sleepwalking? When she was so entrapped by fears she could hardly hear or recognize him?

Her husband would think her crazed. At best he would leave her. At worst, he'd consign her to Bedlam. She'd heard stories of the inmates there. She would happily live a life of spinsterhood rather than risk that fate.

Of course, that wasn't the sort of thing she could tell her family, who so desperately wanted her to be normal again. To be happy.

So Charity kept her fears to herself, as always, and went on searching for the peace that eluded her.

Crash.

Charity jolted awake.

The noise had come from below, somewhere on the ground floor of her mother's London town house. She gripped her sheets, held her breath.

Clomp. Clomp. Footfalls—boots on the wooden floor downstairs. Then, the mutter of male voices.

Immediately, she slipped from her bed and to the window. That was a real crash she'd heard. Not a dream. She pinched herself to be sure. Yes, real.

This time, she would not be captured so easily.

Where were her protectors? Asleep, no doubt. Grown lax, as months had passed and no threat materialized. Not Charity. She had the nightmares to remind her to stay vigilant.

She flung open the lid of the trunk beneath the window, shot her hand to the bottom, and pulled out the knotted rope she'd stashed there.

She paused, forcing herself to breathe slowly as she listened. They weren't ascending the staircase…yet. But if they were after her, it was only a matter of moments. She wasn't taking chances.

A quick loop of rope around the bedpost—just so. She opened the window and dropped the other end out. It uncoiled, the knot at the bottom hitting the exterior wall with a soft clunk. She lifted the hem of her nightdress and swung a leg over the sill.

Hurry. Blood pounding in her ears, she swung the other leg over and shimmied backward. Someone tapped at the door. She scrambled to get the rope between her feet and ducked her head beneath the sill.

"Miss Medford?"

Charity froze, fingers still gripping the windowsill. Penny's voice. Her maid.

"Miss Medford? Is anything amiss? I thought I heard…oh, my."

Charity heard the sound of slippered feet pattering across the room. She looked up as Penny thrust her head out the window.

The maid's eyes grew wide. "Are you sneaking out?" she whispered. "Shall I pretend I never saw you? I'm ever so sorry."

Barely two years older than her mistress, Penny often served as accomplice in Charity's schemes.

Charity shook her head, wincing as her aching fingers started to slip. She clenched the sill harder. "Intruders," she whispered. "Hide yourself!"

"The doors are all locked, miss." The maid tried to reassure her, distress clear in her moonlit expression. "Perhaps you were dreaming again."

"I heard a crash," Charity insisted. Her feet had found purchase on the knotted rope, but she couldn't hang here forever.

"The footmen are downstairs, moving some furniture your

lady mother wanted changed out for the spring season. Likely one of them dropped something. Here, let me help you in."

The explanation made sense. But what if Penny was wrong? Charity might have already lost too much time. "Please, go make certain. Get Matthews—he stands guard tonight."

Charity allowed Penny to help her up until she was half-in, half-out of the window. She flexed her nearly-numb fingers. The ridge of the sill bit into her ribcage, but she wasn't coming any further without proof.

The maid curtsied and hurried out. If she thought her employer's mistrust a trifle excessive, she was intelligent enough not to say so.

Perched on the sill, Charity let her head drop. How much extra, she wondered, did her family pay her maid not to mention their youngest daughter's peculiar antics to anyone outside the house?

More footsteps. Charity sucked in a breath. This time coming up the stairs. Two sets, one lighter than the other. Good. Penny and Matthews.

Sure enough, the maid tapped and burst back in, the solemn Matthews a step behind her. "Not to worry, Miss Medford," Penny said. "Two of the footmen, Mr. Simmons and Mr. Percy, were moving a trunk and Percy backed into a table and sent a pair of candlesticks crashing down. No damage was done, and they are terrible sorry to have disturbed you." She clasped her hands anxiously.

"I assure you, Miss Medford, the premises are secure," Matthews avowed. "I shall inspect the doors, windows, and grounds again, that you may rest peacefully while my eyes and ears remain alert."

Charity eyed him closely. He did appear quite alert. Perhaps he'd not grown lax after all. She eased off the windowsill, letting out a whoosh of breath as her feet hit the floor. Panic gone, she simply felt deflated. Exhausted. Perhaps the exhaustion was a blessing in disguise—if she hadn't been so tired, she might be embarrassed to have panicked, yet again, over such a trivial thing. "Thank you, Penny, Matthews."

"Of course, miss." Penny helped Charity back into bed as the guard bowed and stepped out. "Shall I bring you some tea? Warm milk?"

"No, I shall be well now." She wished it were true. But when the maid was gone, she lay awake, staring at the ceiling.

How many more false alarms would she endure before the moment of truth? The servants might whisper, and Charity's family might look upon her with pity, but none of them could shake what she knew in her heart.

It might take years, but her enemies *would* come for her. The duke still checked daily with the Ministry of Defence— Charity knew that for a fact, because she was the one who'd insisted upon it—but of the five French spies found on English soil last summer, only three had been caught. They no longer lived. The other two had escaped alive. And because they'd once kidnapped her, Charity Medford was the only person in England who could identify both by sight.

March 1816, Grantown on Spey, Scotland

Graeme Ramsey Maxwell scanned the gray, brooding horizon and hoped it wasn't an omen predicting his future.

"Are ye sure ye wish to set out today?" Tom Brevis, driver to the earls of Leventhal since before Graeme had been born, cast a critical eye in the same direction. "Awful early in the year, my lord."

"Not in London," Graeme countered. "The Season has already begun there. I prefer not to miss much more of it, since I've no idea how long it will take to acquire a wife."

Tom pursed his lips. "Somewhat longer than to acquire a horse, I believe." He nodded thoughtfully. "Though a fine lord such as yerself shouldna have a problem, eh?" His wrinkled face broke into a conspiratorial grin.

Graeme chuckled and gave his team of horses one final check, lifting hooves and running a soothing hand over each mane. Undoubtedly Tom and the head groom had both done the same. Everything appeared in impeccable order for his trip to England.

Except that his nephew and ward was nowhere to be found.

"Good work, Tom. Have you seen Nathan?"

"Nay. It'll break the wee lad's heart if ye leave w'out sayin' goodbye, my lord."

"Wouldn't think of it." Graeme had already promised the lad as much. He strode back toward the manor, grimacing at the delay. Tom was right about one thing: this early in spring, the roads could be treacherous. He'd planned to use every minute of available daylight to navigate them.

A search of the nursery revealed only an empty room. Same for the breakfast nook, and the kitchens.

He'd just stepped onto the expansive back lawn when a frantic woman ran up. He recognized her as the gardener's daughter and assistant. "Lord Maxwell, come quickly. Your wee nephew 'as got himself stuck out by the quarry."

"Stuck?" Immediately he set off in the direction of the quarry, slowing his pace only enough for the woman to keep up. "Is he in danger?"

"Only if he tries to move. Got himself on a ledge, and the

pebbles slide whenever the lad tries to ease off."

"Who was watching him?"

"I couldna say, my lord. I was only passing by when I heard his cry."

Bloody hell. "Where is his governess?"

"Beggin' your pardon, my lord, but ye havena hired a new one yet."

"What?" Graeme missed a step, allowing the woman running beside him to catch up.

"Ach. I thought ye knew, Lord Maxwell. Miss Parr run off yesterday. Maisie caught her foolin' with one o' the footmen, and knowin' Maisie, the whole staff would know in minutes. We figured ye'd fired her, but mayhap she run off before ye could get the chance, my lord."

Graeme choked back a growl. He'd been so preoccupied with planning this trip, he'd brushed off the housekeeper when she'd approached him earlier. Likely she'd been attempting to impart this news.

But whether Miss Parr had run off or been fired, she was gone now. Qualified governesses weren't easy to come by in the highlands. He'd dismissed the one prior to Miss Parr after discovering her inordinate fondness for his liquor cabinet.

Just one more confirmation his journey to London was necessary—though technically, it was a wife he sought there, rather than a governess. Someone who could manage a staff and had a talent for producing competent governesses where none existed.

"Very well," he told the young woman. "Go on back to the greenhouse. I'll fetch Nathan. Actually, I'd be obliged if you'd stop at the main house first, and tell Mrs. Saxonberry I've asked her to select someone responsible from her staff to stand in and look after the lad until I return from my trip." No sense delaying his journey just to engage in what would surely be a fruitless search for a qualified, educated, *local* replacement.

"Aye, my lord." She bobbed a curtsy as she turned back.

Graeme lengthened his stride, heading toward the old quarry at full speed. He was ill-prepared for the role of parent, and being thrust into the position with a fully-formed, active six year old—make that a fully-formed, active, *grieving* six year old—hadn't helped matters.

"Nate!" he called, approaching the quarry that had once supplied much of the stone for building Leventhal House. He'd played there as a child too. The place was a natural draw for any adventurous boy.

"Uncle Graeme?" came a quavering response. "I canna get down."

Graeme slowed, spotting his nephew backed against a wall of rock, standing on a ledge about two feet wide and twenty feet up. He blew out a breath, his heart easing its frenetic pace as he realized the lad, while scared, was not in imminent danger.

"All right, now. You're going to be fine. Ease back down the way you climbed up. Go ahead, now."

Nate shook his head, a tear streaking down his dusty cheek. "The rocks are too slippery. I'll fall."

"You must, Nate. You were brave enough to climb up. Show me that same bravery now. Slowly, slowly. One foot at a time…test your footing before you put all your weight into each step."

It was a lot to ask of a six year old. Graeme knew, because he hadn't been much older when his own father had had to give him similar advice.

"You can do it, Nate," he said. "I'm here to catch you if you fall."

Nate took a shuddery breath, then nodded and inched toward the slippery path down. Graeme hovered below, tracking the boy's movement. One step, two. Two more.

Nate's foot slid, sending a shower of pebbles off the ledge. He froze.

"Steady now." Graeme kept his voice calm.

Nate moved forward again, making several feet of progress this time. He glanced over at Graeme with a smile, but the sudden movement was careless. His feet slid out from under him and he shrieked as he landed on his bottom, unable to slow his descent.

Graeme leapt forward, arms out, and the boy tumbled the last few feet into them, followed by an avalanche of gravel. He hugged the child close, then set him on his feet, checking for cuts and injuries.

"Are ye hurt, Nate?"

Nate brushed himself off, winced and held out scraped palms.

"That's not so bad. Just a wee scrape. Count yourself lucky."

The boy wiped his cheek with the back of his hand, smearing dust and tears.

"What were ye doing up there?" Now that he knew the lad was all right, he was not about to let him escape without a scolding. "I've told ye before, the quarry is dangerous. Ye're no' to come here alone."

Hearing his brogue thicken with the moment's emotion, he made a mental note to keep it in check when he reached London. Tucked away in the north, it was easy to let such things slide. But Londoners would expect an earl's speech to reflect his education, rather than the location of his primary holding.

Nate hung his head. "I didn't mean to get stuck."

"Of course you didn't. No one means for an accident to happen—but that's why you must be more careful, Nate."

"I just wanted to hide."

Graeme frowned. "Hide from what?"

Nate looked away.

Graeme knelt down. "What's wrong?"

"You said you wouldn't leave without saying goodbye. I thought, if ye couldna find me…"

Finally Graeme understood. "Ah, Nate." He pulled the lad in close.

"Don't go, Uncle Graeme," his nephew said against his shirt.

Graeme pulled back, gazed down at his puppy-eyed, pleading little nephew and truly did have second thoughts. But he'd made his decision—and a Maxwell never went back on a decision. If there was one thing he'd learned in the years since his father's death, it was that an estate the size of the Maxwell holdings did not run itself. There was always someone who needed his attention, or something that needed to be done. A proud job, but a demanding one. And often a lonely one. He longed for the softness of a woman in his bed, someone to converse with at the end of the day, someone to share the delight of simple pleasures and to hold in times of sorrow. If he waited until all the other demands of life settled down, though, he might very well die a bachelor.

"Come on." Rising, he took the lad's hand and started walking, still trying to decide how to respond.

"Nate," he said, "I know you don't see it now, but this trip will benefit us both. I can provide more for you by going than by staying here. When I come back, I'll be bringing a wife. She'll love you, Nate, I know she will."

"Maybe." Nate trudged toward Leventhal House, its looming mass emphasizing just how small his nephew was.

Graeme sighed. "Of course she will." Never mind that he hadn't yet met this woman, or even identified a likely candidate. "We'll build a family. Turn this old pile of rubble into a home again. And someday you'll have playmates."

Nate cocked his head, considering. "I'll be too old for them."

"Nay. You'll be the one to teach them the very best games."

"Oh." The boy tried to hide his smile, but Graeme could tell he liked the idea.

"Be good while I'm gone, promise? You'll be the man of the house. I'm counting on you to look after Nana."

"Nana thinks I'm you," Nate protested.

Graeme tweaked his nose. "All the more reason to look after her." His mother spent so much time living in the past she didn't always distinguish between son and grandson, but that didn't diminish her fondness for both.

"I mean it, Nate," Graeme admonished, bringing the boy's focus back. "No more adventures at the quarry?"

"What if ye don't come back, Uncle Graeme?" Nathan asked, avoiding Graeme's question with one of his own—one obviously bothering him. "What if something bad happens?"

Graeme blinked. The lad had seen too much for his six years. He'd already lost both parents. It was pointless to assure him such things couldn't, or wouldn't, happen. But at the moment, the distressed look in the boy's eyes, the way his little brows knit together, told Graeme he needed comfort more than logic.

He sighed, then bent down and swung his nephew up onto his shoulders for the rest of the distance to the house.

"I'll come back, lad. I promise."

London, 2 weeks later

Lady Priscilla Medford, Miss Charity Medford's mother, had expressly forbidden her youngest daughter to attend the annual masquerade held by Lord Madrigal—the rakish young lord otherwise known as "the Wicked Baron."

Charity, of course, was going anyway.

Where else but a masquerade could she pretend, if only for a night, that she was someone—anyone—else? Someone who didn't attract stares and whispered speculation everywhere she went. Some of the gossip was innocent enough—the usual wonderings about the exact size of her dowry, for example. But others...others suspected, at least, her connection to the capture of the French spies last year. Though her family had done its best to keep her name out of the papers, one intrepid reporter from the *Tattler* had noted her presence on several visits to the British Foreign Office. No further details had leaked, but even that tidbit was enough to spark the curiosity of the *ton*, whose members' appetite for scandal knew no bounds.

Yes, Charity longed for escape. The only impact of her mother's decree regarding the masquerade was to make her choose her disguise, and her exit plan, more carefully.

It wasn't that Charity didn't love her mother—it was just that she didn't see a reason to *heed* her. Family was family. But everyone in London knew her dowry had been provided by the Duke of Beaufort, her older sister Elizabeth's husband, since her own father had died with naught to his name but a mountain of debt. Even her mother's home had been paid for by the duke, allowing the family to maintain a modicum of dignity. If Lady Medford couldn't even manage her own life, why should she manage her daughter's?

"Penny, come help me dress," Charity called to her maid. "I cannot manage my evening costume alone."

"Of course, Miss Medford." Penny bustled toward her. "Where are you off to this eve, miss?"

"Almack's."

"Oh!" the maid began brightly, then stopped in her tracks as she saw the folds of cloth Charity held out.

Clearly, Penny knew what any qualified ladies' maid should know: unmarried females did not attend Almack's dressed as sultry Indian princesses.

Charity gave Penny her most brilliant smile, dumped the beaded silk into the maid's hands, and slipped out of her shift. Her costume had been ordered weeks ago, and even then she'd had to part with an outrageous portion of her allowance to convince the *modiste* to complete it in time. The daring designs of Madame Bleu were sought after by proper ladies and the *demimondaine* alike. It was debatable whether the jade and turquoise confection made to accentuate every nuance of the female body—Charity's body, to be precise—had come from the design pages meant for the proper clients or the not-so-proper ones. But as long as no one knew who she was, the costume was perfect.

The problem was the mask. A tiny confection of jade-colored silk with holes for her eyes, it would fool no one. That would never do. Anonymity was essential to her plan. Not to mention that life would be infinitely easier if reports of her whereabouts that night did *not* get back to her mother.

Penny gulped, then smiled in return and began expertly draping the folds as though she wrapped her mistress in a sari every day.

Charity smiled in anticipation. The Wicked Baron's parties were legendary. He spared no expense, it was said, to entertain his guests in exotic, tantalizing fashion. The guests themselves sought pleasure above all else. Few unmarried young ladies received invitations to the baron's masquerade—and among those, almost none were expected to attend.

It probably wasn't worth dwelling upon the fact that since she *had* received an invitation, her reputation might not be as pristine as it ought to be. She lifted her arms as Penny pinned the tiny bodice she wore beneath the costume, leaving tempting glimpses of exposed skin above the curve of her hip.

Then again, she no longer counted herself among the innocents. She might not be married, but she'd left her childhood behind the previous June as surely as though a door had slammed on her girlish dreams.

Standing before her looking glass, Charity dipped a finger into a tiny pot and patted the cream beneath her eyes while Penny worked. She frowned. The circles were getting darker. It had been so very long since she'd had a restful night's sleep.

The doctor had told her the best thing was to forget. Well, she'd *tried* to forget…God help her, she'd tried. She just couldn't. During waking hours she could keep busy enough to keep her mind off the horrible memories, but every time she closed her eyes, it all came rushing back.

When what her family referred vaguely to as "the incident" had first happened, the doctor had given her several doses of sleeping draughts. For months, he'd prescribed more—until Charity, fearing he would deem her incurable, had lied about her recovery and told him to stop coming. Those sweet little vials of mercy were long since gone, and she'd had nary a restful night since. She'd been too ashamed to ask for more.

What was wrong with her, her well-meaning family would ask. She was alive, she was whole. Disaster averted. She should be happy.

Except they hadn't seen—or felt, rather, since her underground prison had been utterly dark—what she had. Even Alex and Philippe, who'd rescued her, had not lingered in that awful space long enough to examine the contents of its deepest corners. Nor had they heard the whispered French as her captor slipped her a single, tiny vial before locking her away. She'd flung it away in disgust, but how many more hours would she have lasted before crawling on hands and knees through the utter dark, searching it out with fingertips already bloodied from clawing at the door?

She shuddered, the movement causing Penny's carefully-aimed pin to poke her in the ribs. "Ouch!"

"Ooh. Sorry, miss."

"My fault," Charity told her. Was she such a terrible person, then, to seek this single night's release from the invisible prison that had held her for so long?

Penny adjusted the draping at Charity's shoulder once more, then nodded in satisfaction. "Lovely, miss. The gentlemen at Almack's won't be able to take their eyes off you."

Right. Almack's. Charity dragged her mind back to the present. "Mary Summers is acting as chaperone to her younger sister tonight. She hopes Bess's impeccable deportment will convince the patronesses to grant her permission to dance the waltz." She turned to meet Penny's eye, satisfied by the maid's quick nod that—though they both knew Charity wouldn't be anywhere near Mary or her younger sister that night—Penny knew how to respond if questioned about her mistress's whereabouts.

That took care of one part of the evening's escapade. As to being recognized...she eyed a discarded blue scarf dangling precariously over the edge of her dressing table as an idea began to take shape.

"Penny, one more thing?" She explained what she had in mind, pulling the blue scarf from the table and grabbing a similarly-hued one from the drawer underneath. "If you help me pull this off, the scarves are yours at the end of the night," Charity promised.

The maid's eyes widened and she ran a caressing finger across the silk. Such finery would either make her the envy of all the other maids or fetch a pretty penny at a resale shop. Any uneasiness the poor girl had felt at being party to such illicit behavior had, Charity suspected, just vanished.

Penny pinned the last veil into place, and Charity breathed a sigh of relief. Between the jade-colored mask and the scarves, nearly her whole face was covered.

Now, she just had to give the slip to the men who constantly shadowed her, protected her. One would certainly be waiting downstairs, or in front of the townhouse, ready to follow wherever she went. Guilt pricked her, but she shook it off. Tonight she would be surrounded by throngs of merrymakers, not stupidly sneaking around alone. She'd learned *that* lesson. Disguised as she was, she was safe enough. For the next few hours, she could dance and drink champagne to her heart's content.

She slipped out the side entrance, unseen. Lords Edwards and Blythe, two young rakes, and Miss Allison Hart, an heiress with a wild streak, were her chosen companions thus far this Season. They had two advantages over Charity's previous, more staid group of friends—first, they knew how to cavort from one soiree to another until they dropped from sheer exhaustion, and second, they rarely asked questions. For tonight, they'd already promised to have a carriage waiting down the block.

Chapter 2:
The best laid plans...

Charity entered the Wicked Baron's ballroom surrounded by a Roman gladiator, a Grecian goddess, and an aspiring Lancelot. No one announced their arrival. No line of guests waited to greet their host, either, the Wicked Baron not being one to stand on ceremony—or perhaps the baron was simply astute enough to realize a good portion of his guests would not appreciate having their names announced.

She took a deep breath and firmly quashed the little niggle of unease that rose at the unprecedented lack of decorum. It wasn't as though she'd planned to give her real name, anyway. She'd promised herself one night free from worry, and nothing was going to stop her.

A few steps further, and they entered the ballroom, where Charity took in a scene that spoke of far more than a mere lack of decorum...it spoke of decadence, pure and unbridled.

Instead of the pristine flower arrangements and brilliantly-lit chandeliers found at a typical *ton* event, the baron's ballroom was filled with softly-glowing, colored lanterns and swaths of exotic fabric not too unlike Charity's own costume.

The effect was seductive, multiplied tenfold by an informal stage at the end of the room where two scantily-clad young women swayed and jiggled their hips in a manner that had the male occupants gawking and crowding closer.

Charity, too, found it difficult to tear her eyes away. This masquerade undoubtedly qualified as the most risqué event she'd attended. Not that she would allow anyone else see her shock. The swath of veils arranged artfully over her hair and face were proving useful at hiding more than just her identity.

If this was how the *ton* behaved when they thought no one was watching, then all those girlhood lessons in propriety were a sham. Dancing the waltz too soon? Or favoring a particular partner with a second or—gasp—even third dance? Heavens. How about dancing half-naked and plastered to one's partner, as a good number of the women in this ballroom seemed to be doing? Clearly, this masquerade was not for the faint of heart.

Someone handed her a glass of wine. She adjusted her veil and sipped, then frowned. Sniffed. She caught the spicy aroma of cloves, and beneath it, something more.

She glanced again at the exotic, Eastern flavor of the décor, considering. The laudanum that had first aided her sleep, she'd learned, was a product of the Orient. A sister to opium. And opium, she knew, could be added to wine. Given the apparent theme of tonight's event, it seemed unlikely Lord Madrigal had stopped with mere decorations.

She hesitated, then gulped it down. Just this once. If nothing else, the liquor would give her the courage to see this evening through. If her suspicions proved correct and the wine had been spiked, she might even sleep well when it was over, free of the nightmares that so often plagued her. She feared how easily it could become a habit, but she'd endured so many restless nights that the mere thought of a few peaceful, uninterrupted hours brought tears of relief to her eyes. She blinked them back.

Beside her, Miss Hart eyed the dancers, whose raised arms and undulating hips seemed to hold a promise that extended beyond the stage. "Do you suppose," she asked in a fascinated whisper, "they are...ahem...birds of paradise?"

"Do they sell their favors?" Charity mused over the question, swallowing the last of the spiced wine. The dance ended, and one of the performers sidled up to a man in a black domino. She couldn't hear their exchange, but the man's raised eyebrow and brief jerk of his head toward the door that led to the private rooms of the house—followed by the woman's satisfied smile—told her all she needed to know.

"I should say," she answered slowly, "that if they do not exactly *sell* their favors, they are certainly forthcoming with them."

Miss Hart fanned herself vigorously. "I've seen members of the demimondaine before, at the theater and such, but never have I actually mingled with them." She giggled. "I daresay this shall be a most educational evening."

"Most," Charity agreed, though she couldn't claim to share the heiress's goals when it came to that sort of "education." She desired nothing more than an evening free of the scrutiny that normally accompanied her every move, making the past impossible to forget.

The opening strain of a familiar waltz sounded from the small orchestra. Lord Edwards, her companion in the gladiator costume, turned and bowed gallantly, flinging out one arm—causing a waiter bearing a tray of glasses a momentary look of sheer terror. Fortunately, the servant executed a neat sidestep, and his usual polite mask fell back into place.

"A dance, princess?" Lord Edwards asked.

Charity nodded. This, she could handle. The stuffy patronesses of Almack's might consider waltzing too amorous for some, but compared to the dancing she'd just observed, the waltz was as dry as unbuttered toast. She set her glass aside and followed the young lord as other couples paired off and streamed onto the dance floor around them.

As the waltz began in earnest, Lord Edwards yanked her against him. Charity gasped as her breasts brushed his chest. How dare he be so forward!

But a quick glance around confirmed that her partner had acted no more forward than any other in the ballroom. She should have expected as much. If only she were attracted to Lord Edwards, she might not even mind. But she knew the young nobleman well enough to know his attentions were fleeting at best.

She pressed her lips together as his hand drifted lower on her back, drawing her hips against his. Astute enough to recognize the hardness she felt there, Charity quickly revised her opinion about how much waltz she could handle.

She'd knowingly attended this masquerade—had plotted and schemed her way here. How foolish and naïve would she seem now if she acted outraged by a mere dance? She sighed. Causing a scene would only make matters worse.

They whirled past another couple, and she realized that, intentional or not, she *was* drawing curiosity. She dared another look, and this time locked eyes with the male of the couple she'd just whirled past.

Clad in a domino the shade of rich burgundy wine, he made the gladiator against whom she was pinned seem more gaudy than gallant. His half-mask gave way to a firm jaw, and the domino did little to conceal his massive build. A wide chest and strong arms tapered to a trim waist. Strong thighs. Heavens. She was staring at his thighs. She quickly averted her gaze.

The stranger quirked a brow. Appraising her, in turn. At least *he* danced like a gentleman, she noted, his partner a respectable arm's distance away. Why couldn't she be partnered with him? Who was he? The baron himself? As yet, none of her companions had been able to identify their host.

Charity squirmed. Lord Edwards was beginning to sweat on her. Maybe this evening had been a mistake after all.

The next turn brought them around the other couple, and she observed wryly that her mystery man's restraint in dancing might be attributed to the fact his partner was at least twice his age—though dressed just as scantily as the birds of paradise Miss Hart had commented upon earlier.

This time *she* quirked a brow, smugly satisfied that her veils hid her smile.

Mercifully, the waltz ended.

"I really must see to my hair," Charity begged off, before her partner could suggest they visit the refreshment table, the terrace, or anywhere else.

She hurried toward the retiring room, but when a backward glance confirmed Lord Edwards had turned his attention to a more receptive subject, she veered off, aiming for the card room instead. She'd had enough of dancing—an activity she could partake in at any one of dozens of events during the Season.

The Wicked Baron, absentee host that he was, was said to offer indulgences and amusements far more unusual. Charity had a mind to explore. Not necessarily to partake—she wasn't *that* bold. But after the effort she'd gone to just to get here, she at least wanted to see what all the rumors were about. Aside from the few companions she'd arrived with, no one here knew who she was. No one to judge her. No one to question. No one to be disappointed if she didn't live up to their expectations.

She swallowed thickly, knowing she deserved the mess she'd made of her life. She was all too aware that her own foolish actions had resulted in her capture last year. It had been her ambition to spy on men she knew to be dangerous, just so others would see as much value in *her* as they did in Beatrice Pullington, who'd deciphered a message meant for one of Napoleon's spies and earned the trust of the British government.

Only Charity hadn't been successful like Bea. She couldn't even live up to her own expectations, let alone those of others. And ever since, it was getting harder and harder to stay afloat in the whirlpool she'd set in motion.

Tomorrow. Tomorrow, Charity promised herself as she adjusted the veil that protected her identity, she would get her life back under control.

Tonight, there were too many opportunities to pass up.

"You thought *this* would be a likely place to meet my future wife?" Graeme scoffed.

Ewan MacPherson, his longtime friend and his reason for attending this absurd masquerade, held by an even more absurdly-nicknamed English noble—the Wicked Baron, indeed—caught Graeme's expression and gave a disgusted snort. "Don't look so pained, man. If a wife is all you're after, get yourself to Almack's and have done with it. I just thought you might actually want to have some fun whilst doing the looking."

"Huh. A valid point," Graeme conceded. Fun was a commodity he'd had precious little of in recent years. The two men had forsaken the ballroom for the card room, but after a few hands of five card loo, men at the various tables began standing up and drifting toward the adjacent room.

Standing at its edge now, Graeme could see why. The room was darkened, save for a single lamp positioned to illuminate a screen. In the corner, a turbaned man sat cross-legged, playing softly on a reed flute. Behind the screen stood a woman, her silhouette clearly outlined as she danced to the foreign tune, touching herself in ways no lady would dream of.

The remainder of the parlor was littered with sofas, benches, and chaises, upon which an assortment of Grecian goddesses, faerie queens, and woodland nymphs perched, some attending to a nearby gentleman, others gazing beckoningly toward the doorway.

Graeme rolled his eyes and whispered, "Somehow, I doubt any of *them* are likely to make a good wife and mother."

"You never know," Ewan shot back. "You know what they say about certain widows…"

Graeme just shook his head. He was here now. There would be other, more appropriate engagements at which he might meet a wife. In the meantime, the masquerade *was* an ideal venue for honing his skills at flirtation. It had been an age since he'd courted anyone seriously, and, earl or not, he'd need some finely honed skills to tempt a woman once she realized how far from civilization he lived.

He squared his shoulders. "Very well. Upon which of these mythical creatures shall I lavish my attentions?" He kept his voice low—not that the crowd captivated by the screen woman was paying him any attention.

His friend laughed. "You look prepared to do battle. Just

pick a pretty lass and I daresay you needn't do more than sit down and the rest will take care of itself. Not that brunette over there, though—I've my eye on her already. Hell, Graeme, I know you've done this before."

Graeme just grunted in response. Of course he had. Quite a lot of it, actually. But that was before his father had died. Before he'd inherited an earldom and all the responsibility that came with it. Other lairds had cleared their lands of crofters, making way for sheep to graze and tolling the death knell for the old clan way of life. Graeme had worked long and hard to prevent his own people from having to leave. Not to mention the responsibilities of caring for his young ward, Nathan. He wouldn't trade any of it, but the days of his youthful exploits seemed terribly distant. Ewan, as the second son of a wealthy Lord of Parliament, the Scottish equivalent of the English title of baron, had far fewer responsibilities.

"Ease off," his friend advised him. "One night of fun can't hurt 'ere you consign yourself to matrimonial bliss."

Ewan's tone made clear the two men shared at least one opinion: matrimony rarely had anything to do with bliss. Graeme's own parents had been a rare exception, though that had made his father's death doubly hard on his mother.

Ach. His friend was right. He had grown too serious. He forced himself to smile, the expression growing warmer as his gaze fell on the shapely Indian princess who'd just floated into the room. She'd caught his eye before, while dancing. Her every step, every movement oozed sensuality.

The gauzy fabric of her costume clung to her curves, caressing them like a lover. Her bodice was cut low, the shapely tops of her breasts thrust up for a provocative display, while veils hid most of her face from view. Only her eyes, long-lashed and rimmed with kohl, could be seen. Eyes that beckoned a man to discover more. The combination of sexual appeal with mystery held an allure he couldn't deny.

For the first time, Graeme gave real credence to his friend's advice. After all, what harm could come from one night of flirtation?

"Go on." He nudged Ewan toward the brunette. "Stand too long next to me in a place like this and people will start to talk."

His friend disappeared with a chuckle, and Graeme turned his attention to the Indian princess. She stood a few feet in front of him, paused behind a sofa toward the far back of the room where the shadow woman plied her trade. The sultry princess shifted, her stance uncertain.

Don't leave, he silently implored her.

The shadow woman behind the screen turned in profile, tipped her head back and slowly, deliberately, ran her hands over her breasts and pinched her nipples. Men in the audience groaned and shifted in their seats, but Graeme hardly noticed. The mysterious princess held his focus. Her eyes widened at the provocative display. She cast a glance toward the door, but her feet stayed planted.

He angled himself to see her better. There was something about the way her costume offered tantalizing glimpses of skin, yet obscured most of her face. Except her eyes. The room was too dim to make out their color, but he was drawn to them nonetheless—especially the way they'd widened when she realized what was going on behind the screen. Shock? Yes. But there was something else. Something evidenced by her decision to stay. To continue watching. She looked…captivated.

A surge of lust flooded him. Who was this woman? An actress? A courtesan? *Please*, he prayed as he moved so that he stood just behind her, *please don't let her be a married woman.*

Disguised or not, he didn't fancy lusting after another man's wife—even for a night. Whoever she was, he found her combination of hesitation and interest far more alluring than the unfettered invitations being issued by the other females present.

He bent his head to her ear. "Are you enjoying the shadow play?" he whispered.

She flicked her gaze to him and he saw the flare of recognition before she turned back to the screen. She remembered him from the dance floor. Graeme found this oddly gratifying.

She hesitated, her chest rising and falling with a deliberate breath, before she responded. The slight movement drew his attention to the swell of her breasts. She was slender, but with curves sufficient to hold a man's interest. They were certainly holding *his* interest.

"It is quite... quite... intriguing," she finally responded, her voice so low he had to lean even closer. Not that he minded.

Graeme smiled in the darkness, amused at her obvious struggle to find a proper response to a situation that was anything but proper. It was the response an innocent might give, though that had to be an act. No lamb walked knowingly into a lion's den.

Another moment passed, and still the Indian princess did not move away. Hmm. Proper, yet not proper enough to hightail it to the safety of her home. Unable to ignore her allure, he decided to test her further.

"The performer seems quite enthusiastic. Do you also enjoy such things?"

"I've never—" she cut herself off on a strangled note.

Interesting. He tried a different tack. "Do you dream of *being* touched the way she is touching herself?" he whispered.

She sucked in a breath, but did not tear her eyes from the screen.

Encouraged, he touched her shoulder lightly, stroked her upper arm. Her skin was warm satin. She shivered and leaned back into him ever so slightly. Arousal lit his senses, making him aware of every nuance of her movement. He was nearly hard already, and he'd barely touched her arm. He didn't even know her name. But he knew his reaction was to *her*. No shadow woman could affect him like this. He hadn't even been interested in the other "delights" to be found at the masquerade.

He stroked her other arm, then brought both his hands to cup her rib cage, sliding them down to her waist, her hips. A sigh escaped her, and he pulled her back until her body aligned with his, her bottom nestled against his growing erection.

They were doing far less than some of the room's occupants—indeed, far less than the shadow woman was now doing to herself, but he hadn't felt such an intense pull of attraction in years.

He bent his head to her neck, kissing the sensitive spot beneath her ear, his mind swimming with the heady scent of her—sweet and feminine, a contrast to her sultry costume. He touched his tongue to her skin as his hand skimmed her torso, rising to cup her breast. She whimpered, a sound of need that sent him from semi-aroused to rock hard.

By God, he had to find out who she was before he went mad with desire. But how was he going to stop touching her long enough to suggest they retreat to the card room for polite introductions?

At the front of the room a man stood, pulling his partner by the hand. Her breasts already spilled from her costume and he turned to fondle one as he backed up, tugging her along, presumably headed for more a private location.

The couple stumbled in their haste, and the man bumped against the screen in front. It tipped precariously and fell, knocking the lamp to the ground as well.

The room plunged into darkness, save for tiny flames that sparked up from the floor.

The erotic mood shattered as women shrieked and men rushed forward to stomp out the licking flames. Someone lit another lamp, and the shadow woman, revealed in naked flesh, scrambled to cover herself and ran from the room.

Graeme released the Indian princess, joining the men at the front. Mere stomping would not put out the flames if they caught on the puddle of spilled lamp oil. He pulled off the heavy folds of his domino and elbowed his way through the crowd, then dropped the pile of fabric over the small fire to smother it. He gave the pile a few stomps himself for good measure.

The shrieks subsided as the crowd realized the danger had passed. Men and women alike, engaged moments before in sensual play, now made hasty adjustments to their clothing.

Graeme lifted his head and looked back to the doorway, but his princess was gone.

Charity returned to the ballroom, her heart's racing already beginning to slow. What had she just done? Or almost done? Had it not been for the fiery interruption, she'd have willingly given herself over to the seduction of an enigmatic stranger.

She closed her eyes, breathed deeply, then forced them open again. It didn't matter. The moment was over. Nothing had happened. He didn't even know her name, nor she his. She listlessly selected a spot on the wall against which to stand.

She was tired, so tired. The wine she'd drunk earlier—which she was now almost certain had been laced with opium—seeped through her system, fogging her mind and weighing down her limbs. The initial euphoria, the euphoria that had driven her to the arms of the man in the burgundy domino, was gone. It *had* been the result of the wine…hadn't it?

She gazed across the ballroom, unwilling to admit to herself she was looking for *him*. Unfortunately, he was nowhere to be seen, and even the most outrageous behavior of the other guests could barely hold her interest. That was fine. Tonight she would get what she wanted most. She'd be able to sleep. Just not yet. By the *ton's* standard's, tonight's entertainment had just begun. It would be hours before her companions would wish to return home. That was the trouble with sneaking out. She had no carriage of her own.

She selected another glass of wine from a nearby table and sipped, more slowly this time.

A man dressed as a knight approached, looking hopefully between her and the dance floor. She shook her head. "I find my energy flagging," she admitted.

"A stroll outdoors to revive you, perhaps?"

Charity glanced around. Lord Edwards, Lord Blythe, and Miss Hart had long since abandoned her, melting into the crowd of pleasure-seekers. Who knew when they would reappear? A breath of fresh air *did* sound appealing. They needn't go further than the terrace. She nodded. "That sounds lovely, thank you."

She breathed deeply as they stepped outside, the cool night air a welcome respite from the oppressively stuffy ballroom. Murmurs and giggles floated toward them from the darker corners of the terrace and garden. Nothing unusual there. Her own first kiss had occurred in a garden at a ball.

The knight escorting her exerted a pull on her elbow, guiding her into the dark.

Charity slowed, a vague unease seeping through her opium-aided calm. "This is nice, here on the terrace."

"It will be even nicer if we go further into the garden," he insisted. "Come, there is something I want to show you."

There is something I want to show you? Charity rolled her eyes. Every girl over the age of fifteen knew to beware *those* words. Since her companion appeared well past his teens, he ought to have improved on such techniques by now.

She planted her feet. "Surely you can give me a hint before luring me into the dark?"

He gave her an oily grin. "A hint, is it? I'd be obliged."

Too late she smelled the liquor on his breath, for his grasp on her elbow tightened as he yanked her close, landing a sloppy kiss on the veil covering her mouth.

"Bit of an exhibitionist, are you? Like to be in sight of the house?" He chuckled, the sound making her cringe. "The baron always invites the best sort of women to his parties."

Charity blinked at the backhanded compliment.

"These bloody veils are in the way," the knight muttered, pawing at the gauzy layers.

She stepped quickly back. He was hardly the first man she'd seen become clumsy with liquor or ardor. If her own mind hadn't been so foggy, she'd have registered his impairment much sooner.

A cool sensation tickled the back of her neck as though a breeze had snuck beneath the veils that shrouded her. But the evening was still. Looking up, she once more locked gazes with the wicked stranger who'd whispered to her, touched her, in the shadow parlor. His burgundy domino was gone, but there was no disguising the strong jaw or the heat of recognition in his gaze. She'd seen him, caught that first hint of interest, while dancing. Then…the parlor. Her skin heated at the memory.

He'd touched her, and she'd responded—oh, how she'd responded. It had been mindless—a moment's indulgence brought on by the sensual shadow play and the daze of the opium wine.

Now, he stood in the shadows, his expression once more appraising. Why? Could he not see her discomfort?

The drunken knight had paused to adjust his lopsided armor, oblivious to the silent interaction of the other two on the terrace.

A dark thought made Charity shiver. Perhaps her shadow-room stranger had no intention of stepping in to aid her. Perhaps he was merely waiting his turn. After all, she *was* attending a party known for its guests' loose behavior—and she'd already given him reason to think she would not turn a man away.

She had just enough presence of mind to know she *didn't* have full control of her faculties. And to know that some mistakes could not be undone. It didn't matter how attractive she found him. She dared not let him touch her again.

Finally, her tired brain was roused to action as she realized the danger she was in. She was reasonably certain she could deflect one man. But two? She'd better think fast.

There she was again. His Indian princess, this time with an ardent knight in tow. Though, from her reaction to the knight's kiss, she did not share the gentleman's enthusiasm.

Graeme stopped. He hadn't been able to take his eyes off the mysterious woman from the moment he'd first seen her.

Those brief, erotic moments in the dark had left him entranced, aching for more—though seeing her in trouble now quashed some of that urge.

Whoever she was, she made a highly unlikely candidate for the position of his future wife. But he couldn't walk away. Not when she might need his help.

"A very fine knight you appear to be," the princess loftily proclaimed. "But I shall bestow my favor upon no knight who has not first proven himself in a quest."

"A quest?" The sot fairly panted with eagerness. Graeme grimaced—and tried to ignore the surge of anger that this mysterious beauty might bestow her "favor" upon such a lout. Why should he be angry? He had no claim to her. He didn't even know her name. Although the females at this masquerade seemed to be tossing their favors around rather liberally, Graeme couldn't quell the fantasy of an Indian princess who chose *him*, and him alone, for such an honor.

"What sort of quest?" the knight asked.

Aware the princess was watching, Graeme made a cup of his hands, then held them up as though making a religious offering.

"The holy grail?" She sounded amused. "Yes, of course. The most time-honored of all quests. My good knight, it is the holy grail which I seek."

"But men have searched in vain for hundreds of years, even died on that quest," the knight complained.

"Oh. I see. I should hate to be responsible for anyone's death, of course. In that case, I believe I should settle for a rose."

Graeme wished she wouldn't settle for anything—at least not anything involving the drunken knight.

"A rose for the lady. Indeed. My dear, I shall return

promptly." He swaggered off.

Graeme watched him go, the wisdom of the lady's request sinking in as he observed the man look around in bewilderment, then head a different direction. This early in the spring, he was going to have a difficult time finding a rose.

He smiled. It appeared the damsel in distress had no need of his help after all. She blew out what could only be a sigh of relief, then walked toward the far end of the terrace. This time, he wasn't going to let her disappear without an introduction.

"Well done." He fell into step beside her. If only he could see her face. Did that veil conceal a smirk? Or fear?

"You."

It was not exactly the enthusiastic greeting he had hoped for.

"I thought," Graeme replied carefully, "you might be receptive to a more...proper...introduction."

She tilted her head and gave a low laugh, then waved a hand through the empty space surrounding them. "Proper? Who shall make such an introduction? No one, and nothing, about tonight is proper."

She sighed again. "I saw you, watching just now. Do you wish to pursue me as well? If you do, I must beg of you— please, desist. I am far too exhausted to engage in any further flirtation tonight."

Graeme was spared the necessity of replying to *that* unusual pronouncement, for her pursuer of moments before dashed up, frowning at Graeme. He thrust out his chest. "She was with me."

"I am not *with* either of you," the Indian princess replied, her tone mildly irritated and her accent distinctly British.

The knight dropped to his knees before her and begged, "Allow me another chance to prove myself worthy—a man of culture and refinement. You are the most intoxicating woman to grace this event. If you leave..." He put a hand to his heart.

"Step around him," Graeme advised.

The princess nodded. She sidestepped and passed the over-ardent knight.

"*Je suis desolé*," he called to her.

The princess froze mid-step, swayed, then crumpled.

Graeme managed to catch her just in time.

He swept her into his arms and moved off quickly, though not without one blistering look at the swine who'd given her trouble.

He looked down at her limp form, unable to completely subdue his body's immediate reaction to her slim curves, the weight of her in his arms. Damn. This was a far cry from the introduction he'd hoped for.

What did one do with an unconscious Indian princess whose name he didn't even know? And who, for that matter, was not really an Indian princess at all? And what in the bloody hell had that fool said to cause her to faint?

A breeze lifted her veil. It fell away from her face. Moonlight reflected on a pale complexion, a light fringe of lashes and a pert nose. Beautiful.

Carrying her back through the ballroom would draw too much attention. He headed for a side door—a servants' entrance, most likely.

There had to be a place to set the lass down without placing her person or her reputation at risk. Though, as she'd just pointed out, no one seemed overly worried about propriety in the Wicked Baron's home. Rather the opposite.

He managed the door, easing them both into what appeared to be a private wing of the home. The next door he tried led to a small music room. He spotted a chaise in one corner. Perfect.

As he transferred her weight to the chaise, his mystery lady stirred.

Charity blinked. Heaven help her, what had she done now? Just as quickly, she remembered. The stranger—*her* stranger—watched her anxiously. Well. He'd rescued her after all.

He was handsome, in a sort of unrefined way. Broad shoulders, strong jaw. He was so...so much a *man*. No matter how perfectly tailored his evening wear, no matter how fine the cuts of cloth, the garments could not transform him from strapping warrior to gentleman of leisure.

Even his forearms were thick, corded with muscle and sprinkled with hair. A rush of desire flooded her, so much that she lifted her hand to touch his arm, to feel his skin on hers, before she realized what she was doing and snatched her hand back.

A moment too late.

The door opened, and a giggle turned to a gasp. "Oh dear, terribly sorry!" a woman apologized, nudging the man behind her back out the door.

He peered around her, his gaze taking in Charity and her rescuer near the chaise, then returning to the ample bosom of the woman at his side. "What's the problem?" he asked. "There's plenty of room."

"This lady is not feeling well," her rescuer informed them. "You might find better amusement elsewhere."

The other man looked skeptical, then shrugged. "Come on, Elsie."

His partner giggled. As she left, she called to Charity with a wink, "I do hope he can make you feel better, dear. He looks quite capable."

The door closed, and Charity released a horrified laugh. "She didn't believe you for a second."

He shared the laugh. "I daresay not. Though I spoke the truth. You are not well."

"I am perfectly all right," she insisted. "Better than all right."

Graeme heard her words. But they were belied by the haunted depths of her eyes. He peered closer in the dim light.

Blue. Even in the dark they were blue. And even in the dark, there were shadows beneath them.

Her pupils were tiny dots in those oceans of blue.

He frowned. "We both know better. Have you had too much drink?"

"Only wine."

"Is something else amiss, then?"

"Your concern is kind, sir, but I assure you I am merely overtired. I did not sleep well…last night."

He sensed more to her story, but pushing would get him nowhere. He *did*, however, believe her claim of exhaustion. Even on the terrace, she'd told him she was too tired to flirt. "I wish to help you. Where are the people you came with?"

She scrunched up her nose as though trying hard to recall. "I cannot say exactly. Though they must be somewhere about. They wouldn't leave without me."

Graeme considered that—for about a second. "Well, you're leaving without them."

Her eyes flew open. "I most certainly am not."

He gestured impatiently at their surroundings. "We cannot stay here all night—already we must hope you were not recognized by that pair that interrupted us."

"I don't believe I know them."

"Good. They definitely won't know me. I am not from London."

"Your accent. Scots."

He nodded. "But my anonymity will not save you. Wicked Baron's masquerade or not, I've no intent of taking liberties with the reputation of a woman whose name I do not even know."

She propped herself up and cocked her head. "That makes you a most unusual guest for such an affair, I believe. Nor did you seem to have such reservations earlier. My name is Charity Medford."

"A pleasure to meet you, Miss Medford," he replied, watching her lips quirk in a smile that acknowledged the odd circumstances of their introduction. "It is *Miss* Medford, is it not?"

"Yes."

"A relief, indeed. Graeme Ramsey Maxwell, at your service."

A tiny furrow appeared between her brows. "I know that name. Maxwell, Maxwell...*Lord* Maxwell. You're an earl."

"That I am," he confirmed. "Now, as to leaving." He quashed a surge of regret at the necessity of cutting their strange encounter short. "I shall see you home."

"Pardon?"

"I cannot leave you to fend for yourself, princess, while I search out your friends."

She pushed up on the chaise. "I am quite recovered now. I shall be well able to fend for myself." The arm that supported her weight trembled. She followed his gaze to it and quickly shifted positions.

"Stand up," he ordered.

"What?"

"Stand up."

She put a hand on her hip and thrust out her chin. "Who are you to—"

"Since you insist you can fend for yourself, *stand up*."

She quickly stood. Then swayed.

"As I thought." He pushed her gently back to the seat. "Now that we're through arguing, surely you can see there is but one solution here—we make an unobtrusive exit, and I see you safely home."

How could someone look so mutinous and beautiful at the same time?

"How do I know you'll keep me safe?"

He cocked his head. "You don't. But do I seem inclined to harm you?"

She dipped her head. "I concede your point."

"Good. Then, if I support you, can you manage to walk and appear merely intoxicated, rather than frighteningly weak?"

Her lips parted in surprise, and Graeme gave into the urge that had possessed him from the moment he'd seen her. He'd kissed her neck, yes, but now that he'd seen her lips…

He did it swiftly. Far too swiftly. The merest taste, and he pulled back. God. He could happily drown in that taste.

"What was that for?" she spluttered.

He smiled. "To seal the deal. Come on."

Before she could remember he'd just insulted her by calling her weak *and* having the gall to kiss her, he took her arm and, steadying her, led her from the room. Along the way to the exit, he pointed at various portraits, rugs, and décor, bending his head toward hers and whispering silly commentary. To anyone else, there would seem nothing amiss.

Miss Medford walked with her eyes cast down, only occasionally flicking a glance up to smile at something he said. Almost as though they shared a secret. Almost like lovers.

They took the same exit back to the terrace and had nearly worked their way around to the front, where waiting carriages with drivers lined the street, when a turbaned woman strolling the opposite direction stopped in her tracks.

In a surprised voice that carried clearly through the night air, she exclaimed, "Miss *Charity Medford?*"

Beside him, Charity gasped, then took off running.

Chapter 3:

In which Charity is launched out of the proverbial frying pan and into the fire.

"Your Grace, I beg of you," Lady Priscilla Medford said to her son in law, the Duke of Beaufort, as they traveled home from the Foxbeals' ball in the duke's luxurious carriage. "Charity listens to no one anymore, save perhaps you, as the benefactor whose generosity has propelled her popularity in the *ton*."

Alex Bainbridge, Duke of Beaufort, silently reminded himself that he loved his wife Elizabeth more than enough to put up with her less-than-ideal relatives. "Charity would be quite popular regardless of my support," he replied. "But what would you have me do?"

"Encourage her to marry," her mother pleaded. "Soon. I thought last spring's...*experience*...would have taught her a much needed lesson. But instead, the girl has grown wilder than ever. I truly fear, if we do not marry her off post-haste, she will do something to render herself unmarriageable."

Alex didn't bother to deny this prophesy. Truth be told, he was surprised it hadn't happened already.

"The other day," Lady Medford continued, "she informed me she's rejected six offers. Six! Surely at least one of them came from a respectable source."

Alex raised his brow. Indeed, all six had—but that had been last year, the Season when Charity had first made her bow. He'd quashed the many others that he'd deemed unworthy before they'd officially become offers. With Charity's father in the grave, someone needed to look after his wife's younger sister. Her laughing spirit and zeal for life—traits that won her the affection of everyone she knew—landed her in scrapes more often than not.

But this Season? Charity was still popular, to be sure, but with a different crowd. Not the sort of people amongst whom she was likely to find a loyal husband.

"She has my encouragement, but I can hardly force her to the altar," he pointed out. "Nor would I wish to."

"Perhaps she just needs time," Elizabeth offered.

"You've turned soft since Noah was born," he teased her, referring to their three-month old son.

"Well," Elizabeth argued, "Charity chose to attend Almack's with Mary Summers tonight rather than join us. "What better place for her to go, if we are hoping to see her married and settled?"

"Perhaps," he conceded. Lady Medford nodded her agreement, though the tilt of her head suggested she remained unconvinced.

"Perhaps if you were to specifically endorse two or three young gentlemen," Lady Medford suggested. "You could throw a party, Elizabeth, and be sure they were invited. It would still be her choice, of course…"

Alex didn't point out that, since the last rejection two weeks ago, no one else had come knocking. Instead he tried to reassure the women. "As you said, she is at the marriage mart this very eve. We shall all simply have to hope fortune beams upon her there." He refrained from making any additional promises. As much as he loved Charity, he had a feeling that what his mother-in-law asked now—reining her wild daughter in and convincing her to marry—was a task nigh on impossible.

Graeme took off after Charity as she ran from the masquerade, catching up and ushering her toward his carriage.

"Who was that—the woman who called your name?" he asked after they tumbled inside and slammed the door shut.

"It doesn't matter," she panted. "It only matters that she knew me. I'm not supposed to be here."

Interesting. "I see. Where *are* you supposed to be?"

"Almack's," she admitted miserably. "Though I suppose the hour has grown too late. I ought to be home." She gave him the address.

Graeme paused. Almack's? That place was filled with young innocents and their mamas, and the fops who sought to marry them. Never mind that he'd considered paying a visit to the venerable marriage mart himself. A female guest of the Wicked Baron was an unlikely candidate for Almack's. She'd recognized his name, too. Almost as though she'd studied DeBrett's Peerage.

And then there was the matter of the address she'd just given him. Things weren't adding up. Unless London had undergone dramatic change since his last visit, Miss Medford lived on a highly respectable street, home to some of London's nobles. An unlikely residence for a courtesan, unless she were very discreet. Or very skilled. His gaze fell on the lush curve of her lip.

He swallowed hard, then repeated the address to his driver, cracking the door for just a moment.

When he turned back to her, she seemed to be assessing him. He cocked his head, waiting.

Finally she gave him a weary smile. "It was nice knowing you, however briefly, Lord Maxwell."

"You wish that I should not attempt to renew our acquaintance?" He frowned.

She gave a hollow laugh. "Fear not, my lord. Your gallantry tonight has not gone unnoticed, or unappreciated. But as to renewing our acquaintance, you needn't bother. By my estimate, I have about eight hours to live. Possibly ten."

"What?"

"That is about how long it will take before gossip spreads and one of my mother's friends decides that the morning hour is decent enough for her to take on the 'unpleasant' duty—which of course she will greatly relish—of calling upon my mother to inform her of my whereabouts this night.

"It will happen earlier rather than later," she said knowingly, "for whichever friend it is, she will not dare risk someone else beating her to the opportunity of being the one to relay such scandalous news."

"Ah," Graeme replied. Miss Medford not only resided at a respectable address, she apparently shared that address with her mother. Not a courtesan, then. The more he learned, the deeper the mystery grew. Just who was this beauty—and what *had* she been doing at such a masquerade?

"Actually," she interrupted his thoughts, "could you ask the driver to stop just around the corner? I can see my own way from there."

He chuckled. Having decided to play the gallant, he wasn't about to leave the job half done. That would only rob him of her company sooner and deny him the answers he sought. "Miss Medford, it would be negligent of me to send a lady in distress onto the dark streets of London, alone. I consider it my duty to see you safely delivered home."

She made an expression somewhere between a frown and a pout when he didn't give her the answer she'd hoped for. But a moment later, a smile pulled at the corner of her lips. "You are far more chivalrous than the 'knight' I met earlier."

He chuckled, absurdly pleased.

They sat in silence a moment. Her respectable address, not to mention her disapproving mother, made her off-limits for a liaison in Graeme's book—no matter where they'd met. But he couldn't suppress the desire that rose once more as he studied her slim curves in the shadowy carriage. Not a liaison. But a courtship? Was it possible he'd been drawn to the single true maiden attending the masquerade?

Right now, he just wanted to touch her. He'd nearly decided to abandon caution and reach for her when she lifted her fingers to her lips and squeezed her eyes shut to stifle a yawn.

Graeme blinked. Her earlier claims had been no lie. She truly was exhausted.

"Not too far now. We'll have you home soon, lass," he reassured her.

At his change in tone, she tipped her chin up, and the look of longing he saw in her eyes sent a surge of fierce desire and protectiveness flooding his system.

Her tongue darted out to moisten her lips. He heard the slight catch in her breath, and the desire to protect warred with desire of a very different nature.

The carriage stopped.

Charity blinked and shook her head to clear it, no longer certain she could blame the opium wine for her mesmerized state. No, Lord Maxwell was to blame. There was something about him. She'd felt it the first time she'd met his eye, and every time since.

The door opened, and a footman assisted her down.

Charity's heart sank—and her head cleared—the moment she set foot on the ground.

Lord Maxwell's carriage had indeed stopped in front of her home—as had another carriage just in front of his, from which her mother, followed by her sister and brother in law, the Duke of Beaufort, had just alighted.

"Unbelievable," Charity muttered. She turned back to the carriage, where Lord Maxwell's frame filled the door. "Did I say I had eight hours to live? Make that about five minutes."

"Is something amiss?"

She motioned for him to remain in the carriage. "The trouble is mine, not yours. You've been a gentleman. Now go," she urged, keeping her voice low. "Hurry."

"Charity?" her mother called.

Charity winced, mouthed "save yourself!" to Lord Maxwell, then faced her family. If only she had something besides her flimsy evening shawl to cover her blasted costume.

"Charity, who is that you're talking to?"

"Too late." She heard Lord Maxwell's deep voice just before the sound of his boot hitting the ground behind her.

She shot him a dirty look. This would be difficult enough to explain without a great hulking man following her.

"Good evening, Mother. Good evening, Your Grace. Evening, E.," she greeted her family in a breezy tone. "I was simply thanking Lord Maxwell here for giving me a ride home after my companions became…indisposed."

By now she'd drawn close enough to her family for them to register her unusual garb. Lady Medford's eyes narrowed. "Lord Maxwell." She inclined her head. "I don't believe we've met."

Charity suppressed a shiver at her frosty tone. "Shall I make the introductions indoors, then?" This was sure to turn ugly. At least she could usher them off the street rather than act out this scene in front of the neighbors and their servants. She swept inside, not giving anyone a chance to argue.

As she expected, the small crowd trooped into the house behind her. Once in the salon, Charity made the introductions more thoroughly. "Alex and Elizabeth Bainbridge, the Duke and Duchess of Beaufort. Elizabeth is my sister," she explained. "And Lady Priscilla Medford, my mother."

"A pleasure. Graeme Ramsey Maxwell, Earl of Leventhal."

The group stood awkwardly.

"Perhaps we should be going," the duke offered.

"Oh, no," Elizabeth protested, the corners of her lips quirking in amusement. "This is far too interesting."

Charity gave her a grateful smile. Growing up, they'd gotten into scrapes together. She was on her own now, but at least her sister wouldn't totally abandon her.

"I say. Almack's has changed their dress code dramatically since I last attended," Lady Medford challenged.

"Sarcasm is unbecoming," Charity shot back. "Fine. We both know I did not attend Almack's this evening."

"Masquerades are terribly fun, don't you think so, Alex?" Elizabeth nudged her husband, who shrugged agreeably and headed for the brandy decanter. "What an incredible costume, Charity."

"Although your support for your sister is noted and, I'm sure, appreciated," Lady Medford said, "this particular masquerade was not one I deemed suitable for an unmarried young lady."

"Perhaps we might discuss that *after* we bid Lord Maxwell goodnight," Charity suggested, as her growing anger and embarrassment threatened to destroy the last calming effects of the opium wine. "I'm certain he has no wish to listen to our differences of opinion."

"I am not certain I am ready to bid him farewell just yet. How long have you known Lord Maxwell?"

Charity sighed. "About two hours."

"And what were *you* doing at the masquerade, Lord Maxwell?" The words were loaded with too much bite to hold any pretense of an innocently-asked question.

Lord Maxwell's brows lifted, but he held his own. "Rescuing your daughter. Obviously."

Charity would have smiled at his lack of intimidation, but the idea that she'd required rescuing—true though it was—rankled too sorely.

"Please tell me this was not a 'pistols at dawn' sort of rescue," the duke drawled.

"No," Charity stated emphatically. "Absolutely not."

"You *were* in a carriage alone with him," her mother pointed out.

Graeme took a step back, beginning to feel as though he'd been thrust into the lead role in a Cheltenham tragedy without studying his lines. Perhaps he should have made his escape when Miss Medford had suggested. But he'd never been a coward, nor the sort to abandon someone in trouble. And Miss

Medford was simply too compelling. Even the threat of family introductions, made under highly suspicious circumstances, had not been enough for his instinct of self-preservation to kick in.

"Do not try to fool me, Charity," Lady Medford said. "I am not so old as to have forgotten the type of antics young people sometimes get up to. The sort they regret later."

Miss Medford plunked a hand on her hip. "Oh, for heaven's sake. If you are so in doubt, why do you not simply call for the physician to examine me? He will assure you I am unharmed. *Again.*"

Graeme reached up and felt his jaw. Still closed. Good lord—what kind of young woman was he dealing with that her family distrusted her to the point of needing a physician's word over her own? And, apparently, not for the first time.

Of course, Miss Medford's willingness to submit to an exam suggested truth to her claim of innocence. Which then begged the question—what on God's green earth had an innocent been doing at the Wicked Baron's ball? His head started to spin.

"Come now, Mother." The young duchess, Miss Medford's sister, spoke up once more on her behalf. "I'm certain Charity meant no harm. She was reasonable enough to accept a ride home when it became clear the evening's entertainment was not, perhaps, what she'd hoped or expected. Would you have rather she'd stayed?"

"I'd have rather she'd had the sense not to go in the first place," Lady Medford retorted. She heaved a sigh. "But, failing that, I suppose you are right." Adopting a more pleasant tone, she asked, "So, Lord Maxwell, what is it that brings you to London? Your accent and title, unless I'm mistaken, mark you as a Scot."

Graeme debated the wisdom of answering honestly. Well, why the hell not? The evening couldn't get any stranger. "Actually," he replied, "I came to London to look for a wife."

"Oh, my word." Miss Medford closed her eyes briefly, then opened them and rounded on her mother. "Do *not* get any ideas."

Graeme rocked back on his heels, beginning to enjoy himself.

He'd only spoken the truth. He *had* come to London to look for a wife.

He was, of course, quite certain that Miss Charity Medford did not fit the bill. A wife ought to be nurturing, submissive and controllable. Charity was...not.

Though ravishing and sensual, the chit obviously had a wild streak that ran deep. Hardly an ideal attribute for a dutiful wife, let alone a suitable mother for his young ward.

He'd had plenty of time on the journey south to consider the sort of woman he might court—and who might be convinced to spend the majority of each year in the Scottish highlands he called home. A young widow, perhaps, or simply someone less...beautiful than Charity Medford. Not ugly, of course. Just...*less*. Miss Medford, he suspected, had all of London at her feet. She didn't need him.

Except that she had, tonight.

It was probably too much to hope for a repeat occurrence. If only he could take his eyes off her.

"Brandy?" the duke asked him congenially.

Miss Medford looked between the two men, her parted lips—lips he longed to taste again—registering her disbelief. "Not two minutes ago you considered dueling, and now you're inviting him for a drink?"

The duke tipped his head. "If Lord Maxwell is truly the

chivalrous gentleman you so fiercely purport him to be, it seems the least I can do."

"You're actually *enjoying* this," she accused.

"Fine brandy, my loved ones gathered together…what's not to enjoy?"

Graeme bit back a laugh, though he noticed the redheaded duchess was not so successful in stifling her merriment. With the tension of moments before diffused, even Lady Medford's features relaxed.

Miss Medford, however, threw up her hands. "I must be too exhausted to think clearly, for this all seems absurd to me. Since I cannot be as witty and amusing as the rest of you, I fear I must excuse myself. I wish you all a good night."

Graeme watched her go, disappointed. She'd left the door open, and the soft sway of her hips held his gaze long enough that he saw the way she paused, her whole demeanor drooping as she reached the staircase leading, he presumed, to the family quarters. Whatever else she was hiding, he believed one thing she'd said. Miss Charity Medford was indeed very, very tired.

As for the rest, Graeme was not a man to let a mystery go unsolved. Nor was he—normally—one to make snap decisions.

He hoped he wouldn't regret the one he made now. After all, he knew only three key facts about Miss Medford. One, she was unmarried. Two, she came from respectable family. Third, and perhaps most importantly, he knew from those brief moments in the dark tonight that he'd never again be able to touch another woman without wondering *"what if?"*

Everything after number three was a matter of detail.

"I must be on my way as well," he informed those remaining in the room. "It was a pleasure to meet all of you, as well as the charming—if unconventional—Miss Medford."

"Lord Maxwell," Lady Medford said, "you have my sincere apology if my daughter's…situation…inconvenienced you this evening."

"No inconvenience," he assured her, already moving toward the door. Better to leave before things got awkward again. They would need time to digest his next words. "Scotland is home to quite a few unconventional people. I hope Miss Medford will like it. I rather think I'm going to marry her."

Chapter 4:

In which the word "rather" is analyzed and found lacking.

"I *rather* think I'm going to marry her?" Charity echoed, popping off her bed. *"That* was his proposal?"

She'd already dropped off into a dreamless slumber when her door had burst open and her sister, brimming with news, had shaken her awake. She blinked and shook her head, certain the effects of that evening's heavily-laced punch were still fogging her mind.

Elizabeth bounced on the balls of her feet. "I don't know that it technically counts as a proposal, given that it was uttered more in the form of an announcement than a request. We could hardly ask for clarification, either, as he made this proclamation on his way out the door. This Lord Maxwell may actually share your proclivity for drama."

"Heaven help us both, then. I barely know the man. It's not as though he asked me, either," she muttered. "He could at least have asked permission." She sank back down on the bed.

"I suppose it's a statement of intention, at any rate. Honorable intention," her sister squeezed her hand consolingly.

Charity hated the concern in her sister's eyes. "'I rather think' is hardly a solid foundation on which to rely," she scoffed. "For example, if I were to say 'I rather think I shall cut my hair off short,' it doesn't mean I am actually committed to doing so."

"You needn't be upset. No one has agreed to anything yet. After all, you even said you'd only known Lord Maxwell for two hours. Surely he intends to court you before making a formal proposal."

"I have no idea what he intends," Charity admitted, tugging at her hair. Why *was* she so upset? The man was gallant. Sensual. From what little she knew, straightforward. She could do far worse.

"Do you want him to court you? After all, why not? He is quite handsome. And an *earl*."

"Don't let Alex hear you saying that," Charity mustered the energy to tease. "No. Maybe. I don't know." She scrubbed at her face with her hands, willing her fuzzy brain to *think*. If only she could think.

Finally Elizabeth took pity on her. "Never mind this all for now. Get some sleep, sister dear. You really do look like you need it. We can put our heads together in the morning. I'm sure things will appear more clearly then."

"Right," Charity mumbled. "How am I supposed to sleep now?"

Elizabeth gave her a small smile. "Rest, then, at least. Worrying won't help."

"Right," Charity repeated.

"I'll be back in the morning," Elizabeth promised. "I *should* make you face Mother alone, but I won't."

"You're the best. Really."

Elizabeth chuckled. "Of course. That's what sisters are for."

In spite of Charity's protest that she wouldn't be able to sleep, her body had other plans. By the time Elizabeth closed the door behind her, the foggy entrails of slumber were already curling through her mind, pulling her back under.

"We need a plan." Lady Medford looked around the breakfast room expectantly, as though by announcing the obvious, she'd done her part.

The room's other occupants—Charity and Elizabeth, the latter of whom had arrived early and was gently bouncing her young son on her lap—straightened.

The few hours' sleep had done wonders for Charity. For the first time in days, she felt awake. And only too aware of her precarious situation. Perhaps, though she was loathe to admit it, her behavior *had* gotten somewhat out of hand. She clasped her hands on her lap to keep them from trembling, and managed to look her mother in the eye. "I know it is too late to apologize, Mother. At any moment, some enterprising acquaintance of yours will decide the hour is decent enough to come break the news of my scandalous behavior."

Her mother pursed her lips. "What would you have me say to them? Deny you were even at that horrible masquerade?" She harrumphed. "I do wish I could simply look away and let you deal with your own troubles. But you live under my roof, and I'd like to keep what's left of our family's dignity intact."

Charity shot a quick look at her sister, who was being uncharacteristically quiet. They both knew the Medford family would have very little "dignity" left if it hadn't been for Elizabeth's marriage to the duke.

Elizabeth had had a brush or two with scandals of her own before marrying Alex. Not to mention their father's inauspicious death and empty coffers. So, Charity rationalized, her own escapades were simply following in the family footsteps.

"I accept responsibility for my actions," Charity stated.

Her mother waved a hand. "That is well and good, but it does not help us now. Is there any chance the woman who saw you might be uncertain as to your identity?"

"She called me by name," Charity admitted in a low voice. "And then I ran. Even if she had not been certain, my reaction must have confirmed my identity."

"Oh, Charity," Elizabeth said sympathetically.

"So people will know you were there."

Elizabeth's eyes lit up. "But they do not know *why* she was there. All we really need is a good reason."

"I cannot think of any legitimate reason an innocent would attend such an event," Lady Medford stated.

Charity ignored her mother's unhelpful response. "What are you thinking?" she prompted her sister.

"The gossips always love a good story. Most of them are not above embellishing any *ondit* they find lackluster. All we must do is beat them at their own game. Think creatively. We could say you came looking for me…that you needed to speak with me, something urgent, and were afraid that if you showed up to the Wicked Baron's masquerade as yourself, meaning without a costume, you would not have been allowed in."

"Which is likely true." She *had* been invited, but there was a difference between showing up as a young lady of society and showing up in a mysterious costume…no one would think twice about the latter.

Lady Medford nodded. "Oh, I see. Yes, that just may work. Better yet. Say she came looking for *me*. I am a widow of measurable years, not a duchess and young mother. My presence at such a masquerade, though still not desirable," she glared meaningfully at Charity, "would be little cause for talk."

"Lovely. So I came looking for you," Charity said. For the life of her, she could not imagine her persnickety mother deigning—let alone desiring—to attend the Wicked Baron's masquerade. "Why? Oh. Wait. I have it. What if little Noah had suddenly spiked a fever, and you were terribly afraid, Elizabeth, and even though Alex would of course have summoned a physician, you wanted our mother at your side?"

Elizabeth pursed her lips. "I'm not sure I like using my son in such schemes, but I suppose it does no harm. He will never even know. We can say the fever came and went suddenly, but gave us a scare. You would have borrowed the costume from me, of course."

"Were you seen dancing? Or partaking in…whatever else it is that people partake in at that debauched event?" Lady Medford asked.

Charity hesitated. "Even if I was, I doubt it is cause for worry. I suspect very few guests will retain more than a hazy memory of the night's events."

There was not much more to be said about that.

"Very well. We shall all stay true to that story, should the topic come up," their mother decided. "Next. The Stowells' picnic is tomorrow. It is critical you attend, looking for all the world as though you are the most innocent creature ever to have lived."

Charity's mother's tone bespoke her doubt that her daughter could actually pull off such a feat. "You must stay right by my side, dutiful and doting. Wear something pale, with ribbons."

"And you'll be by my side, as well," Elizabeth put in. "I wish I could offer up Alex's side, but he plans to leave on the morrow for business on the coast." She sighed. "Maybe I could talk him into postponing the trip. With his backing, no one would dare to give you the cut direct."

Charity shook her head slowly. "He has already done more than his share in supporting this family." It was true. He'd stood by Elizabeth when society had scorned her, declaring her not only acceptable, but *desirable*. So much so that he'd offered up what he'd never offered up before—his hand in marriage. Then he'd subsidized their mother, paying for the town house where she and Charity now lived. And finally there was the matter of Charity's own dowry, provided by the duke. The money might mean little to him, but Charity didn't want to be any further in his debt.

"Besides, it's awfully early in the Season for an outdoor picnic. Perhaps it would be best if I went nowhere for a while. Laid low."

"That would only confirm your guilt in the eyes of society," Lady Medford told her. "Never fear. The weather would not dare to insult Lady Stowell by failing to cooperate on the day of her event. She insists on holding it earlier and earlier each year, so that no one else dares attempt to supplant her picnic as the first of the Season."

Charity swallowed, knowing it was true—hiding away would not solve things. There really was no easy way out of this.

"Besides," her mother continued, "I have it on good authority that a certain Scottish nobleman has also been invited to the picnic." She arched her brows meaningfully. "I realize he has not formally declared his intentions, but it would be in your best interests, Charity, to convince him—subtly, of course—to do so very soon."

"You want me to marry Lord Maxwell?"

"Is there a reason he would not make a good match?"

"Nooo…" Charity said slowly. The Scot had been most chivalrous—except, perhaps, those brief moments during the shadow play at the masquerade. In those moments she'd been no better, welcoming his touch, sinking into it, hungering for more. She felt the heat rise to her cheeks.

"Charity?"

A smile played at her lips as she shook off the sensual haze that seemed to come over her at the mere thought of Lord Maxwell. "No, there is no reason to think Lord Maxwell would not make a fine match."

Except for her fears about marriage. How could she share a man's bed, night after night? Unless she discovered a means to keep the terrors subdued, he secret was sure to slip out. She prayed Lord Maxwell would engage her in a leisurely courtship. It would save her reputation, and give her time to come up with a plan.

"We are in agreement, then." Lady Medford sounded satisfied, but stern. "Charity, I do not mean to sound dire, but you must know—Lord Maxwell may be your last, best chance."

Charity was spared the indignity of having to reply to *that* remark when a tap at the door interrupted their conversation. The butler cracked the door. "Lady Medford, you have a caller." His usually expressionless face bore only the faintest trace of disapproval that someone would dare to call at such an early hour.

Lady Medford rose, her mouth pressing into an unflatteringly tight line before she threw her shoulders back, lifted her chin, and schooled her features into an expression of cultured pleasantry and marched toward the front room.

Charity met her sister's eye, her heart hammering against her breast bone. There could be no question as to the purpose of this call. The moment of truth had arrived. She prayed their story would hold up.

Charity was not enjoying herself, in spite of the balmy spring afternoon that lent itself perfectly to picnicking. It seemed her mother had been correct—even the weather bowed in obedience to Lady Stowell's determination to host the first picnic of the Season.

She glanced around at the other guests, most of whom would not deign to speak with her, and stifled a sigh. Somewhere along the perimeter of the property, her guards stood watch. Ostensibly, they were discreet enough not to interfere with her life. But she hadn't missed the plain black carriage, now so very familiar, that followed them here. Nor could she shake the feeling of being watched.

In fact, there was no question she was being watched. Nearly every guest at the picnic was watching her. Waiting for the moment she slipped up, Charity supposed, though what awful deed they expected of her, she couldn't guess. The only difference between them and the watchers she feared most was their intent. The picnic guests would destroy her reputation. The others would destroy her life.

In this part of London, that amounted to practically the same thing.

She'd stood dutifully by her mother through two glasses of tepid lemonade, but her mother kept getting pulled aside by other mothers, who then "whispered" in voices Charity had to pretend not to hear.

"Even if I believe your explanation, the fact remains," Lady Carroll was saying now, "your daughter was seen at an event that is no place for an innocent, seen by heaven knows whom, doing heaven knows what, *and* seen leaving said event, no less, by climbing into the carriage of a man. Unchaperoned."

Charity swallowed, hard. She felt dizzy. But she couldn't seem to look away.

Her mother arched a brow, seemingly unflappable in spite of the onslaught. How did she manage it? "Seen? By whom, exactly? You seem to know an awful lot about it, Lady Carroll, for someone who claims she was not there."

Lady Carroll all but snarled. "And you were?"

"Pfft. Think what you like. I am a dull old widow and all of London knows it. I do enjoy a challenge at cards, however, and most of my acquaintances know that, too. What you may not know is that the young baron has an uncle whose skill at the game is legendary. The opportunity to observe his play is rare for one such as myself."

Charity was reluctantly impressed by her mother's show of solidarity—and her newfound skill at inventing plausible falsehoods. Indeed, the sniping Lady Carroll had no retort. One or two of the others nodded as though they actually found her mother's reasons acceptable. Still, no one made an effort to welcome Charity back into their circle. She drifted away as their hostess, anxious to diffuse the tension, guided the conversation to a new topic.

Tired of trailing after her mother, tired of the scornful looks, Charity wandered toward the edge of the garden, where a handful of children played. Two governesses watched over them, though the young women appeared more caught up in their own conversation than in that of the children. Charity stood for a moment, content to watch the innocent play. Curiosity and joy lit the features on their young faces. She couldn't help but smile, even as a sharp pinch of longing struck her as she tried to remember what it had been like when she, too, had been so carefree.

She knew that for her, those days were gone. There was no getting them back. But if she were ever so lucky to have children of her own—a possibility that seemed far-fetched, considering her fear of marriage—she'd go to the ends of the earth to protect them from making her same mistakes.

Graeme Ramsey Maxwell choked back a swallow of lemonade that was too warm in temperature and too light on alcoholic enhancement. This picnic was a disappointment. He'd hoped to find Charity Medford in attendance, but so far, he'd spotted only her mother and sister. He'd barely even been able to greet them, let alone seek out his true target, for it seemed word of his arrival in London had spread. He could practically see the matrons ticking off a list of his attributes to their daughters. Eligible? Check. Wealth? Check. His estates were in good shape—had they not been, he imagined the London gossips would have known that, too. Title? Check.

"Of course, it's a *Scottish* title," he imagined them saying, "but you can overlook that, dear. 'Tis a title nonetheless. An earl, even."

There was no other way to explain the swarm of mothers and daughters who surrounded him now, feigning interest in sheep and whatever crops they imagined his lands produced. Graeme forced a smile, reminding himself this was, in fact, why he had come to London. There might be a perfectly acceptable young lady amongst this group of hopefuls.

He was about to answer a question about mining when—finally—he spotted her. "Excuse me." He interrupted a woman whose name he'd already forgotten, and strode off. Rude, they would say. He couldn't have cared less.

The rest of the picnickers fell away as his focus narrowed in on the blond beauty lingering at the fringes of the party, attending without really being present. Odd. He'd pegged her as a social butterfly.

Though the scene before him wasn't what he'd expected, he quite liked what he saw.

Charity knelt on the ground, pale pink skirts spread about her, while a little boy gazed at her with something like adoration. Graeme could see why. She didn't notice him watching, so intent was she on unwinding the tangled pull-string of the boy's toy. Her golden hair was pulled up, away from her face, but little tendrils escaped to curl prettily against the flush of her cheeks.

Finally the string came free, and Charity looked up with a triumphant smile. The boy clapped his hands, then clutched the toy gratefully as she handed it over.

She straightened, brushing off her skirts as the little boy ran off. She watched him go, her triumphant smile fading to one more...wistful? Interesting. What made her sad? Did she long for children of her own?

She turned. He knew by the sudden flare of recognition, the faltering of her smile, that she had not realized he was standing there. Then the smile reappeared, more shy now.

He gave her a warm one in return. The scene he'd just witnessed was simple, just a brief moment, yet it did a measure to ease his doubt over whether Charity Medford could be a suitable wife and mother. She was here, at a respectable *ton* event, indicating her eligible status. She'd shown a fondness for children, and she hadn't seemed bothered by a bit of grass on her skirts. That was definitely good, since his home in Scotland boasted far more in the way of grass and dirt than ballrooms and salons. The ballroom, in fact, hadn't been used in years, unless you counted the games of hide and seek with Nathan.

But while the domestic scene he'd observed answered some questions, it raised others—such as why the young beauty shunned the company of the guests closer to her own age. And yet, she seemed happy enough to see him. With that realization came relief. He hadn't known quite how she would react. There were a good many things he didn't know about her yet. Her face was no longer hidden by veils, but she remained a mystery.

"Tell me," he asked as he drew close, "why the prettiest lass at the picnic is off by her lonesome?"

"I'm not alone," she protested. "I like the children."

"I see." Good. He wanted her to like children. But he didn't think she'd given him the full truth in her answer. He waited.

Finally, she tilted her head in acknowledgement. "Also, I found the picnic…stifling."

"Aye. It must have been the conversation, unless I miss my mark, for surely you do not refer to the weather?"

She smiled. No one could deny the weather was as good as anyone in England could wish for on a spring day. "Something like that."

"Speaking of conversations, I must assume your family filled you in on the remainder of ours? After you retired the other night?"

She flushed beautifully. Indeed, she knew what he'd said, then.

"I realize my announcement may have seemed premature."

She flushed deeper, the color blossoming not only on her cheeks, but even on the swell above her bodice. Intriguing. How far down did it extend? And how soon would he have the opportunity to find out?

"For all its prematurity, my statement was no less sincere. I am very much interested in marrying you. That is, if you are amenable."

"To…marriage?" she squeaked.

"That is why I've come to London, in truth. I wish to marry. But we can begin with courtship, if you like. Though the goal remains the same."

"Are you always so blunt?" she asked, rather desperately. "I am not certain how to respond."

Was he coming on too strong? "I liked the way you responded the other night just fine," he told her, keeping his voice low and husky. The art of flirtation was coming back to him.

"My lord, I hardly think…"

"Don't think, then." All right. Too strong. He didn't want to frighten her off. He just needed more time. Needed to know when he could see her next. "Just listen. A few of my acquaintances have planned an outing to Vauxhall Gardens on Friday evening. One of my acquaintances is raving about a performance he saw last week...have you heard, perhaps, of this woman, a Madam Saqui? He tells me she descends from the air while walking a tightrope, all while firecrackers are sent up around her. Perhaps you and your sister would deign to join us?"

Her eyes lit up. "Oh, that sounds..." But just as suddenly, the light dimmed. She lowered her eyes, shuttered. "No, I'm afraid I cannot. Vauxhall isn't sa—. That is...er..."

Odd. Unless he was mistaken, she'd been about to say Vauxhall wasn't *safe*. He gestured, waving off her obvious inability to find the right words. "Not to the lady's liking. No matter. The opera? Cosi fan Tutte is well-regarded."

"Yes, I have heard of it. A *French* opera." Her nose wrinkled and her lovely full lips turned down as she spoke the word "French."

"It is. But if it will put you at ease, let me make this admission: I cannot speak a word of French." The London *ton* would surely consider this a shortcoming of his education, but Graeme couldn't quite manage to sound ashamed.

"Good." She shuddered. "I have nightmares in French."

"Bad instructor?" he ribbed.

She gave him a half smile, a shrug. "Something like that."

Charity Medford was a mystery, indeed. Young ladies in London were schooled in all manner things, many of them useless. He knew French was a part of the curriculum. Charity struck him as intelligent...he couldn't imagine her struggling in school. What about the language distressed her so? He was determined to learn the answer to all the things about her that puzzled him. But he couldn't do that without seeing her again.

"I should hate to be the cause of your nightmares. Cosi fan Tutte is out, then. But I cannot think of any operas currently playing in English. You know," he teased, "you are a difficult woman to court."

"Am I?" She sounded truly surprised.

"No Vauxhall, no opera..."

She blushed. "I suppose you are right. I hadn't realized. You say this outing to Vauxhall will be a large gathering?"

"Indeed. Perhaps you would be more comfortable if your sister were to join you?" Miss Medford's sister seemed a good sort. If he had to choose between sister or mother acting as chaperone, he'd take the sister any day.

As though he had conjured her, the young duchess ran up to them.

"Charity! People will talk."

"But—" Charity began.

Graeme opened his mouth to defend her. Truly, they'd done nothing wrong. Or maybe they had. London society was so strict. No wonder people felt the occasional need to don a disguise and let loose.

But Lady Bainbridge rushed on. "Or, perhaps, they won't. Darling, you have missed the most delicious *on dit* of the Season." She clapped a hand to her mouth. "Oh dear. Lord Maxwell, please forgive my manners."

Graeme bowed slightly, wondering where in the world the Medford sisters had gotten their plucky spirits from. "Not at all, Your Grace. In fact, I am all ears. What is this news we have missed?"

Her eyes sparkled. "Lady Caroline Lamb's book has just come out and—oh, I can hardly even speak of it. Charity, she tells *everything*. I haven't read it myself, of course, but if it is true..."

Graeme was totally lost.

"You mean, about Lord Byron?" Charity asked.

Her sister nodded. "She gave him a different name, but that fooled no one. Lady Stowell acquired a copy, and Lady Hornflower said she had one, but her husband, upon learning of the torrid content, threw it into the fireplace. Of course, I do believe she is even now plotting extra visits to Lady Stowell so that she may finish reading behind his back."

Graeme laughed. At the mention of Byron, he'd recalled a rumor of an ill-fated love affair. More than one, actually. Apparently one such lover had followed the folly of *having* the affair with daring to write about it.

The duchess looked alarmed. "Dear me. I shouldn't say such things in front of a near-stranger. Please forget I said anything, Lord Maxwell."

"I could not possibly, Your Grace. Any time spent with the charming Medford sisters is time to be cherished. But I swear upon my father's grave, I would never repeat a word of it."

She hesitated, looking torn. "Oh, do go on, E.," Charity begged. "What has been said?"

Lady Bainbridge capitulated. "All right. She—Lady Lamb, that is—she has been cast beyond the pale. The patronesses at Almack's have sworn to revoke her voucher. I cannot think of anywhere in all of London she shall be able to show her face."

"Oh, my," Charity breathed.

Graeme noted that her expression, while understandably one of interest, also held a note of sympathy.

"'Tis all anyone can talk about," the duchess added. A look passed between the sisters that Graeme could not interpret.

When neither of them said anything else, he seized the opportunity to change the subject. "Your Grace, I was just telling Miss Medford of an astonishing performer who is to put on a show at Vauxhall on Thursday. I would be very much honored if the two of you would consider joining me. The duke as well. It will be a rather large group of my friends and acquaintances. Some you may know better than I, as it's been some time since my last stay in London."

Another look passed between the sisters. "Charity?" the elder sister asked.

Charity moistened her lips, biting the bottom one nervously. She nodded.

"How delightful. I am certain we shall have a lovely time," Lady Bainbridge said. "I hope you'll excuse us until then, Lord Maxwell. There are several guests casting an evil glare at my sister and I for being so selfish with your company."

The two ladies retreated gracefully. Graeme could not help a longing glance at the delicate curve of Charity Medford's neck, where golden tendrils curled softly against her skin. He wished his lips were in their place.

The picnic had not been a waste after all. Not only had he seen his not-so-Indian princess, he'd garnered a promise of another night in her presence. The courtship was underway.

Miss Medford's sister had only been half-joking about the other guests. Even now, at least two marriage-minded matrons strode purposefully toward him, their eligible offspring in tow. Graeme steeled himself for their imminent arrival.

Chapter 5:

In which Graeme discovers why negotiation is often considered a fine art.

"Let me see if I follow you," Ewan Macpherson said slowly, laying down his cards. "You do not wish to attend the Rutherfords' ball tonight because…"

"I have already decided upon a wife."

"I see." Ewan nodded, his expression making it clear he did *not* see. "And how did you meet this lucky woman?"

Graeme hesitated. "Rather by accident, actually." There was no need to cast Miss Medford's reputation into further doubt by explaining they'd met at the Wicked Baron's masquerade.

"Ah." Ewan picked up his cards again, but made no move to play. "And the young woman agreed to marry you and move to the far, cold north just like that? What do you know of her, Leventhal?"

Graeme shrugged. "It's complicated."

"She comes of good family?"

"Of course," Graeme replied automatically, though the interaction he'd witnessed between Miss Medford and her family made him secretly question the definition of "good." He gestured impatiently. "Play a card, would you?"

"I couldn't possibly. The suspense is killing me." Ewan joked, his grin stretching wide at Graeme's obvious discomfort. "Out with it. Who is the chit?"

"Miss Charity Medford."

Ewan threw back his head and laughed. Recovering, he said, "You really had me going there, Leventhal. Thought you were serious."

"I am."

Ewan sobered, his eyes widening as he inspected Graeme's face for any hint of teasing. "Good God. I daresay you are." He sighed. "The trouble is, your intentions mirror those of a rather long line of suitors, if any of the usual gossips can be believed."

"Miss Medford is...what? Quite the rage, as the Londoners say?"

"Something like that," he said faintly. "Though to hear it, London's darling has developed a wild streak of late."

Well, *that* he could believe.

"Has she agreed to marry you, then?"

"We are...negotiating."

"Ach."

"Ach? What does that mean?"

"Well, you're a fine man, with a fine title, my friend. A name many a lass would be happy to add to their own," Ewan said, finally laying down a card. "But if you don't mind a bit of advice, you might as well continue looking until the matter with Miss Medford is settled. Just in case."

"Your advice is noted," Graeme said drily.

Ewan shrugged. "Noted, and ignored, from the look of it."

"Stubborn as they come, my father used to say," Graeme

replied good-naturedly.

"Then may that trait serve you well."

"You're sure about this?" Elizabeth asked Charity.

Charity's stomach tightened with nerves, but she willed them away. "I am. I want to go." Vauxhall Pleasure Gardens used to be one of her favorites among London's attractions. Now, it made her jumpy. The crowds full of strange faces, the shadows lurking beyond the pools of lantern light, had once seemed romantic and exciting. Now they signaled danger. Logically, she knew she had little to fear. But logic wasn't always enough to quell that fear.

"You must really harbor a *tendre* for your handsome Scot."

A warm flush swept over her. "He isn't *my* handsome anything," Charity mumbled.

"Oh, come off it. The man looked distinctly miserable at the Stowells' picnic—except when talking to you."

"Hmm. I felt rather the same way."

"Oh, but you should be feeling lucky!"

"Because of Lord Maxwell?"

"No. I mean, yes, but also because of Lady Lamb. Please do not think me too awful, Charity, but her social demise could not have come at a better time. Everyone is so scandalized by it, they have all but forgotten the your attendance at a certain highly-questionable masquerade."

"Nothing like a bigger scandal to wash away the smaller one," Charity observed wryly. Her sister spoke the truth. When Elizabeth had led her back to the main crowd of picnickers, several ladies had been so eager to speculate over Lady Lamb's book and the resulting scandal, they'd begun doing so with Charity, completely forgetting that they'd determined her unworthy of their conversation just a short time before.

"Just promise me you haven't done anything else. You haven't, have you?"

"Does that mean I should cancel my outing to go walking in Hyde Park with Lady Lamb?"

Elizabeth gave her sister a shove.

"Oh! Who's improper now? Aren't you supposed to be a duchess?" Charity mocked in a lofty tone.

Elizabeth smirked. "I *am* a duchess. And your older sister. So if you want me as chaperone and not our dear mother, you'd best hear me out."

"Oh, stop worrying. I don't believe I have ever even met Lady Lamb. And I cannot think of anything else I have done that could cause a scandal." She couldn't help but add, "Yet."

Elizabeth rounded on her, but Charity danced away, laughing. "Joking, joking."

The Vauxhall Pleasure Gardens sparkled like a fairyland when Charity and Elizabeth arrived, with brightly colored lanterns lining the paths, and colorful tents and streamers erected around the main stage. Lord Maxwell himself greeted them almost the moment they alighted from the coach, leading them toward a gathering that included a smattering of Scots, English, noble, and merchant. Charity recognized most of the names, if not faces, save for those of Mr. and Mrs. Alasdair Maxwell, who the earl introduced as his cousins. "Respectable lot. You may have even met them before."

"I don't believe so," Charity answered politely. The mousy couple did not look even remotely familiar. She glanced at her sister, who also shook her head.

He shrugged good-naturedly. Quietly, so only she could

hear, he said, "I'm afraid those particular Maxwells are not the sort to leave a lasting impression."

An hour into the evening, after Alasdair Maxwell's third attempt, all equally unsuccessful, to start a conversation about a book of sermons he'd been studying, Graeme leaned over to Charity and amended the description to "distant" cousins. She smothered a giggle.

A troupe of musicians shuffled offstage, and a drum roll from behind the curtains signaled the revelers that the evening's main event was about to begin.

People began to clap and cheer, moving toward their seats or attempting to find better vantage points. The noise level grew—exactly the sort of thing that made Charity nervous of late.

But tonight, it also offered an excuse to lean even closer to Lord Maxwell in order to be heard. She couldn't resist the temptation. He smelled so...manly. Like sandalwood and soap. He dressed the part of an earl, but his body was that of a strapping warrior. His strong jaw held a trace of stubble, which Charity imagined caused no end of frustration to his valet.

"I see," Charity said, struggling to focus on their conversation instead of the firm mold of his lips. "Are you quite certain they are relatives?"

His brow quirked, evidencing his amusement. "Quite. But I aim to redeem the family name by making a *very* lasting impression. The sort you will never forget."

She averted her gaze, a smile playing at her lips. She murmured, so low she was certain he wouldn't hear, "You already have."

He smiled broadly and took her arm, guiding her toward their seats. Perhaps his hearing was sharper than she'd expected. He'd tucked her hand into the crook of his arm with a possessiveness that bespoke more than mere manners. Nothing that would even draw the attention of the rest of the group. Yet her breath escaped in a little *whoosh*, and she could feel the sizzle of attraction between them. It was there, humming, like a living thing.

As they sauntered toward their seats, Elizabeth gave her a smirk. With Alex still out of town, Graeme's friend Ewan MacPherson had gallantly offered to act as her escort for the evening. "Best mind your manners, MacPherson," Graeme teased him now. "That's a duchess walking beside you."

"And a bonny lass she is," MacPherson replied irreverently. He preened, turning toward Elizabeth. "Do you think being seen with you might raise my social standing?"

She gave a choked laugh. "You are too bad."

"It might," Graeme put in, "but if you walk any closer together, you'll only enjoy it until her husband returns and calls you out."

Since the pair was walking at a perfectly acceptable distance, and since Ewan's social standing really needed no improvement, the whole group was laughing by the time they took their seats.

Madam Saqui was, quite possibly, one of the more astonishing performers to grace the stage at Vauxhall this season. But Charity was not paying the least bit of attention to her.

Heavens. Just Lord Maxwell's presence beside her made her feel alive again. The fog of the past months receded, and all her previous, desperate attempts to escape the monotonous torture of her day to day existence seemed just that. Desperate. She *had* been worried about facing Vauxhall tonight, but the determined joviality of her companions had actually worked. She was relaxed, and having a wonderful time.

Just realizing that nearly made tears well in her eyes. It had been so long since she'd felt like this. But seated next to Lord Maxwell, it came almost naturally.

Too soon, the performance ended. Charity clapped enthusiastically with the others, all the while trying to think of a way to extend the evening without being obvious. Elizabeth, as usual, was a step ahead of her. "Shall we walk about? I should so enjoy the chance to stretch my limbs."

The men eagerly agreed, and while one or two of their group wandered off to explore the other activities at Vauxhall, the majority of them strolled toward the gardens. Lord Maxwell took Charity's arm, leading them. Elizabeth walked just behind, doing a masterful job of tripping up her escort and distracting the group by occasionally pausing to examining a particularly lovely lantern or statue, giving Graeme and Charity the opportunity to drift farther from the main group.

Charity was not unaware of the effect Elizabeth was having. She was just torn between appreciation and the sisterly desire to give her a good ribbing regarding her chaperoning skills—or lack thereof.

Still, when Lord Maxwell gave her elbow a quick tug, pulling her around a corner and behind a hedge that marked the end of the lit portion of the paths, she didn't protest.

In the dark, she could just make out the trace of amusement on his features. "Her Grace will come looking for you soon, I'm sure." He didn't sound sure. Stopping, he turned her to face him. "All things considered, though, I could hardly pass up this opportunity."

She leaned in, accepting the invitation for what it was. Somehow she'd known since the picnic that he would not let another encounter slip by without stealing a moment alone with her. It might—*might*—even have been the reason she'd swallowed her misgivings about Vauxhall in order to be here tonight.

"I have been waiting to do this for days," he told her, his already-low voice dropping even deeper.

He heard the catch of her breath. "Days?" she whispered.

"Days," he confirmed. "Since the night we met. Since that first, brief taste of your lips left me hungering for more."

Her soft "oh" was swallowed by his kiss. His lips were so firm, so deliberate. The sensation filled her, subsuming her senses until the world outside of his touch slipped away.

Graeme kissed her thoroughly, ignoring the impulse to hurry. He'd waited long enough to want to enjoy this moment. Though that control came with a price. The taste of her intoxicated him, and blood rushed to parts too long ignored. His inner youth urged him on, wanting more, but he quelled the blood-pounding desire to plunder, choosing instead to seduce.

He smoothed his hands over her bodice, coming up to cup her breast. Damn. This gown was far more constricting than the Indian princess costume she'd worn the other night. He missed the warm, soft feel of her flesh.

He traced the smooth swell of skin above the fabric, dipping his fingers beneath the edge the scant inch the gown would allow. His fingers grazed down the curves at the sides of her breasts, coming back to her waist even as she pressed against him, her breathing shallow.

His own breathing accelerated as he took her lips with another kiss. She welcomed him, her lips parting as he drove inside, his tongue stroking hers as he took what she so sweetly offered. God, she was a passionate little creature. His hands continued their caress, shaping the curve of her hips, slipping up her back to the delicate bones of her shoulder blades, pulling her hard against him.

He held her there, one hand at the small of her back, the feel of her hips snug between his thighs, his erection pressing against her stomach nearly sending all rational thought from his mind.

Theirs was hardly a proper courtship. But there were some lines a Maxwell did not cross. Which really only reinforced what he already knew: he was going to marry her. And he was going to have to do it soon.

Somewhere further down the path, a twig cracked.

Charity leapt, snapping suddenly to her senses. She squinted into the darkness, only to see one of the duke's men make an apologetic gesture and silently disappear once more.

She blew out a breath.

"Are we being followed?" Lord Maxwell asked, incredulously.

Charity swore mentally. Aloud, she simply sighed. "The duke's guards. They are only making sure I...stay out of trouble."

"You have guards." It wasn't a question.

"Yes. Sometimes."

"Why does your family mistrust you so?"

She gave him a coy look. "Perhaps because I do things like this?"

He laughed, but didn't drop the matter. "You aren't doing anything a thousand other young ladies haven't also done before you. I bet you any lass with a Season under her belt knows the pathways at Vauxhall."

He wasn't going to allow her to flirt her way out of an explanation, apparently. From behind the next row of hedges, they heard giggling. "You may be right," she admitted. "Perhaps that is why the guards did not leap upon you and drag me away when we kissed." She sighed, tempted to just tell him everything. But then he would know she was tarnished. It was so unfair—she'd been trying to do *good*, and look where it had gotten her. She settled for a half-truth.

"It is not entirely a matter of distrust. My family only wishes to protect me."

"Lass, they seem a tad overprotective."

"They have their reasons."

"Such as?" he prompted, when she didn't elaborate.

"What have you heard about my family?" she hedged.

"Very little, to be honest. I know of the duke. He is well-respected."

"Yes. It is largely due to him that the other rumors have faded. When my father passed away, we had very little money left."

"I do not care about that."

She gazed at him. "Perhaps not, but my mother certainly did, especially with two unwed daughters. All of London seemed to know our circumstances. She and my uncle conspired to marry Elizabeth off to a distant relative who had no breeding. He cared only that our father had held a title. Nasty, he was."

"And the duke swept in to her rescue?"

"If only. He wanted nothing to do with her, at first. They did fall in love eventually, but her first suitor was none too happy to be thwarted. He conspired to get my sister alone, and he treated her abominably. And *then* the duke swept in to her rescue."

"So it all ended well."

"It did, but neither of them has forgotten. Add those memories to the duke's involvement in politics, and the threats he received during the war, and, well, he does his best to protect us all."

Whew. Charity was actually rather proud of herself. She'd left out the most critical detail, of course, but she'd managed to make her "guards" sound like an almost reasonable precaution nonetheless.

"I see." He drew her close again. "So, what you are telling me is that, if I were to kiss you again, those two great oafs would not do me bodily harm?"

"I rather doubt they could, even if they wanted to."

"In that case…" His words broke off as his lips captured hers.

For long moments, they kissed. Never had she met a man who kissed the way he did. She wanted it to go on forever.

But instead he broke contact with her lips, holding only her gaze as he asked, "So, how soon can we be married?"

Charity stumbled, still reeling from the kiss. "M-married?"

"Lass, ye canna kiss a man like that unless ye intend to marry him."

"Oh. Oh, I, that is, I should be honored," she stammered, desperately trying to gather her wits from the ends of the garden to which they had apparently fled. The brogue in his voice gave her the shivers—in a very good way. He wanted to marry her. Charity's heart swelled until she felt giddy. *Yes, yes, yes*, her heart wanted her to say. Her mind, less quick to forget her troubles, forced her to ask, "But why the hurry?"

"Because," he growled, "kisses such as those lead to other

activities. And those other activities are best suited to a marriage bed."

Charity let out a strangled laugh. "Oh, my. I see. Well, let me think. I suppose, for a proper engagement, and to plan a wedding as it should be done...perhaps a year?"

"What!?"

"Oh, but Lord Maxwell," she continued, warming to her story, "the best venues must be reserved well in advance. And then there are the invitations to send out, gowns to order—the popular French dressmakers are months behind, and of course no fashionable lady would be seen in a lesser creation at her own wedding, and then there is time to hire the extra staff..." She nattered on, fully aware she sounded like an imbecile.

"No."

She came to an abrupt halt. "No?"

"Too long."

She eyed him doubtfully. "I suppose I could push to get things done faster, but I truly don't see how it could be less than nine months." Nine months was still enough time. She'd be better by then. Healed. The horrors of the past forgotten, just like her doctor, and her family, and herself, wanted.

"Nay, lass, I'm afraid not." He tucked her arm into his and began to lead her back to the common area.

Charity felt a great weight drop in her chest. Please, God, don't let him leave her. No man had ever swept her off her feet—literally—the way he had. She did want to marry him. She was just scared. She bowed her head.

He used two fingers to tilt her chin back up. "Do not look so sad, lass. You shall have a lovely wedding, if it is important to you."

She bit her lip, uncertain how far she should push. "Do you not agree, Lord Maxwell, that a lengthy engagement would only serve to increase the…ah, *anticipation*, for the activities to which kissing can lead?"

He gave a bark of laughter. "Lass, that level of anticipation may very well be the death of me."

Chapter 6:

In which Graeme discovers why difficult negotiations are sometimes aided by subversive plotting.

Graeme regarded his breakfast the following morning with a surliness the food had not earned. The townhome he'd rented for the Season had come with a small but perfectly adequate staff, including a cook.

His glance fell upon a copy of the latest gossip sheets left near his plate. He ignored it. Trivial people poking their noses into one another's business. He had problems enough without borrowing those of others.

His biggest problem came in the form of a stunning, sensual blonde. She'd become his obsession. The taste of her lips, the curve of her breast, the soft moan when he cupped it… Why on God's green earth did she want to *wait* to marry?

This was not something Graeme Ramsey Maxwell, Earl of Leventhal, Viscount of Kirkaldie, and one of London's best matches of the Season, had planned on. To be honest, he hadn't really given much thought to the *process* of getting married. He'd rather thought he would come to London, select an agreeable and attractive young lady, and that would be that.

He had failed to consider that he might select a young lady with ideas of her own. A glaring omission on his part. Stupid. If he wanted his marriage to work, he had to choose a woman spirited enough to thrive in the Highlands. Since women with spirit tended to also be women with ideas, he should have seen this—or something like it—coming. Besides, there was really no question. Once he'd met Charity Medford, no other woman would do.

No wonder his driver had remarked that acquiring a wife would take "somewhat longer than to acquire a horse."

He was fine with her having ideas. It was just this one *particular* idea, of waiting a year to be married, he could not abide.

His gaze landed once more on the newspaper. He might not find it interesting, but from the prominent placement his servants had given it, much of London clearly did. Perhaps it merited a moment of his attention after all.

"Marry him. Don't marry him. Marry him." Charity idly plucked the petals from a daisy she'd found growing in the tiny yard in back of the house, wondering what to do about her most prominent suitor. Or rather, *when* to do it.

She'd be a fool not to marry Lord Maxwell, for reasons more important than the one her mother had honed in on so quickly—namely, his title. Charity was not nearly as title obsessed as her mother, even if having a duke for a brother-in-law had saved them a time or two.

More interesting by far was the fact that Lord Maxwell had been attracted to her *before* he knew her name...before knowing she had a dowry befitting a duchess, or that she'd once been considered the catch of the Season...or even that her popularity was waning as she gained a reputation as one who would accept no offer and who perhaps acted recklessly at times. Graeme hadn't known any of that—meaning his attraction was real.

There was no judgment in the way he looked at her. After months of pretending to ignore the skeptical looks, the whispers passed behind the protective screen of ladies' fans, it was just so...so wonderful to have someone look at her and see none of that.

Even if it was nothing more than physical lust, it was lust for *her*. Best of all, a marriage to Lord Maxwell offered one thing she yearned for deeply, and which she could never have in London: freedom. Even if her fears about the return of the French spies would never entirely subside, at least she could be somewhere where every site, every street corner, did not remind her of the danger. Of her foolishness. She could have the freedom to be herself again, not someone whose life was defined by everyone else around her.

If only he loved her. He'd called her "my love," that once. But that was just an endearment. It wasn't the same as actually saying he loved her.

Then again, he'd promised her marriage.

She returned to her room, still at loose ends and bored with the garden, if it could even be called that. Penny stood near the wardrobe, sorting and folding Charity's winter garments for storage.

"If a man offers marriage, and calls one by endearing terms, would you say that constitutes a declaration of love?" Charity asked.

The maid paused and cocked her head. "I could not say, miss, but if a fine lord called me sweet things and offered his hand, I'd not waste time wonderin' what he meant," she answered practically.

Charity laughed. "Yes, you're right, I'm sure. My mother would agree, anyhow. 'Don't be such a silly twit,'" she imitated her mother's voice. "'Ladies of the *ton* marry for titles, or wealth. Both, if you're lucky. Romance is only for novels.'" But her sister had married for love—and Elizabeth, in Charity's opinion, was a far happier person than their mother.

"Oh, I don't know about all that, miss. I think Lord Maxwell is quite romantic. Why, he practically declared for you the very night you met."

Charity's heart warmed. "He did, didn't he?"

"Never you worry, miss. Every bride-to-be gets at least one case of the jitters." She returned to her folding.

Bride-to-be. Is that what she was? Lord Maxwell's bride-to-be? Charity stopped in front of the looking glass, pretending to experiment with a new style of braid, her head spinning. No formal engagement had been announced, but of course the whole household was abuzz with the news anyway, believing the matter all but settled. Only Charity knew better. She hadn't agreed to a shorter engagement, and, as yet, Lord Maxwell hadn't agreed to a longer one.

Graeme strode into White's that evening with a plan that didn't make him proud.

After all, he *had* come to London to find a wife, he reasoned. Charity Medford was available for the position. She was unmarried. She was willing. She was of good family. And there was no denying the frisson of attraction between them.

It was just her absurd insistence upon a lengthy engagement that had him flummoxed. Men were the ones who were supposed to be hesitant to settle down, who needed time to sow their oats.

Christ. That wasn't it, was it? She wanted more time to play before settling down? No, he knew the attraction between them was stronger than that. There was something else…he just couldn't put his finger on it.

"Leventhal, come join us."

He recognized several men at the card table and greeted them in turn, but politely declined to join them.

So what if Charity was a bit wild? She would settle into a more wifely role once she got used to the idea—he hoped.

He did *not* suppose she would demonstrate great enthusiasm at moving to his remote home in the highlands. Then again, she might. He'd seen the tension between her and her family. If it were him, he'd have leapt at an excuse to move far, far away from a mother like that.

Regardless, he would have to bring Charity to Scotland. Leventhal House was his home, his kingdom, where the local men, women, and children respected and relied on him. Where, without a partner, he was too often alone.

Graeme shoved that thought away. They could work out the details of how, and where, they would live later. First, he had to marry her.

Where *was* Ewan MacPherson? Surely this was not the one night his friend would choose to finally abandon his favorite haunt. To his knowledge, Ewan had spent virtually every night here since the night he'd sworn off matters of the heart. Somehow he seemed to find more steadfast companionship in a deck of cards than he had with the last of his ladyloves. Graeme was counting on him being here.

Finally, he spotted his friend among a group of men crowded around a gaming table.

"MacPherson. Thank God you're here."

Ewan looked around. "Where else would I be?"

Ignoring the question, Graeme announced, "I need your help."

"You need *my* help? With what?"

"Come have a drink." Ewan already held a drink, but both men recognized the invitation as code for "I don't want anyone else to hear this."

His friend stepped reluctantly away from the dice game he'd been observing. A rousing cheer went up from the table just seconds later, and he looked back longingly.

"They'll be playing the next night. And the next."

"True." Ewan shrugged, settling into a seat at the corner table Graeme had selected. "What has the great and mighty Lord Maxwell so flummoxed as to seek out my help?"

"A certain Miss Medford."

Ewan slapped his knee, laughing. "Oh, now this begins to make sense. I warned you, did I not?"

"I prefer to forget that."

Ewan poured himself some brandy from the bottle the waiter discreetly left at the table. "But, Leventhal, she seemed quite taken with you the other evening at Vauxhall."

"She was."

"Did you argue with her since then?"

"No."

"Never tell me she turned you down flat."

"No, not that either."

"Then what is the problem?"

"The problem, MacPherson, is that she thinks it perfectly reasonable for our engagement to last a full year."

Ewan choked on his brandy. "You, I suppose, do not."

"Nay. I do not." He lowered his voice. "So that is where

you come in. I need you to write an anonymous letter to the *Tattler*, expressing concern over what you saw at Vauxhall the other night."

"I saw nothing at Vauxhall. Nothing of concern, anyway."

"Then would you like me to explain what you *could* have seen, had you happened upon the same path where I strolled with Miss Medford? Shall I tell you how soft her lips are, and how they simply tempt a man to lose control?"

Ewan raised a hand, shaking with mirth. "Nay. Please, desist. I am quite certain I have the gist of it."

"I am certain you do. And you, as an overbearing, gossipy matriarch, simply *must* relay your concern for London's youth, lest other young ladies get it into their heads that such appalling behavior is to be tolerated."

"I as a *what?*"

"I think it would sound better coming from a woman, don't you?"

Ewan just gaped at him.

"After all, a man would simply congratulate me for stealing a kiss so thoroughly and move on."

"She's going to kill you."

"Nay. Because *I* am not the overbearing, gossipy matriarch who is going to write the letter." He lifted his glass to Ewan. He wasn't proud of the plan, but he *was* confident it would work. "I am the one who is going to come to her rescue."

Charity awoke earlier than usual on Monday morning. Or maybe "awoke" wasn't an accurate description, since she wasn't certain she'd actually slept.

Thoughts of Graeme had kept her awake. Good thoughts, of how he was determined and gallant, and *very* good thoughts, that made her nipples tighten and ache to be pressed against his hard chest, and scary thoughts, about their engagement and how long it would last and how her life would change very, very soon.

Charity went straight to the breakfast room, where that day's copy of the *Tattler* waited for her mother's reading pleasure. Picking up a scone from the sideboard, Charity swiped the gossip rag and scanned it. Today might be the day her engagement was announced. They hadn't come to an agreement on a wedding date, yet, but she had essentially agreed to marry him. The way they'd left things at Vauxhall, she hadn't been confident they'd come to any understanding. But then Elizabeth had sent her a note, stating that her husband had received a calling card from Lord Maxwell the day after the Vauxhall outing, requesting a formal audient. The Scotsman's insistence on that matter of propriety made her smile, especially as propriety hadn't kept him from kissing her with more seductive power than London's most notorious rakehells. She already knew the duke would approve, which was why she was eager to see the paper today.

Her smile fell away, though, as she discovered that, while the paper did indeed contain mention of her, the mention came not in the form of an engagement announcement, but in a letter to the editor:

Dear Readers,

It is incumbent upon me, I feel, to warn the mothers of London, that they may keep their daughters safe from impropriety. This author has, like many others, often taken part in the festivities at Vauxhall Pleasure Gardens. Just two nights ago I attended a wonderful performance. But, oh! Dear readers, the pleasure of those gardens was thereafter tarnished forever to me. Whilst walking the paths, my sister and I lost our direction, straying into the unlit portion of the gardens. Dear readers, these gardens are not, as I had thought, off limits when unlit. Or, if they are, they have gone too long without policing. The improprieties I witnessed there! My heart nearly failed me. A certain Miss M was spotted in the dark, with no escort aside from a certain Scottish earl—though indeed, this author cannot be entirely certain of their identity, given that their faces were joined so closely only their hair could be seen. Such lack of comportment must be routed from our youth, lest we mothers find ourselves with daughters rendered unfit for the station to which we strive to raise them. Mothers, protect your daughters!

With sincerest concerns,

Mrs. E

"No. No, no, no." Charity dropped her head into her hands, the scone rolling unheeded toward the edge of the table. She stayed that way a long time.

Why, oh why did she never seem to get away with *anything* anymore? It was only a kiss.

That was no mere kiss, her mind argued. "Not helping," she muttered to herself.

The creak of a door and footsteps alerted her that her mother was awake. Hurriedly she stood. She grabbed the *Tattler*. On second thought, she set it back in place. Everyone would know soon enough. Better to let her read it here.

Still, Charity was smart enough not to stick around for the carnage. She retreated to the safety of her room.

She expected she'd have, at best, twenty minutes or so to gather herself before her mother stormed in, face white with rage.

Twenty minutes passed, and then another twenty. And another.

The curiosity was killing her. Charity crept back into the

corridor, feeling sheepish for sneaking in her own home, but too nervous to stop. She snuck down the stairs and around corners until she had a line of sight into the breakfast room. The remnants of Lady Medford's breakfast served as evidence she'd eaten, but the lady herself was nowhere to be seen. The gossip rag lay open to the page of doom. She'd definitely read it, then.

She was ruined. Coming so close on the heels of her last scandal, there would be no escaping the backlash of this one.

Worse, there would be no engagement announcement. Lord Maxwell was sure to hear the flood of rumors that would resurface with the publication of this letter. He could do so much better than someone like her.

The duke might pressure him to go forward with the engagement. After all, he'd been mentioned in the letter too. But he was a man. A noble one, at that. Different standards applied.

She'd rather be put on the shelf than know her husband had been forced to marry her. Somehow, she knew this was not a storm that would blow over. This was the death knell for her chances in the marriage mart.

Chapter 7:

In which Charity learns why Scotsmen are so often considered stubborn.

For once, both Charity's mother and sister agreed with her. She didn't see them until late afternoon, and the house was eerily absent of other callers. If she'd lived five hundred years ago, she'd have thought someone had put the mark of the black plague on their door.

Only when Elizabeth arrived with her baby in tow did their mother show her face. Charity gave her nephew an extra-long hug, inhaling his sweet, innocent scent. What she wouldn't give to go back to her worry-free childhood days.

No one bothered trying to pretend the matter away.

Elizabeth did at least try to convince her the engagement could still happen. "He may not even see this letter. How many men actually read the *Tattler*?"

Charity shook her head. "It won't matter. He was mentioned as well. Certainly *someone* will think to tell him."

"You two are all but engaged already. Perhaps, if the duke

talked to him, they could agree to put out the word that the engagement became official on Thursday and that…kiss…was celebratory. It was just a kiss, right?"

Charity cringed. "Yes. Maybe more than one. But nothing more than that."

Lady Medford, for once, kept her mouth shut. In fact, she had it shut so hard her lips were turning white and Charity was afraid her face might crack.

"Even so," her sister said. "I daresay duels have been called over accusations less damning than what that letter in the *Tattler* contained. If you're telling me the letter was true, I think Alex *should* have words with your Lord Maxwell."

"No duels. Don't even think of it. Elizabeth, please, please, tell the duke not to put any undue pressure on Lord Maxwell." She knew her sister too well. If there was a way to fix things, she would try to do it.

"Why ever not?"

She lowered her eyes. "I just…I don't want him to someday look back on this past week and think it was one giant mistake that ended in a forced marriage. And then I'll be stuck somewhere in Scotland with a husband who resents me."

"Oh." She thought about that. "I wish I could say you're being silly, but you have a point."

"A good point," Lady Medford cracked her lips long enough to add.

Charity blinked. She'd been certain her mother would absolutely insist on pressing for the engagement. Instead, she was once more standing by her daughter's side. After years of conflict, Charity didn't know what to make of that. "Lovely. We are all in agreement."

"Sarcasm does not become you," her sister chided gently.

Charity sighed. "Very little does these days."

Little Noah, lying on a small quilt near the sofa, stretched up his arms and cooed. Before Elizabeth could reach for him, Lady Medford scooped him up, not even cringing when he took the fingers that had been in his mouth and patted her cheek. Having a grandson who was heir to a dukedom had gone a long way toward mellowing out persnickety Priscilla Medford. "I had hoped to see both my daughters make good matches," she said finally. "But I have begun to think, Charity, that your penchant for trouble would make you a difficult wife."

She almost laughed. It probably would.

"I also know the pain of feeling trapped. You are too young for me to wish that upon you. But if Lord Maxwell were to come to you of his own accord…"

"He won't." Tears welled, threatening to spill over her lashes. The last thing she'd expected was for her mother to actually be *nice* to her. "Why should he? Nearly every encounter we've had so far has resulted in awkward moments and embarrassment for him."

"Perhaps it is time to give some serious thought to a life in the country. You would not be turned away at any of our estates," Elizabeth offered.

"Maybe," she managed past the lump in her throat.

"Cousin Lily did finally leave Montgrave around Christmas time, but I'm sure if I wrote to her, she would return in a heartbeat. You'd have company."

"Cousin Lily who filled the liquor bottles with water after consuming their contents in secret?"

"Charity! You weren't supposed to repeat that."

She gave a horrified laugh. This was what it had come to. Crazed Charity and tipsy Cousin Lily, rusticating the years away as guests of the benevolent duke? "I will think about it," she promised. Maybe when her emotions settled down, the idea would hold more appeal. "Right now, though, I just want to go lie down." She felt like she could sleep for a year.

In fact, she did sleep for much of the next few days, which was a strange blessing indeed. Somehow, being a confirmed pariah lifted the strain of being a near-pariah. She had nothing to worry about, because no one had any expectations for her to live up to at all. As long as she stayed tucked away in her room, and the duke's men maintained the guard, she was safe.

The deep loss that left her chest hollow and aching was another matter. The night of the masquerade, Lord Maxwell had swept into her life, swept her into his arms, and nothing had been the same since. She'd been almost in love with him. Maybe more than almost. But whether he'd ever had that audience with the duke, or what the outcome had been, she didn't know. She'd heard nothing from him personally since the night at Vauxhall. Unless she missed her guess, he'd finally learned the truth about her.

By the following Friday, Charity had accepted her fate. She spent the entire day and well into the evening in her morning dress, reading books and beginning to wonder, *really* wonder, what she would do with a life in the countryside. She couldn't imagine just mouldering away as a permanent guest in one of her sister and brother-in-law's houses. Perhaps she could go to America and become a teacher. One of her cousins had done so, some years ago. She should write her a letter. See how the adventure had come out.

A tap on her door signaled the entrance of the butler. "Miss Medford, you have a caller."

"You must be mistaken."

"No, miss. Lord Maxwell is here."

Charity popped to attention, going from listless to heart-thudding anticipation in the span of a second. *Lord Maxwell.* What did he want?

"He says you have an engagement at the theater." His carefully-schooled expression gave no hint that he'd noticed her attire was anything but appropriate.

"I do? Oh!" She *had* agreed to attend the theater tonight, but that had been ages ago. Another lifetime. She'd been certain, with all that had happened, the plans had been canceled. "Tell him I am running just the tiniest bit late, and will be down shortly."

"Yes, miss." He bowed and left.

"Penny! Help!"

The maid rushed in, and Charity stared worriedly into the looking glass. At least she hadn't been crying in the past hour. Her face was pale, but not blotchy. "I have to get dressed."

"Your blue silk is pressed. Will that do, miss?"

"Perfectly." She wasn't even certain what Graeme would say. Perhaps he just wanted to formally end things. She might not be leaving the house. But she could hardly see him *en dishabille.* Faster than they'd ever managed before, Penny got Charity dressed with her hair pinned up. The hurry brought a flush back to her cheeks, at least enough to confirm her standing among the living. Pearl earbobs, a present from Elizabeth on her last birthday, completed the look.

Charity flew down the stairs and stopped dead at the entrance to the salon.

Lord Maxwell stood in full theater-going attire. He wore a black jacket and trousers with a stark white shirt and cravat, his form filling them so perfectly, so *thoroughly* that her mouth went dry.

"Miss Medford, you are a vision."

Was it possible? Had he somehow spent the last week

hidden in a cellar and not heard that his almost-fiancé was unfit for polite company?

She lifted her chin ever so slightly. Meeting his gaze, she saw the knowledge there. No, Lord Maxwell hadn't been hidden in a cellar, under a rock, or anywhere else news didn't travel. He was just too honorable to ignore a prior commitment. Still, he'd kissed her just as thoroughly as she'd kissed back and they both knew it. But she could be honorable too. There was no sense in ruining a second life. She would go down with whatever dignity she had left.

"Lord Maxwell, I fear there has been a mistake."

Graeme hated his role in causing the paleness in her face. It had been so hard to stay away this week, when he wanted to spend every waking moment wooing her. Now she stood like a vision, pale but determined. Beautiful. Not to mention stubborn.

So stubborn that her benefactor, the Duke of Beaufort, had given his approval of Graeme's request, then told him he'd have to work out the details with Charity herself. Knowing where she stood on that matter, he'd tried to up the ante by publicizing their courtship.

His ploy had hurt her. But if the second part—the part he'd set into motion tonight—worked as planned, he would make it up to her in a thousand ways. He could spend the rest of their lives making it up to her, and would do so gladly.

He cleared his throat. "Nay, no mistake. We made plans to attend the theater, did we not?"

"I thought—" she started, then stopped. "You should not be seen with me."

He'd been dumbfounded when, during his next audience with the duke, Beaufort informed him that, *Tattler* or no *Tattler*, he would not insist on an immediate marriage. "*I* would, *actually,"* the duke had confided, *"if I thought there the slightest chance that Charity could be dragged to the altar and made to comply. Unfortunately, though her virtues are many, compliance is not among them."* A diplomatic way of saying that in spite of any fondness he might hold for his sister-in-law, he'd written her off.

"I have every intention of being seen with you."

She looked tempted. And tempting. Still, she protested. "You should save yourself while you still can."

He stepped closer, holding back a smile. "You told me that once before. Lass, it is too late. Even then, I was already lost."

She took a shivery breath.

He closed the distance between them, his hand coming up to caress the bare length of arm between the tiny sleeves of her gown and the top of her gloves.

"Charity." Her eyes widenened at his use of her given name. "I can offer what you seek."

"You have no idea what I seek." It was hardly more than a whisper.

Something solid to hold onto. A modicum of wisdom made him keep that thought to himself.

A distinctly female shriek echoed from somewhere above, followed by a voice whose words were indistinguishable, but whose tone was clearly that of a mistress berating her maid. In answer to Charity, he suggested "Peace?"

A reluctant giggle escaped her. But when she said, "Peace, indeed," he caught a wistful tone to her words.

"And protection," he offered, struck by the fierceness of his desire to shield her from hurt.

Charity, quick to recover, tossed her head. "What makes you think I want your protection?"

He laughed. "Nothing in all this world has led me to believe you want my—or anyone else's—protection." A husky note entered his tone. "But, lass, I'm going to give it to you anyway."

She said nothing, just stared at him with those huge blue eyes that were somehow both soft and wary. Finally she tipped her head in acknowledgment. "How very chivalrous of you, Lord Maxwell. Allow me to collect my wrapper, and I shall be down directly." She turned to go, but he heard the last words under her breath. "If only it were that easy."

He clasped his hands behind his back and took long breaths, trying to quiet the thumping of his heart. So far, so good. He'd feared, especially given the wait when he first arrived, that she would refuse to leave the house entirely.

He heard female voices above, and the berating voice of moments ago let out a happy squeal. Lady Medford approved, then. He wondered if she'd feel the same way tomorrow.

Charity returned a few minutes later, a light wrap covering her gown, a confection of blue silk that brought out the fathomless blue of her eyes. He saw dainty slippers poking out from beneath her gown. Perfect attire for a night at the theater. Not at all suitable, though, for what they were actually going to do.

"Miss Medford, I fear the evening has turned chilly. Will you be warm enough?"

She glanced at her attire. "I shall manage. The theater is often quite warm."

Insisting she bring warmer clothing would only draw suspicion, so he let it go. "Shall we be on our way, then?" He took her arm, escorting her from the house and down the short walk to his waiting coach. A footman assisted her up, and he followed quickly after.

She turned to him in surprise. "I thought you said your cousins would be joining us?"

"Yes. About that."

This was it. The telling moment. Suddenly he realized he should have practiced a speech. They were still too close to her home. He needed to buy time.

"I do hope you'll forgive the impropriety, but we travel alone tonight."

She was silent for a moment. "I have been alone in a coach with you once before." He could hear a note of amusement creep into her voice. "I had not thought to make a habit of it."

He reached for her. "'Twould seem to me a fine habit to make."

Her face fell. "Lord Maxwell, I understand that the way we met might have conveyed the wrong impression about the type of behavior I typically engage in. And whatever rumors are being bandied about…"

"Nay. It is I who have conveyed the wrong impression. What I meant was, it won't matter once we're married." He drew his fingers along her hair, her chin, guiding her lips to his. Her body belied her words, for she did not pull away. He heard a soft sigh as he settled her more comfortably against him.

"But we are not married," she murmured against his lips. "And my reputation is already in tatters."

He kissed her once, then again, unable to resist. "A problem for which, fortunately, I know the remedy."

She gave a muffled laugh, and the remainder of her protest was swallowed by his kiss. He took her mouth fully, shaping her lips with his, delving inside to taste her. Her sharp intake of breath fueled his desire, as did the way she grasped him as though she were drowning and he the only rock amidst the swirling water. His tongue tangled with hers as he stroked her back, feeling the soft curve of her hip.

He pulled back just enough for air. God. Who was this

minx? A few kisses and he was practically panting, imagining her naked and writhing beneath him.

"We can't," she murmured, though her fingers running through his hair, clutching him to her, said they most certainly *could.*

"Aye, we can."

"We haven't time. We must be nearly to the theater by now."

He followed the instructions of her fingers, rather than her words, and bent his head to hers once more.

Minutes later, the carriage hit a bump—just enough to jostle them apart. Just enough for Charity to regain her senses. She was breathing hard. So was he. He would have reached for her again, but she pressed her face to the small window. "Shouldn't we have arrived by now?"

He could avoid the truth no longer. "About that," he said.

She turned her face back to him, and in the dim light he could see her eyes widen.

He took her hand. "Your sister told me you had a flair for drama. This should be right up your alley."

Chapter 8:

Sometimes, reckless seduction achieves what proper "negotiations" cannot.

"What? What should be up my alley?" Charity demanded. "Where are we going?"

"Gretna Green," he informed her with more confidence than he actually felt. "We're getting married."

"We're doing what?" she screeched. "No! We most certainly are *not.*"

"We most certainly are," he countered.

"This is madness."

"I prefer to think of it as daring. And you, Miss Medford, are known to be daring, are you not?"

"But—"

"Our courtship is public knowledge. More public, as you yourself admitted, than is healthy for a maiden's reputation. Once we are married, no one will question how the marriage came about. Or what we were doing alone together in a carriage. Or anything else they might think we have done."

"Oh, yes they will." How could this be happening? Her situation had gone from dire to...to...

"Not for long. Some other scandal will come along to distract the masses. Just think of the stories you can someday tell our grandchildren."

"Grandchildren?" she squeaked. She sucked in a breath and fought the urge to tug at her hair. What he said was true—the first part, at least. A rushed marriage invited speculation, but rarely resulted in prolonged censure.

But that didn't mean she was ready for it. "This is not a traveling carriage," she pointed out.

He laughed. "And here I thought the notion of marriage was what you objected to. Never fear, beautiful one. My traveling coach is being readied. 'Twill be no more effort than stepping from one to the other, and we will be on our way."

"I have nothing with me. No trunks, no clothing..."

His smile grew. "Another problem that can be easily rectified. We will send for your things to follow us. Ach. Look. Here we are."

Sure enough, the carriage stopped along the drive to a well-kept townhouse. A footman hurried to open the door. He assisted Charity down, with Graeme following scant inches behind her.

"As I said, a quick transfer of vehicles, and we shall be on our way. Look, your carriage awaits."

Just ahead on the drive, a lacquered black traveling coach and team of six stood, the horses huffing and shifting their hooves as though eager to be off.

Charity couldn't breathe. Graeme held her hand, tugging her along so that she nearly tripped in the fluster of consternation...but not holding her so tight that she couldn't have wrenched her arm free if she'd wanted to.

Did she want to? She couldn't even think. This past week had thrown her from dizzying heights, down to the depths of despair, and back up again. She'd thought her engagement over before it was ever officially announced. When he'd returned tonight, she'd been afraid to hope. Part of her still feared he'd come only because he was a man of his word. She hadn't realized he was serious. No. That wasn't it. She'd known he was serious about marriage. Just not that he meant to marry *now*.

Before she knew it, Graeme himself was helping her into the traveling coach. She couldn't say he tossed her in, exactly, but it was hardly her most graceful entrance.

She landed with an *oomph*. Graeme landed across from her, and the coach took off at a pace that was surely unsafe on London's busy streets.

This was not her first experience with being kidnapped. Though, if she came willingly, Charity supposed it couldn't quite be called kidnapping. This time, she knew one thing for certain, deep in her gut: Graeme had no intention of hurting her. From the very first night they'd met, he'd had the opportunity to take advantage. Yet he'd done nothing but protect her, even defend her. He admired and believed in her when the family and friends she'd grown up with did not. Reminding herself of that, she took a few slow breaths and tried to quell the nerves that raced through her.

"I left instructions with my secretary," Lord Maxwell informed her. "If I have not returned by tomorrow at noon, he is to deliver a pre-written note to your family, informing them of my—or rather, of *our*—intentions."

She considered this. "You do not wish them to fear for my safety."

"Precisely."

"Nor do you wish them to catch up to us."

"Smart lass."

She couldn't help but laugh. "I suppose it is as gentlemanly a gesture as one can make, given the circumstances."

"I try."

She could only imagine the pandemonium in her mother's house when *that* letter was delivered. She was almost sorry to miss it.

Charity had never in her life been able to say "no" to an adventure. She was certainly attracted to Lord Maxwell. Very much so. In fact, it was her inability to resist him that had landed her here in the first place. His solid strength, coupled with that smoldering gaze she often found focused on her, seemed to enthrall her. She longed to touch him, to sink gratefully into all he offered until she was lost. She supposed, all things considered, insisting on immediate marriage was the only gentlemanly thing he could do.

If it weren't for her fears of marriage in general, of revealing her troubles when one of the uncontrollable nightmares came on, she'd have no qualms about marrying Graeme Ramsey Maxwell.

As if he could read her thoughts, he said, "All will be well."

"But..." Her ability to reason was shrinking in the face of his confidence. Finally she could come up with only one word. "Marriage!"

"Aye, marriage." His smile fell away as he searched her face. "Of course, I could never force you to speak the vows. I see I have taken you by surprise. You are nervous. Understandable. But think on it, love. If, by the time we reach Gretna Green, you decide you truly are against this marriage, I will relinquish my claim."

"By the time we reach Gretna Green," she muttered, "it

will not matter." The trip to the little town just over the Scottish border would take three days, even traveling fast. By then, she'd have spent so long in the sole company of Lord Maxwell, with no chaperone, relative, or even a maid present, any remaining shreds of her reputation would be destroyed. If she refused to marry him at that point, even her own family would likely cast her out.

He peered at her, then nodded. "You have a point. It is a risk I am willing to take." He sat back, looking so smug she had to stifle the urge to wipe the look off his face with the back of her hand.

"You're actually enjoying this," she accused.

"What's not to enjoy?"

"You're kidnapping me!"

He cocked his head. "Now, now, lass. No need for such dramatics. Do you wish me to stop the carriage?"

That silenced her. If she said yes, she had no doubt he would, in fact, stop. He would let her go. She *trusted* him.

It was a tough realization to swallow. It meant she had a role in whatever actions they took next. If she said nothing, if she continued on with this hare-brained scheme of his, she would have to own that choice.

One word from her, and he would stop the carriage. She knew it. But what would she go back to?

She would return to a life where she was nothing but a burden to her family. Confined by their protection, yet fearful because no amount of protection could guarantee her former captors would not someday find her. Alex's men had found no trace of them. Most likely they were in countries far away, living new lives. They probably never thought of her. They might not even know she'd lived.

What if all her fears were for no reason? She could be living in a trap of her own making. If she went home now, she would almost certainly end up a spinster. Her own actions had ensured that. Lonely, with nothing but her fears—and tipsy Cousin Lily—for company. Compared to all that Graeme offered, there really was no choice.

She scuffed the toe of her slipper on the floor of the carriage.

"Charity?"

She didn't respond. Couldn't. She felt two strong fingers beneath her chin, the touch both easy and firm, commanding her to look at him.

"Do you wish me to stop the carriage?"

"No."

It was barely a whisper. She couldn't hear it herself over the clattering wheels of the coach, but the movement of her lips was enough. He dropped his fingers and took her hand in his, instead.

"Try not to worry, lass. These things have a way of working out."

"They do? How would you know? If you had done this before, you would already have a wife, and therefore have no need of hauling *me* off to Gretna Green."

He chuckled. "I assure you, I have never 'hauled' any woman to Gretna Green—nor entered vows of marriage in any other venue—before. I have never even desired to do so. You are the only woman who has ever driven me to such lengths."

She smiled weakly. "I suppose that is a compliment."

"Of the very best sort."

She had no response to that, so they rode in silence for a while.

Charity assumed she would spend this journey on the edge

of her seat, her knuckles white from gripping the edge, her head sore from her nervous habit of tugging at her hair. Instead, she fell asleep.

Outside of London, the coach slowed to a pace that allowed the driver to navigate around the inevitable ruts and pits left by spring rains. Graeme's driver was skilled, and the gentle rocking of the carriage lulled her like a babe. Charity stared out the small window as the lights they passed grew fewer and further between. Eventually, she felt her head begin to nod.

Graeme noticed too, shifting quickly to sit beside her. He eased her head onto his lap. She was too overwhelmed to protest. Besides, it felt nice, she thought sleepily. He smelled good. And he was stroking her hair, making her want to stretch and purr, like a cat. She couldn't remember why she was supposed to be mad at him. Oh…yes. He was abducting her. But he was going to marry her. And she wanted him to. That made it all right.

Charity shook awake a short time later, as the country road grew bumpier, the ruts unavoidable. Still, she awoke cradled in Graeme's arms, his body shielding hers from the bumps as best he could. She opened her eyes slowly and found him gazing down at her.

"Why me?" She spoke the first words that popped into her head.

"Why what, lass?" His voice sounded rough, as though he'd been asleep too.

"You are an earl. You have your choice of women. Why me?"

"Fishing for compliments, are we?" he teased.

She pulled back in mock outrage, but doing so deprived her of the delicious heat of his body. She snuggled back closer.

"How is it," she asked, "that an absurd solution such as running off to Gretna Green, and the Scottish wilderness after that, seems entirely reasonable when proposed by you?"

He chuckled. "Three reasons. One, I am a Scot. Runaway marriages are practically a time-honored tradition for my people. I am only doing what any respectable Scotsman would do. Two. You, my sweet, have a penchant for adventure, and I dare not guess how exotic a suggestion would have to be before you would truly deem it absurd. And, three," he paused, cupping the side of her face and gazing intently at her. "Sometimes, you just know."

"Mmm."

He tipped her chin up, brushing her lips with his. "And then, there's the kissing…"

"Oh, yes, the kissing," she murmured against his mouth. He tugged at her bottom lip playfully, then traced the edge with his tongue until she reciprocated. At her capitulation, he plundered her mouth, coaxing and stroking as heat pooled in her center and moved lower, down to her woman's core, suddenly aware and aching.

Too soon, he tore his mouth from hers, shifting focus as he trailed kisses along her jaw, until he reached her earlobe and gently nipped it with his teeth. His tongue traced the delicate line of her ear, until he found the spot just behind her earlobe. Desire shot through her as he lingered there. Her head dropped back, giving him greater access.

He cradled the back of her neck in one hand, as his other came up to cup her breast.

She moaned. Too much. Not enough. Too much fabric in the way. She wanted that large, rough hand touching her where she needed it most. She didn't dare say anything, though. Ladies didn't think such things.

Thankfully, she didn't need to say anything. He was of the same mind. His nimble fingers worked the laces and hooks that held her bodice in place, until he'd loosened them enough to tug it down, freeing her breasts to his attentions.

"So beautiful," he murmured.

Charity registered, in some distant corner of her mind, that this was not how ladies were supposed to behave. Especially not *before* they were married. But, after all, they were in a carriage rushing pell-mell toward Gretna Green, which, when one thought about it, only one step away from actually *being* married. And Charity was not one to quibble over trivialities.

Especially not now, when Graeme's large thumb scraped over her nipple, his palm cupping and pushing her breast up to meet his mouth.

Charity closed her eyes and stopped thinking. Oh, God. He drew her nipple into his mouth and sucked. Desire arced through her, and she grew moist. She shifted, needing more, running her hands restlessly over him.

She found his erection, and at his sharp gasp, she knew. She ran her palm over him, marveling at his hardness. Wanting to see, to touch. She stroked him and watched his eyes grow dark.

He took her other nipple in his mouth as she stroked him, his other hand playing with the one he'd lavished first. Their movements became frantic. She couldn't tell his moan from hers.

Finally he moved her hand. "You have to stop that, or I will lose control."

"Lose it, then," she invited him, too caught up in the sensations he made her feel to be shocked at her own audacity. "Only, don't stop."

He smiled. "I never said I was going to stop. Only that we

had to stop *that.*"

She paused, curiosity getting the better of her. "You don't want me to touch you?"

"Oh, I do," he assured her. "But if you keep touching me now, we will be celebrating the wedding night before the wedding."

Heat filled her cheeks. But then he assured her, "Don't worry, sweetest. There are other ways to give and take pleasure."

He dropped to his knees on the floor of the carriage, his hands finding the hem of her gown and sliding beneath it. He took her ankle in one hand, smoothing over her calf, pushing up her gown, exposing her undergarments—what little of them she wore. The theater gown was cut in the daring French style so favored among the London set this Season. Beneath the supple fabric, Charity had worn only a short corset to lift her bosom, and the thinnest of her muslin petticoats as a concession to propriety, or the possibility of an evening chill.

If Graeme continued touching her…

She twisted away in sudden panic.

He looked up. "Too much?"

She thought about that. He kept his hand still on her calf, awaiting her answer. The heat in his gaze reignited her own desire. "No. Not enough."

"Ach, lass. You definitely must marry me." He returned his focus, his hands moving higher, massaging her thighs.

"We shall have to send to London for the remainder of your clothing," he murmured. "I find I quite like these new styles. They have not made it to the highlands just yet."

"No, I imagine not," Charity breathed, just before his fingers reached the apex of her thighs, and her ability to hold up her end of any conversation evaporated.

His fingers skimmed the folds of skin, teasing. He brought his lips to the inside of her knee and kissed her there. He trailed kisses higher, and again higher, until his lips reached the same folds his fingers caressed and took their place.

"My lord?"

"Trust me."

She did. Oh, she trusted him. Even when he was touching her in ways she'd never imagined. And when he began to lick, long, slow strokes in her most intimate place, she was lost. Her eyes closed and her head fell back. He traced her shape, then settled in, licking and massaging, over and over until her body felt like it had melted, her limbs all turned to liquid, all but the singular sensation of his tongue at her cleft. The sensation built, the ache and need spiraling, until she was twisting on the carriage bench, grasping his shoulders. More. More. If only—

Waves of pleasure rocketed through her, again and again, until she shuddered and lay still. Limp. And utterly content.

Charity's eyes flickered open. Graeme raised his head. He looked quite...pleased.

Graeme stayed on his knees, heart pounding. He wasn't certain he could move if he tried. His need to make love to her was so intense it crippled him. He bowed his head, willing his raging erection down. He met with no success.

She was so damned sweet. So damned passionate. He knew from the way she'd hesitated that she'd never had a man taste her before, but the abandon with which she'd given herself over to him once she'd realized...God. He'd never get tired of her passionate abandon.

He'd gladly bring her to pleasure a thousand times before finding his own, if it meant hearing that sweet cry of ecstasy, watching her beautiful skin flush from head to toe.

But his young English beauty was not finished. She pushed herself up on her elbows until her eyes were level with his. "Your turn," she said.

For a second he forgot to breathe. Then the blood rushed from his head and centered at his groin. His already-hard cock pulsed with the surge of fresh arousal, straining against his breeches.

"Tell me what to do," she whispered.

"What to…" he repeated stupidly, the fog of need so thick his brain struggled to form a sentence.

"How to make you feel like…that," she clarified, an impish twinkle in here eye replacing the languid, satiated glaze of moments before.

Sweet Jesus. She was asking him to tell her how to make him come. "Do whatever pleases you," he rasped. "As a general rule, if you liked a particular touch, I will, too."

Her tongue darted between her lips, moistening them, and he watched her gaze drop to the bulge in his trousers.

Graeme hardly dared to breathe. He shifted himself back up onto the bench beside her.

"Earlier, you seemed to like this." She reached for him. Stroked him. A shudder ran through him.

Her fingers lingered at the laces holding his breeches fastened. "But, if what you say is true, then I think you will like it better if this clothing is not in the way."

"Aye," he agreed hoarsely.

She unfastened the breeches slowly. He couldn't tell whether her fingers were fumbling or if she was simply drawing out the act. Either way the torture was exquisite.

He shifted his hips, making it easier for her to tug his shirt up and away from—

Ach. Her small fingers closed around the length of him. He pried his eyes open and found her studying his member with wide eyes.

Tentatively she moved her hand, and pleasure shot through him. "Good?" she asked softly.

He nodded. He couldn't speak. She rubbed him again, pushing the fabric of his breeches further down to explore him fully. Her other hand stroked his inner thigh and cupped his balls.

She looked at him questioningly, then slid to her knees on the floor of the carriage, where he had been moments ago. She bent her head.

He nearly came undone. Maddeningly, she had taken his words to heart. *If you liked it, I will too.* She kissed the inside of his knee, her palms braced on either side of him for balance. His cock ached with the loss of touch, begged him to bury himself deep inside her. But he knew the path she was following. The same he'd done to her. Which meant that in mere moments…

Her lips touched the inside of his thigh. Then her tongue. The sensation was foreign. Exotic. He never wanted her to stop, and yet if she didn't touch him again soon, he might very well go mad.

She did touch him. Her lips brushed the head of his cock tentatively. He groaned, his eyes drifting closed again. Her tongue traced the length of him.

She paused. He was prepared for her to stop. Amazed she'd done this much. Well-bred young ladies, he'd been told, did not do such things. Naturally she might find it…disturbing.

He steeled himself against the knowledge he was likely to spend the next hour with a painful erection.

Then her mouth closed around him. He heard his own cry

of pleasure. She gave a low hum of satisfaction in return, and the vibration against his cock was too much. His body clamored for release.

She flicked her tongue against the sensitive head and sucked, the way he'd drawn her clit into his mouth just before she came. The memory of her taste as she came, shattering against his mouth, combined with the hot wet sensation of her mouth on him, pushed him over the edge.

With sheer will he pulled from her mouth, just as he came, his seed spilling out in a hot rush, his body racked with a tidal wave of pleasure. His head fell forward and he rested it on hers.

When he could move again, he drew her up, pulling her into his arms and onto his lap. "Charity, my love." He tucked her head under his chin and stroked the soft skin of her arms. Would she regret what she'd just done? God, he hoped not.

"Did you...that is, did I make you feel the same as what you did to me? Should I have gone about it differently?" She sounded uncertain, but hopeful.

"Love, ye made me feel everything you felt and more. You are more than a man could dream of."

She turned her head into his right arm and he could feel her smile. "I think you flatter me."

"Not a whit. How did I get so lucky? To think, I almost didn't attend Lord Madrigal's costume ball."

She gave a muffled laugh. "I was not exactly supposed to be there, either, if you recall. So it was really I who am the lucky one, for you were the one good thing that came of my rash decision."

He hugged her tighter. "Then 'twas fate."

"You believe in fate?"

"I do. Don't you?"

She absentmindedly tugged at a lock of golden hair. "I don't know."

He bent his head to whisper in her ear. "Wait until the wedding. Wait until I can take you to bed and make love to you, join our bodies as one, the way a man was meant to love a woman. I daresay I can convince you to believe in fate."

Chapter 9:

In which Charity dares, as all brides should, to hope.

Three and a half days later, Charity was not looking her best. They'd stopped occasionally to change horses, to eat, and to stretch their legs, but that was it. They'd passed long hours kissing until her lips were swollen, her breasts aching, her body straining for more. He'd pushed her over the brink of pleasure more than once, and yet she'd wanted more. Wanted *him*.

But he wouldn't make love to her. Yet. "When ye marry me, I will take you to bed and make love to you," he'd promised. "And I will do it again the night after, and every night after that." He'd whispered naughty descriptions of what they would do in that bed, how they would luxuriate in each other's touch, until she was half senseless with desire.

By day three, though, the wait for a bed had become torture in more ways than one. Charity had caught snatches of sleep in the coach, wrapped in Graeme's arms or with her head on his lap. He'd done his best to make her comfortable. She knew his muscles had to be stiffer than hers, his exhaustion warring with the restlessness of having been cooped up for so long.

Yet she wasn't so very tired as to not care about the fact that she was arriving for her wedding in a gown—*theater attire*, no less—she'd been wearing for three days straight, with her hair unwashed and unkempt.

The only saving grace had been that the interrupted nature of her slumber meant she'd never had a chance to fall deep into dreams. No night terrors. No paralyzing fear. No shrieks of despair, sure to frighten her new fiancé more than anyone.

As every mile that passed, she'd fallen harder for him, become more and more certain that this crazed rush to Scotland was the right thing to do. She couldn't lose him now. Somehow, she would find a way to keep the nightmares at bay.

Finally, the coach rolled to a stop in the yard of a little inn bearing a sign that proclaimed it "The Dog and Anvil." Graeme stepped down, then turned to help her. Charity stumbled out, blinking in the bright sun. The air smelled clean, the ground still damp from a spatter of rain the night before. Lord only knew what the innkeeper must think. She surely looked a fright. Probably smelled one, too.

Graeme looked back down the road, as he'd done each time they'd stopped. This time, he looked at her curiously. "We've arrived. It does not appear we've been followed."

Charity had thought of this already. By the time Lord Maxwell's message had been delivered to her mother, they'd have had at least twelve hours' head start. But a single rider on horseback could have traveled faster than their coach, making up the time. So Graeme was right. They hadn't been followed.

Which meant...what? That her family supported their elopement? Well, of course they did. They had all encouraged Lord Maxwell's suit. Even though Charity had asked them not to pressure him, they were unlikely to protest if the Scot was the one doing the pressuring.

Charity gazed around the inn yard again. The unobtrusive but ever-present guards she'd grown accustomed to were also absent. The duke would not have overlooked this detail. If Alex hadn't sent them to follow her, he must think her safe enough under Graeme's protection.

She was free.

It was an odd feeling.

The door of the inn opened, and a bearded man of indeterminable age came toward them, arms open in a welcoming gesture, a broad smile cracking through his beard. The innkeeper.

Graeme smiled back in acknowledgement, but held up one finger.

The man raised his eyebrows, but a quick glance at the luxurious traveling coach must have told him all he needed to know about his newly-arrived guest, for he retreated just as quickly.

Graeme Ramsey Maxwell saw the confusion on his bride-to-be's pretty features. But there was one thing he needed to tell her before they took their vows.

He placed his hands on her shoulders.

"If we're going to do this, there is one thing you ought to know. I should have told you earlier."

Charity gave him a questioning look.

"I have a little boy."

Her lips parted in surprise. "A...a natural child?" she stammered. "I hadn't considered..."

Graeme mentally cursed himself. Lord. She thought he meant he had a by-blow, a child born of a union outside of marriage. And she was wondering why on earth he'd been so indelicate as to mention it, let alone doing so moments before their wedding.

He'd approached this all wrong. He shook his head, held up a hand. "No, no. Nathan is not my own...though he *is* mine, now. My sister's son. She and her husband have both passed on, leaving the lad an orphan. He came to live with me when they died."

Understanding lit her expression, and she visibly relaxed. "Poor soul," Charity said softly, and he saw in the tilt of her eyes that the sentiment was genuine.

He gave a rueful chuckle. "That boy has had to deal with more than anyone his age ought to. He loves me, but he won't say it. He's afraid. Everyone he's loved, he's lost."

"He had no siblings?"

"No. I've come to think of him as a son, though Nathan would only become heir if I had no sons of my own. But I want him to know, always, that he is loved and welcome. That I raise him out of love, not just duty. I need to know my wife will feel the same."

"Of course. How could I feel any other way? He is lucky to have you for an uncle," she said. "When my father died, my uncle also came to help my mother. But I am quite certain *he* did not feel the same way about the responsibility."

"I'm sorry to hear that."

She shuddered. "You have no idea. If it hadn't been for Alex..."

"Don't tell me the lofty duke has won your affections in addition to those of your sister," he teased.

She laughed. "My undying gratitude, yes. But my affections...seem to have settled elsewhere. Though on no less worthy a target."

"Ach. That is a great relief. I shouldn't enjoy having to compete with the duke." There was a kernel of truth behind his teasing tone—not because he doubted his fiancé's loyalty, but because everyone she was related to seemed to have an opinion about her every action. Though Charity's sister and the duke seemed nice enough, Graeme couldn't help but be glad they all lived a considerable distance from his primary home.

She looked at him through her lashes, clearly enjoying their flirtation. "I do imagine you would hold your own in such a competition, my lord."

"I shall have to sharpen my skills, just in case His Grace comes for a prolonged visit." He was clearly joking now.

Not to be bested, she leaned forward, blushing madly, and whispered to him, "I believe the skill of your tongue will serve you better than the skill of your lance, when it comes to maintaining my, ah, affection."

"You have yet to experience the skill of my lance," he returned, loving it when her eyes sparkled and she let out a burst of shocked laughter. It was all he could do not to snatch her up right then and there and carry her into the inn. But they hadn't raced all this way just to put the wedding night before the wedding.

"I think," he suggested, "we had best go inside and satisfy the innkeeper's curiosity before he falls through that window."

She turned quickly, laughing as the innkeeper's form ducked out of sight.

She nodded. "Indeed, we should. But why did you wait until now to tell me of your nephew?"

Guilt twinged him. "I should have told you earlier, but I wanted to be certain you were completely convinced that we would suit. Convinced of the wisdom of marrying me, before adding extra responsibility into the equation."

"You thought I would reject you because you took in your sister's poor little boy?" She sounded incredulous. "Who could be so cold-hearted?"

He could think of a few women, but that was neither here nor there. "Not really. But I wanted to be sure your choice was about *me*. Call it selfish if you will, but when a Maxwell marries, that marriage is forever. Long after Nate is grown, and any other children who come our way, you and I will still be together. I want us both to be happy with that choice."

"When a man speaks like that, how could a woman refuse?" The words could have been teasing, but for the way Charity looked up at him. What he saw in her eyes gave him hope. Dreaminess, yes, but also trust. Desire. Respect. It was a foundation on which a man could build.

Together, they turned toward the inn.

"Lord Maxwell! Welcome, welcome. When ye said ye were headin' to London to find a wife, I did no' expect to see ye again so soon."

"I stayed here on my way down," he explained to Charity. To the innkeeper, he said, "As luck would have it, I met the woman of my dreams almost the same night I arrived. This is Miss Charity Medford, who has done me the honor of agreeing to become my wife."

"Did ye now?" the man chortled. "Ach, I do so love a good love story. But mayhap the story should wait. Do I take it right, that your arrival here means ye wish to be wed, my lord?"

"Indeed, we do, Mr. Partridge."

"And ye, lass? I mean, Miss Medford?"

"Yes."

He clasped his hands together, obviously proud that the Scottish lord had chosen *his* inn for the nuptials. "Well, then, welcome to Scotland, ye lucky lord and lady, where we hold that the only thing necessary to host a wedding is the willingness of the bride and groom."

The ceremony was simple. All she and Graeme had to do, he explained, was speak a vow to one another, declaring themselves husband and wife, in the presence of witnesses, and the deed would be done.

In England, weddings were far more complicated. Parents had to give consent for a bride or groom under the age of twenty-one, banns had to be read for three weeks in a row, or a special license obtained, a clergyman arranged to officiate...and that was for even the most basic of weddings.

In Gretna Green, though, weddings were a business, with various establishments competing for the patronage of the runaway couples who came to be married there. Mr. Partridge, puffed up until he resembled the bird with whom he shared a name, did his best to make each and every wedding—but this one in particular—special.

"An honor, indeed, Lord Maxwell. Shall we proceed immediately?" He, too, glanced down the road, as though at any moment a rider might appear at breakneck speed, bent on stopping them. "Or shall I have your things brought up to your room, so that you may refresh yourselves?"

"There's nothing to be brought up," Graeme informed him.

"Ach. I see." He seemed to take this as confirmation that resistance was, indeed, on the way. "Then, let us be about our business. Would you prefer to stand near the fireplace, or in the flower garden?"

"The flower garden," they answered unanimously.

He nodded approvingly and escorted them to a small but cheery garden at the back side of the inn. He stopped near a trellis where climbing roses had just begun to bud.

"Have you rings?"

To Charity's surprise, Graeme produced a small pouch and shook two golden rings into his large hand. The sun caught them, and the unmistakable green of an emerald winked at her from his palm.

"I did, after all, come to London in hopes of finding a wife," he reminded her.

Her eyes grew misty. Their wedding might not be traditional, but he'd planned for the most important things. A lifetime together, he'd promised her, and the rings that symbolized that promise.

Graeme was an honorable man. She could have done far worse. "I don't deserve you," she told him, though she barely managed more than a whisper. "But I do want to marry you."

"As I do you. And don't be silly. You deserve everything your heart desires," Graeme replied chivalrously. "Since fate was kind enough to place you in my path, I am honored to be the one who gets the chance to fulfill those desires."

Mr. Partridge smiled widely. "There is little more that must be done. If ye will join hands, I'll read the blessing." He pulled a small book from his vest, opening it to a dog-eared page. The book was only for show—it was clear as he spoke the words, short and traditional, that he knew them by heart.

Graeme held her gaze through the prayer, sliding his ring onto her finger at the end. When it was her turn, her fingers trembled, but she managed to get the gold band over his knuckle and onto his ring finger, where it gleamed proudly.

"Lord Maxwell, Lady Charity, I now pronounce ye husband and wife."

Never letting go of her hands, Graeme placed a soft kiss on her lips. Charity closed her eyes.

Maybe, just maybe, the nightmare of the past year had finally given way to a beautiful dream.

With the ceremony over, Charity was at a sudden loss for what to do. The urgency that had propelled their actions for the past several days had suddenly disappeared. She was married.

That is, until Mr. Partridge asked, "My lord, will ye be stayin' here for the night?"

And her newlywed husband replied, "Aye."

Then it hit her. *She was married.* She would share a bed with her husband. As much as she longed for the intimacy that would entail, she had not yet let go of her terror of what came after. *To sleep, perchance to dream...*

Charity sprang into action. "My good Mr. Partridge, could you tell me where we might find shops in Gretna Green?"

"You wish to shop? Now?" Graeme asked incredulously.

The innkeeper chuckled. "Never met a lady yet what didn't love to shop."

She batted her eyelashes at Graeme. "My lord, have you forgotten? Our trip here was rather...sudden. I find myself lacking certain amenities."

"Oh. Oh, right. Certainly."

She could tell from his expression that he had no idea what she meant, but feared it had something to do with womanly matters that were better not discussed in mixed company. Not exactly the truth, but it suited her purposes.

She turned the full force of her charm to the innkeeper. "An apothecary and a dressmaker—are those available?"

"Of course, my lady. But you must be exhausted from your travels. Perhaps you could tell my wife what you are after. She will gladly see to it that anything you require is promptly delivered."

"Mr. Partridge, you are heaven sent. I definitely need a few things, but the idea of climbing back into the coach so soon was nearly enough to give me the vapors."

"Me, too," Graeme joked, making them all laugh.

The owner of The Dog and Anvil knew his business well. Within minutes, Charity had given her order to his wife, who had cheerfully suggested a couple items she hadn't even considered. Obviously the good woman had seen more than one unprepared bride arrive at her doorstep.

With that settled, the innkeeper led them upstairs. "The finest room we have," Mr. Partridge told them proudly, opening the door to a bedroom that boasted a large bed hung with burgundy. Matching drapes framed a large window. Charity barely took in the rest of the room, registering only that it was, indeed, quite nice for an inn. Her eyes kept going to the bed. That is, until the proprietor strode forward and threw open the door to a small adjoining room and she saw the one thing she wanted even more: a bath.

"I'll have the staff bring up hot water directly," he promised when he heard her soft exclamation. "Then, after you've had a bit of a lie down, I do hope you'll grace us with your presence for dinner, my lord and lady. The Dog and Anvil boasts the best chef in Gretna Green, we do."

"'Tis no boast," Graeme agreed. "Why do you think I stay here?"

The innkeeper's chest swelled once more. "Right ye are, my lord. Blessings to the happy couple, then."

Charity could have sworn he all but winked at Graeme as he shut the door behind him.

She stared at Graeme. Her *husband*. Why was it that after nearly four days in a carriage, *he* still managed to look so tempting?

"Should we—should I—that is, I mean, do you wish to—" she stammered. How did one properly ask one's newlywed husband whether he wished to exercise his marital rights?

Would he wish to get to it, right away, or wait until bed time? Was there a correct time of day for marital relations? They hadn't worried about such things while pleasuring one another on the journey here, but then again, they'd stopped short of the marital act. She'd gleaned certain key elements from her sister, and her faster set of friends had a number of ideas on *improper* relations, but obviously, her education in such matters had been incomplete.

A tap on the door signaled the arrival of a pair of footmen bearing large buckets of steaming water. Charity's gaze followed them longingly to the tub.

Graeme laughed. "Don't worry, my sweet. Have your bath, before the water cools. We've all the time in the world now."

She glanced at him doubtfully, but was unable to resist the steamy tendrils that curled so beckoningly through the air.

The servants trooped up the stairs twice more, and the tub was filled.

Charity moved toward it as though in a trance. Graeme came up behind her. His arms closed around her and he bent to whisper in her ear. "I have only one condition. Let me play at lady's maid and assist you. I have a pretty good idea how that gown fastens."

She felt a smile playing at her lips. Of course he did, given the number of times he'd managed to *un*fasten it on the way here. "You are one ugly lady's maid," she teased.

He put a hand to his heart. "My lady, you wound me with your cruel words."

She giggled while he made short work of unfastening her bodice, amazed how he always knew the right thing to put her at ease. The gown slipped down to pool at her feet. The short corset came off next, and finally her shift.

Graeme's hand skimmed reverentially over her hip. Desire threaded through her at his touch.

Without warning, he scooped her up and plunked her into the tub. She shrieked in surprise.

"If I hadn't done that," he growled, "your bath would have grown ice cold before you ever set foot in it."

Charity sucked in a breath at the intense desire in his eyes.

Graeme stalked over to the soap and washrag. They were not the luxurious scented soaps Charity had at home, but they were of good quality. After all, the inn did specialize in weddings, she remembered.

Graeme plunged the cloth into the hot water, wringing it over her back. She sighed as the hot droplets sluiced over her skin.

"You have no idea what this is costing me," he muttered.

She started to push up from the tub.

"Don't you dare."

"But you just said—"

"I know what I said. And I am painfully hard with the desire to finally, finally make love to you."

Charity drew a shuddery breath as his blunt declaration fueled her own desire.

"But I also know that I intend to lick every inch of your body, and the taste of your freshly bathed skin is a pleasure worth these minutes of torture."

"You intend to…" Her nipples hardened at the images his words brought to her mind.

"You have beautiful breasts." He proceeded to wash them.

Charity squirmed, needing more, and he chuckled knowingly. "Wanton."

"Wretch," she retorted.

He continued running the soap over her body, unable to resist leaning in for kisses that left them both breathless. His shirt was soaked. Finally he pulled back. "Can you manage your hair on your own while I undress?"

She nodded, her voice strangled by desire.

She gave her hair the fastest washing of her life, then hopped out of the tub as Graeme stalked toward it, fully naked and sporting a massive erection.

Her knees threatened to give way.

While Charity's bath had been lengthy, sensual and luxurious, Graeme's was entirely opposite.

The bath was a delay he deemed necessary, since he'd arrived in his home country smelling quite ripe, and he wanted his wife to enjoy making love. He had no doubt she would, so long as he took care not to handle her too roughly the first time. She'd already proven to be a creature of passion.

"Do you wish me to help you?" she purred.

"No, thank you," he managed in a strangled voice, looking away lest he be tempted to lick the last droplets of water from her delectable breasts. "I'll manage. As much as I would welcome your ministrations, the distraction would be…overwhelming."

She gave him a smirk and sauntered off. He shut the door to the small bathing area and proceeded to scrub himself in the most perfunctory manner possible. Satisfied he would not offend her, he blotted the drying cloth over his body. There.

He couldn't take another minute of delay. He wrapped the drying cloth around his hips and opened the door.

Charity stood combing out her hair. She'd borrowed his

spare shirt, which clung to her still damp body.

She dropped the comb.

Graeme gazed at his newlywed wife, her hair damp and skin still flushed from her bath, and his erection threatened to pry loose the cloth at his hips.

Still, he couldn't help but subject her to a bit of teasing, after the pleasurable torture of watching her bathe. "So, my wife, what shall we do now? Would you like to go shopping? Or perhaps a game of draughts?"

"You tease." She giggled. A girlish sound, fresh and natural. And totally belied by her body, which screamed *take me*. The sweet curve of her breasts was clearly visible through the thin cotton of his shirt, the dusky tint of her nipples pushing temptingly against their covering. The garment hung nearly to her knees, and beneath he could see the outline of her legs, the slight shadow at her cleft where they came together. The place his body clamored to be.

"I, tease? Nay, my sweet. It is you. Your every move has teased and taunted me from the moment we met."

She gave him a saucy look. "I was not teasing. I was...enticing."

"Ach. Lass, perhaps I am not as schooled in the new forms of flirtation. What, exactly, is an enticement, if not teasing?" He was enjoying this verbal parry with her, even more because he knew it where it would end. In bed, with him deep inside her.

"An enticement is...like a promise," she decided.

"I see. Then, Lady Charity, I believe it is time for you to make good on your promises."

He stepped forward, slid his hands beneath the shift and lifted it over her head in one fluid motion. He clasped her to him, skimming his hands over the smooth skin of her back, the sweet curve of her buttocks. Her breasts pressed against his chest. Her hand came between them. He felt a tug, and the cloth at his hips fell away. His erection pressed against her stomach. The feel of skin on skin, head to toe, sent a rush to his head more intoxicating than whisky. He wanted to step back, admire her glorious body, but he couldn't let go, couldn't stop his hands from squeezing her bottom, pulling her tighter against him.

He seized her lips in a kiss, his tongue delving into her mouth and finding hers, parrying until they both gasped for breath.

"Bed." He guided them toward it, scooping her up and onto the mattress. Her legs wrapped around him, pressing her moist center against his hardness. He followed her down, groaning as she bucked her hips against him. He kissed the sensitive flesh at the base of her neck, filling his hands with her breasts, cupping them, brushing the pad of his thumb over her nipple. She cried out, arching into him. He slid further down, capturing her nipple in his mouth and drawing on it tightly. Her head thrashed from side to side.

"Now, Graeme. Please," she begged him.

Now, definitely. Any more anticipation would only torture them both. He guided the head of his cock to her entrance. God, she was so slick. So ready for him. He pushed into her, straining every muscle in his body to keep from going full force. She sheathed him with impossible tightness. The urge to drive deep, thrust until he was buried to the hilt, nearly overwhelmed him. He gritted his teeth.

"More," she whispered.

"I don't—want to hurt you," he panted.

She gazed up beseechingly, desire darkening those endless pools of blue. "Graeme, I want all of you."

That did it. He pulled back, then thrust home. She tensed with a sharp little cry. He stilled. "Too much?" He started to withdraw, guilt penetrating the haze of lust.

"No!" Her small hands held him to her. "Just...be still just a minute...there." The tension left her body. Still holding him, she wiggled beneath him. "Graeme..."

He knew what she wanted. Needed. The same thing he did. He started to move again, slowly, and her eyes darkened with need.

He stroked her, long and deep, until she was thrashing again, reaching for the peak. She wrapped her legs around him again, inviting him deeper. His own limit was growing near, but he held off, needing her to come before him. He brought his fingers between them, rubbing the sensitive nub in front of her entrance, now slick with moisture. Her hips bucked, and he stroked her faster, inside and out. Her eyes closed and her back arched as she came undone, pulsing and throbbing around him.

Just in time. Graeme threw his head back as he found his own release, coming long and hard, before the strength in his arms gave way and he collapsed, gathering her to him and rolling to the side.

Slowly, their breathing calmed. He buried his face in her still-damp hair, amazed at his own reaction to their lovemaking. Amazed by the deep sense of belonging that filled his chest. He would never grow tired of this woman. Fate had handed him a gem indeed.

Charity fell asleep curled against Graeme's chest. Secure, she slept dreamlessly, awakening only when the tantalizing smell of roast pork wafted up from the dining room of the inn.

Her stomach growled. Or maybe it was Graeme's. With her body pressed so tightly to his, she couldn't be sure. They were both famished.

Clothing, however, was a problem. She wasn't wearing any. The thought of putting on that same blue theater gown...ugh. Fortunately, Graeme peeked outside the door to find two parcels neatly wrapped in brown paper. The good Mrs. Partridge had delivered. One package contained a simple but well-made cotton dress of cheery yellow. A shift accompanied it, along with a lace garment she lifted from the paper. It spilled over her arms, soft as baby's breath, and sheer as mist. There could be only one purpose for such a thing. When the older woman had suggested a nightshift, Charity had pictured something far more practical. Silly her. Smiling, she tucked it back in the paper.

The second package was much smaller, but brought Charity just as much relief as had the sight of fresh clothing. She turned away from Graeme as she unwrapped the paper, hating herself for needing it, hating herself for lying to Mrs. Partridge about having cramps, yet terrified of ruining her chance to hold onto Graeme's love. Even though he hadn't spoken the words, she'd felt it in his touch. The paper fell away and she released a breath she hadn't known she was holding. The shameful answer to her secret prayers. How ironic that, months after her rescue from that dark cellar with a single vial of poison as her only companion, the relief from such memories came in a similarly-shaped vial.

Chapter 10:

In which Charity learns that the honeymoon is sometimes the first true test of strength in a marriage.

Hiding in plain sight. It was so deceptively simple. Jasper Morton was proud of himself for thinking of it.

Escaping to faraway lands, like André Denis had done, might have been safer. But that required the ability to ease smoothly between cultures. Jasper didn't have that. He was a two-bit thief and he knew it. A common thug.

So he'd headed north.

Jasper didn't especially like life on the run. He hadn't really liked being a spy, either. But the problem with being a petty criminal was, sometimes you fell in with folks even worse than yourself. He'd done a few odd jobs for André Denis, and before he'd known it, he'd been sucked in. He had little understanding of the world of politics and intrigue. But he understood orders, and how to follow them. And Jasper had a talent for making things, and sometimes even people, disappear.

When their little group of informants had been

compromised last year, they'd split and run. He'd heard about the ones that got captured. Not too hard to get the news when every inn across the country was abuzz with it. He hadn't even considered trying to follow Denis. For one, Denis held an "every man for himself" kind of philosophy when it came to taking risks. He'd have sold out Jasper in a heartbeat if he thought it would save his sorry butt. It would have been only too easy, because Jasper knew he'd stick out like a sore thumb anywhere outside the British Isles.

North, though still risky, was his best option. Smaller towns, where everyone knew everyone. But there was also a certain stoic acceptance among the locals. If a man kept to himself, earned his keep, and didn't bother anyone, he was unlikely to be bothered in return. Jasper was counting on that. Most people who moved north had some kind of story. Bad debts, family trouble, you name it. It wasn't too hard to come up with one of his own. He barely even had to lie. He just had to focus on the rough upbringing rather than the string of crimes that followed it.

There was plenty of work to be had, even if it came mostly in the form of odd jobs. For the first time in years, it was honest work. There were no quiet knocks on the door in the middle of the night.

Jasper had almost grown comfortable. He could forget the past, and the past would forget him.

On the way from Gretna Green to Leventhal House, the Maxwell family seat, Charity and Graeme took a more leisurely pace. They stayed an extra day at The Dog and Anvil, allowing Charity to shop for a few additional provisions. She needed stockings, a sturdier pair of shoes, and a few other things, knowing that her trunks might be weeks in arriving.

Once on the road, they stopped often to stretch their legs and take in the countryside.

Charity peppered him with questions, and Graeme told her all about his lands and the people of his home.

"Many of the crofters are related. Have been for generations."

"A clan?"

"At one time, yes. Most of the clans have broken up now, what with the crofters heading south and to the coastal towns for work. I can't compete with the railroads and the coal mines, but my family and our lands have fared better than most. Many of the families date back to the clan days."

She could sense his pride in this.

"We have excellent weavers, and the wool from the Leventhal sheep is always in demand. Add in a bit of mining and stone masonry, and we manage to find steady work for all who wish to stay."

It was so odd to hear a noble speaking in such terms. In Charity's experience, noblemen spent their time on leisurely pursuits. Gaming and spirits, and occasionally horses. She knew of a few who'd invested in shipping ventures, but hardly any who were directly involved in how their people made a living. It sounded almost like a feudal system, but in a good way.

Only once did Charity slip up. The second night after leaving Gretna Green, they stayed the night at a well-traveled inn—one very accommodating, but less luxurious than the others they'd stopped at.

From their room, the occasional murmur of voices could be heard, and outside, the arrival and departure of riders. Charity made sure to take her medicine before bed, attending to that and other necessary matters in privacy. But it wasn't enough. In the dark of night, a rider pulled up in front of the inn—someone the staff at the inn must have recognized and deemed unwelcome. A man shouted. Another angry voice responded. Argument ensued.

Charity snapped from slumber to panicked action. "They're coming! Hurry, hide."

The only window looked down on the yard, where two dark figures gesticulated angrily. Too dark to make out their features. Not too dark to know they were angry. Angry was bad. Scary. No escape that way. She would have to hide.

"What is this place?" she worried aloud.

Her body moved sluggishly, her limbs and mind still woozy from laudanum. Her head swung wildly as she searched for a hiding place. How had she forgotten to make a plan? She always had a plan.

She crawled under the bed, squeezing as small as she could, hugging herself, unable to distinguish whether she shivered more from chill or terror. Maybe they wouldn't find her. Maybe.

Only when Graeme's head poked over the side of the bed did reason penetrate the haze of fear. "Charity?"

Graeme. Husband. Traveling.

Flaming hot embarrassment erased the chill. She was naked and shivering under a bed in an inn in Scotland.

"I—I thought someone was robbing the inn. I heard men arguing."

"My sweet, come back to bed. You are safe here. I don't know what the argument was, but it seems to have ended."

She listened. It was true. The night outside had fallen still again. If she strained her ears, she just make out hoof beats in the distance as the unwelcome rider retreated.

She wedged herself back out from under the bed, painfully aware of each inch she had to scoot until she could climb back under the covers like a normal person.

Her eyes welled with tears. Her husband must think her such a fool. He pulled her over to rest her head on his chest. The tears spilled over.

"Don't cry, love."

"I—I'm sorry. I overreacted."

He stroked her hair. "Maybe a little, lass."

"I was frightened."

"This is a strange bed, and you have had a tumultuous few days." He made the excuse for her. Made it sound almost reasonable. "You must have just been too tired to think straight."

Too tired to think straight. Yes, that was it. If only that were *all* of it.

"You needn't worry. I won't let anything happen to you."

She nodded against his chest. Oh, how she wanted that to be true. He didn't seem too worried about her irrational behavior. She didn't deserve such a good man for a husband.

Graeme's breathing soon returned to the even rhythm of slumber, but Charity stayed awake in his arms. He'd excused her this once, but what would happen the next time? Or the time after that?

She would have to do better. Try harder. Tears leaked from the corners of her eyes.

They continued on toward Leventhal House the next morning, and the strange episode was not mentioned again.

Charity knew when they finally got close to Graeme's homeland, because his whole body shifted to alertness. He kept an eye on the window, drinking in the sight of his lands.

Curious, she knelt on the opposite bench, her nose pressed

to the glass. The sky had grown steadily darker since they'd set out that morning. Thunder rumbled in the distance. The shrubs and trees growing at the edges of the road were foreign to her. Wild, stalky plants with odd-shaped pods, dotted here and there with pale blooms. The hills rising in the distance, covered in moss and rock, seemed to impose their greatness over anything humans might try to construct. Charity shivered, hoping the people would prove friendlier than the land.

To Graeme's eyes, his homeland had a wild, primitive sort of beauty. Untamed. He observed his new bride. The place suited her perfectly, though her scrunched-up nose and distinctly unhappy pout suggested Charity might not agree with his assessment. He reminded himself to give her time. She'd already adjusted from a dream of a long engagement and large wedding to an engagement that lasted only long enough for their coach to carry them over the border, and a wedding with a single, near-stranger as the only guest. She'd come through with remarkable good grace. He could afford to give her more time on the many other adjustments their marriage would require of her.

No London girl knew what to think of the highlands upon first sight. To her, the surroundings would seem strange, the customs foreign. In time, though, the strangeness would wear off, and the charm would shine through. He hoped.

Leventhal House had been built to blend with the landscape, using rock quarried locally. He heard Charity's indrawn breath as it came into view.

"Welcome home, my lady."

She tore her gaze from the window. "It's huge."

He laughed. "You said the same thing last night."

Her eyes popped wide and the first smile he'd seen in hours cracked her face. She batted at him with a pair of gloves she'd been clutching. "That is too bad of you, Lord Maxwell."

"Well, *Lady Maxwell*, the manor house is of good size for a reason. My ancestors had a mind that we Maxwells would reproduce rather liberally."

Her mouth fell open. "My lord!"

"I think ten or twelve is a reasonable goal. How soon do you think we will get started?"

By the time the coach stopped and Charity took her first steps onto Maxwell land, Graeme had her giggling so hard she had a hard time keeping upright.

Her infectious laughter rang out, signaling their arrival to all. The staff rushed to greet them, and soon the normally-stoic faces of the servants were wreathed in smiles as well.

It was not, perhaps, the most *dignified* way to introduce one's new wife and mistress of Leventhal House, but Graeme had a feeling it was, in this case, the *right* way. There was nothing his home needed more than good cheer.

"Uncle Graeme!" Nathan came running pell-mell from the grounds behind the house, ending with a flying leap into his uncle's arms.

"Oomph." Graeme exaggerated his stagger as he absorbed the little boy's weight. "You've gained a full stone, I'd wager."

He giggled. "I have not."

He set the boy down. "Nathan, I'd like you to meet my new wife, Lady Charity."

He settled down, eyeing her with a mix of interest and trepidation. "A pleasure to meet you, Lady Charity," he recited, as though he'd practiced.

Charity stooped to his level. "No, the pleasure is mine. Would it be all right if you call me Aunt Charity?"

Nathan nodded. "Aunt Charity."

"May I hug you?"

He shrugged. "I guess so."

Graeme knew his nephew was trying not to get his hopes up, but the smile tugging at his mouth gave him away. As Charity gave him a hug, the boy looked up at him and mouthed "she's pretty."

Graeme nodded and winked. "I am a lucky man, don't ye think?"

He introduced her more formally to the butler, housekeeper, and other staff, then insisted on giving her a tour of the house himself. Nathan tagged along for most of it, before finally getting bored and running off to play.

Graeme seized the opportunity to finish the tour by stopping to kiss Charity in each and every room.

The rain that had threatened earlier had now begun to fall in earnest, bringing a chill over the burgeoning spring. Graeme led Charity back to the library, which boasted three walls stacked floor to ceiling with books and other oddities, and a fourth with large windows overlooking the grounds. A fire burned merrily in the hearth, dispelling the gloom outdoors.

"Ooh, I think this room is my favorite," she exclaimed, moving over to stand by the fire.

"It is?" He pulled a face of disappointment.

"You don't like it?"

"Oh, I like it, lass. 'Tis only that I'd hoped the bedroom would be your favorite."

She laughed and teased him right back. "The bedroom? With that huge, enormous bed? I cannot possibly imagine why anyone would need such a monstrously large bed. Unless your ancestors were giants. Were they?"

"Nay, not to my knowledge. There would have been tall

tales about that, and I do not remember any. Their virility was legendary, however. That I know. All sorts of tales abound."

"Letch!"

He grabbed for her and she laughed again, sidestepping.

"Since you seem to lack imagination, I will make it my task to show you *exactly* why we need such a huge, enormous bed." He caught her up and this time she didn't resist, but kept her back to him as she leaned into his embrace. Her bottom rubbed up against him in a manner that had him rock hard in a second.

His hands slid up over the curve of her breasts, skimmed her shoulders, and found the pins that bound up her luxurious pile of golden hair. He pulled one, then another, but her hair remained stubbornly in place. Frustrated, he muttered, "How does it *do* that?"

She turned and peered up through her lashes. "A woman never reveals her secrets."

"Will you take it down?" He nibbled at her throat, feeling her pulse leap reflexively at the touch.

"Now?"

"You have somewhere else to be?"

"When you put it that way…" She deftly plucked several more pins out, sending her locks tumbling down, one after another, in a cascade of gold. The firelight reflected off the shiny mass. Graeme sank his hands into the strands of silk and tilted her face up to his.

Do you like your new home? He wanted to ask, but it was too soon, everything too new and strange. Instead he kissed her. The question could wait until he was sure he'd won her over.

She kissed him back, her tongue tracing his lips. He parted them and sucked her in, never able to get enough of the taste of her. He heard the tiny *ping* of the hairpins hitting the floor as they slipped from her hand.

He bent lower, licking a path along her collarbone, eliciting a shiver and a tiny moan. He kept one arm around her, still buried in that beautiful hair, and used the other to tease her nipple through her gown. "Make love to me," he murmured against her neck.

"Here? Now?"

"Why not?"

"My lord. We only just arrived. And we're in the library. What will the servants think?"

"They'll think I brought home a beautiful woman for my wife and am doing exactly what any warm-blooded man would do."

"But—but—" she sputtered.

He waited, knowing from her expressive blue eyes that, once again, she was torn between passion and propriety. It was one of the things he loved best about her.

In the end, she gave in and did exactly as he'd hoped.

Graeme pointed out the library window, across the grounds. The "tour" had taken a delightful detour—long enough to leave them both satiated, and long enough for weak rays of sunlight to finally break through the clouds.

"Just over that hill is the dowager house. I'll take you to meet my mother this afternoon, now that the rain has let up."

"She lives there alone?"

"She has a maid. Cook sends over meals, and Nathan and I walk over to visit."

"But the manor is so large," Charity said. "She could stay in the main house."

He shook his head. "I told her the same thing, especially

before I married. She chose the dowager house, though. It helps her remember."

"Remember?"

He hesitated. "My mother...sometimes has trouble keeping track of time. Not like she gets busy and loses track, but like whole years slip away. At Leventhal House, where she and my father spent so long, it's harder for her to remember that he has passed on, or that Nathan is my sister's son, and not me."

"Oh, I see." Charity pictured an elderly, lonely woman whose mind was starting to go, and felt sorry for her.

When they visited later that afternoon, Charity was surprised to find that Graeme's mother was not much older than her own. She was sweet, and very welcoming of her son's new wife, even if she did seem to have trouble remembering Charity's name and finally just settled for calling her "dear."

"When my father died," Graeme explained on the walk back to the main house, "something inside her just cracked, and it never mended quite right. I lost a bit of her at the same time I lost him."

"How awful. She loves you, though."

"True. She wants Nate and I to be happy, even if she cannot always remember which of us is which."

No wonder Graeme was so protective, Charity reflected that evening, having been introduced to nearly everyone who lived or worked at Leventhal House. Aside from the responsibility of the earldom, he had both his mother and Nate to care for. It also explained why he'd come looking for a wife. It had to be lonely at the top, with all those people looking to him for their well-being.

She'd done the same thing, in a way. Looked to him as the answer to her problems. Guilt pulled at her chest, now that she understood how much more than that Graeme needed in his wife. His people would look to her, now, too. Charity swallowed. Would she prove worthy of the role?

Chapter 11:

"The evil that is in the world almost always comes of ignorance, and good intentions may do as much harm as malevolence if they lack understanding."— *Albert Camus*

The first few days at Leventhal House passed in a blur of activity. Charity was too exhausted to even decide whether she liked it or not. She liked little Nathan, and she liked Graeme, and she *really* liked the moments spent alone with her new husband.

The rest was, honestly, a bit overwhelming. She longed for her own clothing, and a familiar face or two. She wrote to Penny to ask if the maid would accept a transfer of position. With the slow pace of the mail coaches, Charity knew it would be weeks before she'd have an answer.

The highland home was busy by day, but at night, it was far quieter than Charity's native London. The stillness helped her sleep, though. That, and the carefully-measured doses of laudanum she made sure to take before bed. So far, though her dreams were sometimes troubled, she'd not experienced another breakdown.

As grateful as she was for that, she'd nicknamed the medicine "the vile vial." When it was empty, she was not going to get more. Not this time. It was only too easy, as she knew from last summer, to come to rely on it night after night, needing more and more to find relief. She hated the lingering lethargy, the fog that crept into her mind and stayed like stagnant water in a bog. The doctor had dismissed her concern, but she'd felt herself, her mind and soul, slipping away. She didn't dare tell anyone. They'd just take it as a sign she was descending further into madness.

Against doctor's orders, she'd stopped taking the medicine. That had been a mistake. Horrible aches and restlessness plagued her until she'd caved once again.

The next time, she tried weaning herself slowly. That worked better. The sleeplessness and panic attacks had come back, but by then, the staff at Lady Medford's house had been trained to calm her down. How embarrassing.

Additional visits to the doctor had yielded no useful advice. "You need to forget. Thank heaven you are alive and unharmed, and put the rest out of your head." *As though it were that easy.* Charity had concluded that the doctor was an idiot with a truly odd definition of "unharmed."

Doing things her own way hadn't gotten her much farther, but at least she was in control. Most of the time. Until that one night at the Wicked Baron's Masquerade, when everything had been too much, and she'd given in to the temptation of opium-laced wine. Look where that had gotten her.

Well, actually, despite a few awkward moments, it had gotten her a husband. So why should she be surprised that she needed a tincture of opium in order to *keep* her husband?

Charity tugged at her hair. No. She didn't need it. Tonight's dose was the last. She would *not* purchase more. Surely she was stronger than that. She was almost certain now that Graeme loved her. Somehow, she'd find her way back to sanity, or she'd make him understand.

She was beginning to think the doctor had been wrong about more than just the laudanum. He and her family had all recommended keeping the whole matter to herself. Eligible bachelors, they'd said, would not look kindly upon a woman whose behavior put her in compromising situations. Their reasons made sense, and yet it would be so much easier if she could just tell Graeme what had happened, and how sometimes little things that didn't bother anyone else bothered her greatly.

Finding the opening to such a conversation, though, was a challenge.

"There are still so many things about you I have yet to learn," Graeme told her over breakfast the next morning.

It was almost the perfect opening. *Why, yes,* she could respond. *Did you know that last summer I was drugged, kidnapped, mishandled, then left to die?* But when she opened her mouth to speak, what came out was, "What do you wish to know, my lord?"

"Do you like to ride?"

An image of their lovemaking last night flashed before her. His broad chest, the trail of hair tapering down his taut stomach to where her thighs straddled him as she rode them both to completion.

Clearly, that was not what he was asking. Her brief hesitation must have given her away. His eyes darkened with heat. "I so love the way you think, my wife."

"I have received considerable education in the art of riding recently," she replied demurely. "I find I like it very much."

That was all it took. Strong arms hauled her from her chair

and over to his. "Do you now?" he asked, his voice turning husky. Pushing her skirts out of the way, he settled her atop his lap, straddling him, face to face. "Very much?"

She nodded, already breathless with anticipation. This wasn't the discussion she'd intended, but the sudden flare of need sent all other thoughts scattering to the winds. His unquenchable thirst for her fueled her own desire. This handsome, powerful man she called *husband* couldn't get enough of her. Nor she him.

The position he'd placed her in put her breasts nearly in line with his mouth. He kissed her jaw, then her neck, her collarbone. She barely registered his nimble fingers at the tie of her wrapper or her chemise—until he tugged the edge of the fabric down and the heat of his mouth covered the tip of her breast.

She couldn't help it. She cried out, and ground down against the burgeoning hardness that pressed up against her most intimate place.

Graeme groaned. He used his hands to rock her hips back and forth. Charity grew slick as her need spiraled higher. She rocked against him as he tugged on her nipple. More. She needed more.

Her husband knew it. Needed it just as badly. He was adjusting his trousers, loosening the laces, when a discreet cough came at the door. "Leave us," he growled, his grip tightening like a vise when she would have shimmied away.

"Graeme! They'll all know."

"Mmm. They probably already do. My reputation as a masterful seducer is growing even now."

"You're terrible."

He finally freed his shaft, and with a single movement, lifted her and settled her atop it. She sank down slowly, savoring the way he filled her. He rocked his hips again, and she forgot to care what anyone might think.

She gripped his shoulders, grinding down harder as she moved against him, sensations building, spiraling higher and higher until she shattered atop him, shuddering and drawing him deep as he, too, found release. Her head fell back as he pumped into her, long and hot and hard.

Long moments later, Graeme recovered enough to lift his head. "I hope this won't leave you too sore for an altogether different sort of ride."

She shifted experimentally. "I shall be fine, my lord."

"Good. Believe it or not, there is much I still want to show you. I had in mind a ride out through one of the villages. The crofters are all anxious to meet you. A bit further on, there is a high knoll that will be covered in wildflowers this time of year. Shall we explore it?"

She agreed, and they spent the afternoon visiting crofters and frolicking like children on holiday. The balmy breeze and sunny sky had wildflowers unfurling in the meadows. She asked Graeme the name of each and every one, delighted when he knew most of them.

He introduced her with pride to the highlanders who herded sheep and wove their wool. With every passing hour, Charity knew she'd fallen deeper in love with her husband. The dashing man who'd romanced her away from London was noble in more than just title. His dedication to his people and his land was a tribute to his character.

Unlike her own, the character of Graeme Ramsey Maxwell was not besmirched. More than ever before, her family and her doctor's advice made sense. *Keep your secrets.* If her husband knew the full extent of her transgressions, he would know he had chosen a wife unworthy of the role. He would look down on her. How could he not?

Better to start fresh. She would spend every day from now on doing her utmost to be the best wife he could ever ask for. With any luck, he'd never find out that she hadn't been that way when he'd married her.

Graeme's lovemaking that night was fiercely tender. "I love having you by my side."

"I love being there."

He gathered her close in his arms. In the dark, she could feel his smile against her cheek. "Whatever compelled you to attend that ridiculous masquerade, I shall be eternally grateful."

She smiled too. "As shall I. There are probably very few couples who can say they met their future spouse at the Wicked Baron's ball."

"I should think not. An event more likely to destroy a marriage than to spark one. But I am not so foolish as to question fate." He trailed kisses down to the hollow between her breasts, and Charity lost track of the conversation.

Afterward, she lay still. Making love to Graeme was everything she'd imagined and more. No two times were the same, but every time was wonderful. She stretched her toes beneath the sheets, her body deliciously sated, if a bit sore. Beginning with breakfast, it had been a most passionate day. Graeme's arm lay heavy across her as he drifted toward slumber.

She didn't dare join him there. She *should* be exhausted after all they'd done, but anxiety had her twisting the sheets between her fingers. She shifted, nudged him. "I'm feeling a bit restless tonight. Shall I return to my suite now?" *Say "yes,"* she prayed.

But his arm tightened, holding her close. "You're staying right here. If you think I'm going to let you go, you're mad."

Therein lay the problem. Graeme had nailed it, though he

didn't realize it. She *was* mad. Those seemingly endless hours last summer, locked in the bowels of the earth, had knocked something loose inside her head. How was she to keep her secret if he insisted on sharing a bed?

Charity pressed her lips together, worried. Plenty of married couples slept separately. Perhaps later in the marriage, when the newness wore off…but if they were ever to get that far, she would have to make it through tonight, first.

She took a deep breath to steady her fears, forcing her body to relax. She laid her head back on his chest, where it fit so well. It would be all right. She would simply have to stay awake. Sleepless nights were nothing new. She could do this.

She brushed a hand along the side of his jaw. His strong features looked peaceful in repose. "I love you," she whispered.

He didn't hear her. She hadn't expected him to. She bit down on her tongue, needing the pain to keep her awake. It was going to be a long night.

If only she weren't so comfortable, tucked securely against Graeme's strong, warm body, his heavy arm holding her close.

A horrible shriek rent the night air.

Graeme came awake with a start, throwing a protective arm over his new wife. Only she wasn't beside him.

Fists pounded at the door. "Who's there?" No answer. He thrashed out of the covers, trying to keep calm in spite of the acceleration of his heart. He stumbled to the window and threw back the curtain. Faster than lighting a candle in the dark. Moonlight streamed in, illuminating a woman on her knees at the door, sobbing. *Charity*. What the hell?

The door wasn't locked. Why didn't she just open it?

"Charity?" he asked uncertainly.

Her head whipped toward the sound of his voice. "No! No, don't leave me here. I'll do anything, anything." She reached for the door again, clawing at it, her hands sliding slowly down the wood panel as though all her energy, all her soul, was draining away.

"Sweetest, no one's left you. Did you have a nightmare?" It was the only explanation he could think of—though she appeared very much awake.

"They left me! I don't want to die down here."

"Down where?" Their room was on the second floor.

She didn't answer him. She crumpled forward until she was nothing but a heap on the ground, her shoulders shaking.

He took a step forward, then another. "Charity?"

She buried her head under her arms, but he thought he heard a muffled, "Yes."

Frowning, he held out a hand. She took it without looking at him, and he helped her up from the floor. She walked unsteadily toward the bed, sitting down carefully, as though her body were made of fragile glass.

A sinking heaviness settled in his gut as snippets of conversation, oddities of her behavior that he'd labeled as mere quirks, came rushing together to form an altogether different picture. *Damn.*

"So. This is what you've been hiding."

Charity opened her mouth to deny it, but the words caught in her throat. She'd failed. Again.

She'd *known* better than to fall asleep. Now there was no avoiding the truth.

Her husband of less than a fortnight laughed bitterly. "I wondered, on our journey here, why no one tried harder to stop us. It seemed too easy. Now I understand. They were all back in London, laughing at me."

Fear choked her, cutting off her breath until she felt dizzy.

"Foolish Lord Maxwell," he mocked himself, "too enamored with a young woman's beauty to bother finding out much about her before hauling her off to Gretna Green. Stupid Scot."

"No," she whispered. *Please, please God, don't let this be happening.* "That's not it."

He slapped a hand to his forehead. "They even warned me—or tried, at any rate. Ewan MacPherson told me the gossips believed you a bit fast, perhaps troubled. I took little heed, thinking it no more than the usual gossip started by females jealous of another's beauty. And then the duke, he tried too. Any man would have insisted I marry you without delay after that piece in the *Tattler*. Instead he took pity on me. Gave me an out, a chance to save myself. Idiot that I am, I thought *his* behavior was odd. And so I find myself here."

His shoulders dropped as the initial rush of anger passed. He gazed at her face, looking into her eyes as though searching for something lost. "Indeed, your beauty is beyond question. I have married a beautiful madwoman, have I not?"

"No," she said again, this time with enough conviction to be heard. "I am not mad, not truly. Only...the nightmares?"

He reached out, stroked the side of her face sadly. Pityingly. "Charity. That was no mere bad dream. I have even heard of sleepwalking, but this..." His gaze found the door she'd been clawing moments ago. "This is different. As though you were under a spell."

"I can explain," she offered. It was past time. The embarrassment couldn't possibly hurt more than the pain that stabbed her now, as she felt Graeme's withdrawal like a physical loss. She was losing him.

He shook his head. "It does not matter the cause. I had hoped to find a wife who could also fill the role of mother to Nathan. But I cannot risk his safety, should you fall under such a spell when I am away."

He stared out the window, where the gray light of dawn crept slowly over the land. "Even more, I had hoped to one day welcome children of our own...but I have seen what madness can do to a person. My family has suffered already. To pass that curse down to a child would be too cruel."

"It—it doesn't work that way. Only when I sleep. When I dream," she insisted.

He scrubbed a hand over his face, shook his head. "That went beyond dreaming, my sweet. You were *clawing* at the door." He lifted her hand. The ragged edges of her fingernails bore testimony to his words.

Burning shame heated her cheeks.

"That night at the inn," he realized. "It happened then, too, didn't it?"

She nodded miserably. "I wasn't always this way."

"But can you stop it—whatever it is—from happening?"

"No." Defeat infiltrated her tone.

He squeezed his eyes closed as though to shut out the pain of her words. "Then I'm not sure the reason matters."

She had no response to that.

He opened his eyes. "Look. I wish this wasn't happening—to either of us. I don't know what else to say right now. But I definitely can't go back to sleep." He shoved up from the bed, tugged on trousers and boots, pulled a loose linen shirt over his head, and left the room.

Charity remained sitting on the bed. She hugged her knees to her chest, wondering how she could feel so cold with her heart still racing the way it was. Teardrops fell with tiny splashes on her knees. She hadn't known she was crying.

She couldn't say how long she stayed that way. Every indrawn breath seemed an effort that lasted a century.

Occasionally she would hear a sound below. A door opening, a boot step on the stairs. What was he doing? What was he thinking?

She didn't dare go to him. Not when he'd made it so obviously clear he wanted to get away from her.

Embarrassment and shame washed over her, a relentless tide that threatened to drag her under. How would she ever explain? She'd waited too long. If only she'd told him earlier…he'd given her the perfect opportunity that night at Vauxhall, when he'd spotted her guards. She'd been too cowardly to confide their true purpose.

Charity rested her forehead on her knees as the bitterness of defeat sank into her bones. She spent the rest of the night sitting like that. Awake, and shivering.

Chapter 12:

In which Charity seriously debates the wisdom of the expression "'Tis better to have loved and lost, than never to have loved at all."

Only when the pale light of dawn penetrated the gloom of the bedroom suite did Charity force her wooden legs to the floor and down the stairs. She cinched the tie of her wrapper tight against the morning chill as she entered the breakfast room.

Her husband had already eaten, from the look of it. Was he avoiding her? Would it help if she just gave him some space? She reached for a bread roll out of habit, but discovered she had no appetite for it.

Maybe she should find him. Maybe the words would come to her more easily then. She could salvage this yet. Her fears were only making it worse. But she didn't hear his voice, or his movements, anywhere.

She found Mrs. Saxonberry in the long-unused ballroom, directing two footmen who were moving out the miscellaneous items stored there. "Is Lord Maxwell about?" she asked tentatively.

The housekeeper turned to her and froze, but not before Charity caught the tiny flicker of alarm in her expression. Belatedly she realized how she must look. "My lady, I believe he went to meet with the weavers this morn."

"Thank you." She beat a hasty retreat up the stairs and into her dressing room, where the looking glass confirmed her fears. Pale face, wild hair, puffy eyes with dark circles beneath them. That was no way to convince her husband that what he'd seen last night was a mistake.

She beckoned to one of the upstairs maids, having no lady's maid of her own as yet. "I should very much like a bath, and some assistance with my hair. Can you help?"

"Aye, my lady. I'll ask the footmen to carry up the water. You'd best let me fetch Maisie for your hair, if you don't mind my sayin', my lady. She's only a downstairs maid, but she's a true wonder with hair."

"Lovely." If Graeme had gone to the weavers, she had some time. She would make herself presentable, and come up with an explanation for the unexplainable.

He *loved* her. She knew he did. After the initial shock, he'd been more sad than angry. If he didn't love her, he wouldn't have been so hurt. Right? She prayed it was true. If he loved her, he would forgive her for deceiving him. He would let her explain. Help her to heal.

If he didn't…she didn't want to think about that. Even that brief flash of anger last night, directed toward her, had felt like the very earth beneath her was crumbling.

When the bath was ready, Charity sank gratefully into the lavender-scented water. Steam suffused her face. She breathed it in, each inhale deliberate, as though somehow the tendrils of steam carried answers that could be absorbed by mere breath.

Graeme cared about her, she repeated to herself. She just had to tell him the truth and hope he didn't turn from her in disgust. There'd been no room in their whirlwind courtship for telling tales of past woes. Last night, he'd been too upset to hear her out.

If he knew, he might not look at her the same way anymore. She didn't want his pity. Or worse, his scorn. She wanted him to look at her the way he had the night they met—with desire.

She pushed herself up and clambered out of the tub just as Maisie, the downstairs maid, arrived to help with her hair. Maisie was a natural chatterbox and overcome with excitement at the opportunity to play at lady's maid to "a real true lady." Her enthusiasm required very little input on Charity's side, for which Charity was grateful.

The only spare gown she had was a pink frock they'd purchased from a garment shop in Gretna Green. It hugged too tightly at her breasts, and hung too loose at her waist, but it would have to do. She'd feel more confident in one of her own gowns, which had been sewn for her body specifically and chosen for their ability to lure a man into proposing marriage. The proposal was over and done with, but her need to be alluring was greater than ever. Unfortunately, those gowns were all still back in London.

Nonetheless, by the time Maisie helped her with her hair and tied a cream-colored ribbon beneath her bust, the result was quite fetching. Charity looked in her glass and nodded in satisfaction. There was no sign of the madwoman Graeme was convinced he'd married.

Her heart hammered like it was trying to escape the confines of her chest when she heard his voice downstairs. She smoothed her skirts one last time, and tried not to trip as she flew down the stairs to meet him.

Graeme looked up to see his wife standing at the bottom of the stairs. It hurt to look at her. God, she was beautiful. If there was any other way...

Graeme closed his eyes. Steeled himself. He knew what he'd seen. And it explained so very much. From the first night they'd met, the signs of trouble had been there. He'd just been too enchanted to see them.

After last night's debacle, he'd spent the remainder of the dark hours trying to think of a solution. He'd come up empty.

He tipped his head towards the door to his study. "I was just going to review the ledgers. You may join me, if you wish." Even though it would be torture, to look but not touch. To want and never possess.

One would think that last night's episode would be enough to make him want to steer clear of her. After all, he'd seen what madness could do to a person.

His mother had suffered for years. True, her afflication had not manifested until the death of his father, and some days were better than others, but it was painful to watch. Probably even more painful to bear. Unlike the tales he'd heard of his Great Uncle, who'd been mad as a hatter and happy that way, his mother—or some small piece of her—seemed to know when she wasn't making sense. Only she couldn't figure out why. Which made it doubly hard.

Graeme believed himself entirely sane, but how could he be sure the propensity toward madness did not lurk somewhere within his blood? Such things were said to run in families, and his family had already seen its share. Everyone knew red hair often skipped a generation. What about insanity?

If he fathered a child with a woman he knew to be mad, no matter how normal she seemed most of the time...the risk was simply too great. He couldn't bear the guilt of knowingly causing the pain that child would experience.

And yet, seeing Charity standing there, he could not turn her away.

She followed him into the study and settled herself in a large chair opposite his desk. She curled her feet under her, looking for all the world like an innocent child.

Graeme opened the ledger book to the most recent accounts. Mentally, he added numbers, but they meant nothing to him. Instead he counted every breath she took, every slight shift of position.

His home, his kingdom, even the vast space of the highlands seemed to close in on him, crushing his very lungs. The happiest day of his life had been the day he married Charity. From the moment he'd met her, he'd been so certain that she was the one. That they belonged together. That their partnership was *right*. His conviction rooted deeper when he'd seen how Nathan took to her, as well as the staff at Leventhal House. He'd had everything he could possibly want. Except maybe a child of his own, and he'd planned to waste no time in that endeavor. Until now.

What was he *doing*? How had all his best plans, his good intentions, come to this?

How had he damned himself to be more alone than ever before?

He knew only too well, he could not stay here and *not* touch Charity. He hadn't been able to keep from touching her from the moment they'd met. And knowing how touching lead to tasting, and tasting to lovemaking…

Graeme growled in frustration as his body grew hard with the direction of his thoughts. Yes, he had to leave. Soon.

Hell, it could already be too late.

As if summoned by the direction of his thoughts, a discreet knock at the door signaled the arrival of his driver, Tom Brevis.

"The coach is ready, me lord."

He gave a nod. "Thank you."

Graeme watched the door close again, then turned his gaze to meet Charity's injured one.

"You're leaving." She didn't sound surprised. She didn't sound hurt. She didn't sound...anything.

Was he the one feeling it all? He cleared his throat. "For a time."

She bit her bottom lip. "Because of—" She swallowed audibly. "Because of last night?"

He sighed.

"I can explain," she offered. "Please. Let me tell you why that happened."

He was tempted. Sorely. Instead he stood. The ledgers could wait. "I cannot do this. I need some space. Some time to think. I'm sorry. I never meant to hurt you."

"But you are," she whispered. The sound barely escaped.

He heard it. He just couldn't listen anymore. The crushing disappointment threatened to drown him, suck him down into delusions of his own...delusions where everything was fine, where he could make love to the beautiful creature before him without fear he was damning the futures of his unborn children.

His emotions were too raw, his brain too sleep-deprived, to discuss anything further. He raised one hand, palm up, in a helpless gesture, then shook his head and stepped from the room. He just needed time. And distance.

Charity watched as her husband's shiny black coach pulled away from the drive and down the long lane to the main road. It would have been easier not to watch, perhaps, but she couldn't help it.

Vise-like pain gripped her heart, squeezing until she couldn't breathe through the ache.

Surely he would stop. He'd realize that this, too, was a kind of madness. Running from your problems didn't make them go away. She should know. She was an expert at running.

He would turn back. Allow her to explain. Forgive her. Love her.

Help her.

Because the terrifying truth of it was, Charity feared her husband was right. She'd kept her secret out of fear that suitors, and then Graeme, would look at her and see a defiled creature, rather than a lady of unstained virtue. It was a good reason—especially when one's husband was built of such noble character that a normal person could never hope to measure up. But that fear was not the one that gripped her now.

She was afraid that, somehow, while in the dank confines of her prison, something inside her had snapped and broken. Something that, maybe, couldn't be mended.

She was afraid she might, indeed, be crazy.

If she'd managed to talk to Graeme, he might have overlooked what those men had done to her. But obviously, he could not simply overlook crazy.

The coach bearing her husband away did not stop.

It rolled out of sight, but Charity stayed by the window, refusing to give up hope. He *would* stop. He would realize his mistake, and turn around. He had to.

But one hour passed, and then another. And Graeme did

not return.

Sometime during the first hour, the strength in Charity's legs gave way, and she sank to her knees, fingers still gripping the window sill in futile hope. After the second hour, her fingers too gave up, and she bent forward, her body keening in a long, silent cry.

Oh, God. Oh, God. She'd lost him. Lost everything. Her stupid inability to forget the past, to let go of old fears, had cost her the most wonderful husband and lover a woman could ask for. She rocked back and forth, body racked with painful shudders, an ache too profound for tears. Why, oh why, couldn't she be *normal* again? All she wanted was normal.

No. Not true. All she wanted was Graeme. And she'd lost him.

Chapter 13:

In which a nurse clucks her tongue, then gets down to the business of caring for her charge, which, as it turns out, isn't such difficult business at all.

Charity drifted like a ghost through the house. The servants' actions indicated no knowledge of what had caused their master's sudden departure. If they thought it odd he had business so urgent it would cause him to abandon his wife less than a fortnight after the wedding, they did not show it. The staff was as solicitous as ever. If they thought Charity was overwrought, if they noticed how she had to struggle through thick grief to find the words to answer even the simplest questions, they did not remark upon it.

In the space of a few short weeks, Graeme Ramsey Maxwell had gone from a dashing stranger to the very essence of her world. With him gone, the floor had fallen from under her feet. Every minute, every hour stretched out before her like an empty eternity.

Luncheon was served, but she forgot to attend. For supper,

the staff sent up a tray to her rooms. Graeme had not returned.

When the servant who delivered it turned to leave, Charity tried desperately to stall the man. *Donough*, she remembered, having only learned everyone's names. But "Thank you, Donough," were the only words she could find to penetrate the deep blanket of sadness that smothered her.

He bowed and left. Loneliness engulfed her.

The master chamber, with the enormous bed they'd joked about such a short time ago, now seemed to mock her tiny presence. The cavernous space echoed her lament at the loss of its master.

On one of her first nights here, she had giggled with mirth at Graeme's proclamation that it was a good thing they had this hallway to themselves, for no one else would get any sleep if he kept making her cry out in ecstasy.

Would he ever do so again? And now that she knew how amazing it was, how would she live without it? Without *him*?

With Graeme gone, the entire upper hall was eerily empty. Every creak, every whisper of the wind, raised the hair at the back of Charity's neck.

No guards. No strong, protective husband. Anything could happen here.

Her dinner grew cold.

The evening dragged on, and the hour grew late. Still, fear kept her awake. Fear, and the awful coldness of the empty sheets beside her.

Even the nursery was far away, in the opposite wing of the house. Mayhap she could suggest moving it. Not that she expected a seven year old and his caregiver to act as protection. It would just be comforting to know there were other humans nearby. And it would ease her mind, a little. The two of them had lived here longer and knew the noises of the house. If they slept peacefully, maybe she could, too.

Besides, Nathan was family now. She and Graeme were the closest thing to parents that the little boy had. Families *should* be together. Even families with flaws. She could tuck him in at night, read to him from her favorite storybooks and learn his favorites too…

But Graeme might be angry. He'd made it clear he thought her "illness" rendered her unfit as a mother. The last thing she wanted to do was anger him. If only they could reconcile. If only he would come back.

The following morning, Graeme had not returned. She hadn't really expected he would. When he hadn't returned for dinner the night before, intuition had told her she was in for a long wait. Another day stretched endlessly before her. She was too heart sore to even attempt a façade of normality in front of either Graeme's mother or young Nate, so she simply avoided all company. She didn't know them well enough yet to break down in front of them—which she surely would. Solitude was both her shelter and her prison.

It occurred to Charity to go after her husband, but he hadn't told her where he was going. Added to which, she really wasn't certain of the best protocol. She couldn't run to him and promise to never let it happen again. If she had that kind of control, there wouldn't be a problem in the first place. Would it be better to give her husband some time and space to think? That was what he'd said he needed, after all. She should respect that.

Was it too much to hope that, given the time and space he'd requested, he would come to terms with the fact that although she had these spells, she was still the woman he'd so passionately desired that he'd whisked her off to Scotland and married her barely two weeks after they'd met? Or had his disappointment and confusion turned to anger and bitterness toward her for knowingly deceiving him into that marriage? She prayed it wasn't the latter. If only she knew what he was thinking. Or where he was.

The only other indication Charity had as to Graeme's frame of mind came on the second day of his absence, via the arrival of Leventhal House's newest resident, sent there by the earl himself.

Charity's devastation at Graeme's departure was complete. No other feeling could penetrate her grief—at least, not until she met the new resident and learned her husband had sent her a nurse. Then, the fires of indignation pierced her consciousness.

She had come down to the lesser parlor upon learning from Mrs. Saxonberry that Lord Maxwell had hired a new member of the staff. She'd been prepared to greet a maid, or perhaps a gardener. A governess or tutor, perhaps, for Nathan.

"My name is Ismay, my lady. Ismay Boyd. I'm to be your nurse."

A *nurse?* The woman standing before her was young, perhaps only a few years older than herself, and yet her face appeared careworn.

Charity quirked a brow. "Miss Boyd, I think you are mistaken. Perhaps you mean you are to be nurse to young Nathan, my...nephew?" Nathan was legitimately her nephew, now that she and Graeme were married, but it felt somehow wrong to call him that—as though it pointed out his orphan status. What an odd little family they were turning out to be.

Miss Boyd shifted uncomfortably. "Nay, my lady. The earl—your husband, that is, he hired me to help your ladyship.

Are ye recovering from an illness, my lady?"

"Not exactly," Charity replied stiffly. *Ooh*, when she got her hands on that man... What was she thinking? If she ever got her hands on him, it would be all she could do not to throw herself into his arms and beg him to understand.

She took a deep breath and focused on the young woman in front of her. Her frustration with Graeme wasn't going to help right now. She straightened her posture, suddenly thankful for the years of etiquette training her mother had forced upon her.

Ismay Boyd shifted again. "He said ye had pride, my lady. I promise, I come qualified. I been a nurse since I was sixteen, and carin' for folk long 'afore that. I'll understand, if the illness is of a nature ye might not normally speak of..."

"What, exactly," Charity asked, "did my husband tell you of my 'ailment?'"

The two women squared off. Ismay's features took on a thoughtful expression, as though she was considering the kindest way to answer. She needn't have bothered. Charity read the truth in her eyes.

"He thinks I'm insane," she said dully.

The pity she read in the other woman's eyes made her want to claw them out just so she wouldn't have to see it anymore. Except then she really would be insane.

"I don't need your help."

"He said you would say that. He also said that the rest of the household doesn't know. I thought, maybe, that if you were to allow me to help you—just a little bit—they might never find out."

Charity was reluctantly impressed. Ismay Boyd knew how to manipulate a person as well as any aspiring miss in London. She couldn't deny the woman's point. Even if *she* knew she wasn't crazy, others would not understand her behavior. Her husband included. It was only a matter of time before the others discovered her secret. If everyone started treating her like a madwoman, she might very well become one.

Not to mention she had a feeling that, even if she tried, she couldn't send Ismay Boyd packing. Better to capitulate, no matter how it rankled to give in. At least that way she'd have some company in this godforsaken wilderness.

"Truly, I am not a madwoman, Miss Boyd. But I do sometimes have terrible nightmares," she confessed.

"Oh, my lady." Ismay's compassion sounded genuine.

"And I have trouble sleeping." In for a penny, in for a pound.

Ismay gave her a gentle smile. "Lack of sleep could drive even the sanest person to act mad now and then."

"When it first started, my physician back home prescribed laudanum. That helped some. For a while. Perhaps it actually helped too much. I didn't want that to become my life…drugged out of my senses every night."

Ismay nodded. "I 'ave seen that, indeed, an' far too often. 'Tis no life for a young woman such as yerself, my lady. I am no physician, but I'll do my best to help. And I thank you for trusting me enough to tell me."

There was plenty more she *hadn't* told, but Charity didn't feel like pointing that out just yet. A more pressing problem had just occurred to her. "What position does the housekeeper believe you are interviewing for?" *Please don't say nurse. Please don't say nurse*, she thought fervently.

"The earl told her I was training to become a lady's companion." Ismay smiled. "Imagine that. Me, a lady's companion. It sounds quite lovely, if a bit above my station."

Charity couldn't help but smile. She and Miss Boyd could

share their secret, and both women might even benefit. It almost reminded her of her youth, when she and Elizabeth would share secrets and come up with harebrained schemes together.

"In that case, I shall be happy to instruct you."

From a certain, absurdly-impersonal perspective, Charity could not fault her husband's kindness. He hadn't locked her in an attic. He hadn't sent her back to London, or, worse, had her carted off to Bedlam. Other men might very well have done so. It was why she'd feared marriage in the first place.

By telling his household that her nurse was actually a lady's companion-in-training, he'd protected her further and, unwittingly, given her a companion that kept the wrenching loneliness from becoming too much to bear.

But, oh, it stung to know Graeme had gone from looking at her with desire to looking at her with pity. He thought her incompetent. So much so, he'd sent her—no matter what rest of the household thought Ismay Boyd to be—a *nurse*.

In truth, Ismay had very little to do. Her meager belongings were quickly settled in the maid's quarters next to Charity's room. After the first lonely night, Charity had decided to move to the bedroom belonging to the lady of the manor. And why not? She was still the lady of the manor, since her absentee husband had not actually cast her aside. At any rate, it was too painful to think of sleeping in the bed she'd shared with Graeme without him there.

The arrangement suited Charity and Ismay both. "This way I can wake ye if the dreams get to be too bad," Ismay promised.

Charity nodded. From Gretna Green, she had written to

London to send for her things, and offered her lady's maid a handsome pay increase if she would come work at Lord Maxwell's home. Her trunks were on the way, but Penny was not. A note from Elizabeth indicated she'd taken employment elsewhere rather than live among the "wild folk." So the little maid's room was empty. She'd been considering offering it to Maisie—who was indeed a hair-styling wonder, in spite of her tendency to prattle—when Miss Boyd had shown up.

"A true lady's companion, though, would take affront at being assigned the maid's quarters. Perhaps we should station you in one of the lesser bedrooms." Charity clasped her hands and peered down the hallway, wistfully. The idea of having someone close by was so appealing, she hated to sacrifice it.

"Ach. But, you see, I am only a lady's companion *in training*," Ismay declared, mischief lighting her eyes.

"Oh, yes, I nearly forgot," Charity replied, relieved. Not only would she have someone nearby, but that someone had promised to help keep her secret. Maisie's penchant for gossip would have meant trouble for them both. It rankled to realize that Graeme had found a way to provide everything she needed most—except himself. His acts were kind and lordly, yet oh-so-infuriating. "Well, then, perhaps when you complete your training," she told Miss Boyd, "We shall promote you to a nicer room."

"Aye, my lady. No hurry. Don't ye worry. These quarters is far nicer than some."

After the matter of sleeping arrangements was settled, there was little else required.

"What shall I do first?" Ismay asked, to which Charity simply held up her hands in a questioning gesture.

"As I said, I am not truly a lunatic. At least, not very often. If I was, do you think his lordship would have married me in the first place?"

"My lady, I do not know what to think, in truth."

Charity blinked. Fair enough. Of course the madwoman would claim she was sane. She could tell Ismay watched her closely over the next couple days, relaxing bit by bit as Charity's behavior stood tribute to her claims.

"This job is too good to be true," Ismay announced by the third morning, enunciating carefully, as though she were indeed training for a higher station. The two women practiced speech and reading each morning, in keeping with the farce. "Never have I had such luxury."

The two women sat in the library. Charity had selected a volume of poetry—Lord Maxwell's library being somewhat short on the novels she generally preferred—while Ismay embroidered a lace cuff.

"You said you've been a nurse for some years. Is it usually quite hard, then?"

"I shouldn't speak so of my work. The things I've had to do…well, when a person is sick, you do what must be done. Much of it indelicate." She wrinkled her nose. "Let us not speak of that. My lady, may I ask a question?"

Charity nodded warily.

"I have heard you tossing and turning in your sleep each night, and I know sometimes you stand at the window for long hours before seeking the refuge of bed, but, my lady, this hardly seems to merit my presence. Is it possible you and your earl had a misunderstanding?"

A rueful smirk lifted Charity's features for the first time in days. "That would be one way of putting it."

"Perhaps, if the two of you were to talk…"

"Do you know where he is?"

Ismay looked surprised, then sad. "No, my lady."

Charity let out a long sigh. "'Tis a misunderstanding between the earl and I, to be sure. But that is only part of it. You have yet to see the full extent of my troubles."

Ismay's careworn face showed only concern. "What else should I be looking for?"

"As much as I would like to castigate him, my husband is not entirely without cause in sending you to me. You'll know when you see." She left it at that.

After the noon meal, Charity let herself out the back entrance, heading for the gardens. She'd sent Miss Boyd to visit Graeme's mother. Guilt pricked her for not going along, for she suspected the older woman must suffer from loneliness. She just couldn't face a family visit yet. Her feelings were still too raw. What would she say if Lady Eleanor asked about her son? Or how she was enjoying married life? As confused as she often seemed, Charity suspected the dowager countess possessed an uncanny ability to understand emotion. It was a theory she didn't feel quite ready to test.

At least Miss Boyd would give her some company this day.

The gray sky cast a shadow that seemed to drain the color from the earth below.

The growing season was shorter here, so the vegetable garden was mostly contained in a long greenhouse. The open-air kitchen gardens, as they were, contained a mix of herbs and flowers. Charity recognized buttercups, violets, and sweetbriar—bright spots of color cheerily defying the dreary sky. Peppermint poked up among the buttercups. The other plants, she couldn't name.

Ahead of her on the path, Nate's small figure appeared. He used the toe of his boot to kick a round stone, turning it over and over.

"Good morning, Nate," she called.

He slowed until she caught up. "Morning, Aunt Charity." He kicked the stone again and it rolled a few feet.

"What are you playing?"

He shrugged. "Nothing, really."

It struck her that he looked bored. Or lonely. And why not? He had no playmates here. The town and the crofters' cottages were too far for a child his age to walk alone.

"What game is your favorite?"

He had to think about that for a while. "Hide and seek, probably." He meandered a few steps and gave the rock a half-hearted kick. "I like it best when Uncle Graeme plays, though."

"I'll bet," Charity managed, before the lump that had settled in her throat when Graeme left choked off her words.

"He was supposed to stay this time," Nate mumbled, looking at the ground rather than her.

Tears welled in her eyes as a fresh wave of guilt assailed her. It was *her* fault he'd been abandoned again, even if Nathan didn't know it. She stooped to wrap her arm around his thin shoulders in a hug. To her surprise, the little boy didn't pull back, but turned in to receive her hug more fully. She knelt, wrapped both arms around him and gave a squeeze. "I know. He's an important man, your uncle. He has many responsibilities to oversee."

He drew back and gave her a look that was way too old for his seven years. "People always leave."

Her heart ached for him. For herself. Even for Graeme. The melancholy threatened to drag her under if she only let it.

"Mrs. Saxonberry says I'm to have a new governess," Nate offered. "Uncle Graeme sent word. Do you think she'll be nice?"

"I'm sure your uncle wouldn't hire a governess who wasn't."

He looked skeptical. "Governesses don't seem to like it here much. But mayhap she can teach me some new games before she leaves."

The poor woman had been dismissed before she'd ever arrived. Nate must have seen quite a stream of them come and go to be that nonchalant about it.

Something told her this little boy needed her as badly as she needed him—all comments about unfit mothers aside. She thought for a minute, then stood and brushed off her skirts. "How about you and I play hide and seek? I used to be quite good at it, actually."

He eyed her doubtfully. "You?"

Charity reached deep and summoned a smile. "Try me."

Jasper Morton was well on the way to forgetting the past, and to the past forgetting him, until he trundled into the local inn one evening for supper and found the whole establishment chattering excitedly about the comely new lass in town.

"Evenin,' Munro." The innkeeper greeted him, as he did each and every patron.

Jasper silently chortled as he made for his usual spot along the wall, close enough to the fire to be on the fringes of conversation, but not in the thick of it. His one last theft—before he'd resigned himself to a life of legitimate labor—had been to burglarize a church registrar. He'd stolen the birth record and matching death certificate of a baby born the same year as himself. Then he'd burned the death certificate.

He was now Willard Munro. It was the smartest move he'd ever made. The best part was that the real Willard Munro had died twenty-odd years ago, before ever even learning to speak his own name. Absolutely no one would be looking for him.

He accepted the mug of ale the innkeeper brought over, leaning back against the wall until the wooden legs of his stool tipped up. The conversation swirled around him.

The new lass, it turned out, was not really a lass. She was a lady. And she was not really in *town*. She was at Leventhal House, the family seat of the Earl of Leventhal, having recently married the earl himself.

Normally Jasper did not trouble himself with such matters. The nobility moved in circles quite removed from his own—except in rare instances.

"From London, she is," one of the patrons affirmed.

"Don' know why his lordship 'ad to go all the way to London to find himself a mate," one of the women grumbled.

"Ach, Bessie, mos' every lord does that. Besides, she's right pretty to look at, to hear tell."

"O' course she is. Lord Maxwell is a handsome one, and not one o' them lords what gambled all their lands and fortunes away three generations ago, still hangin' on to a title."

"What about his wife? Is she of noble blood as well?"

Another woman jumped in. "Aye, indeed. But her pa was only a baron."

Jasper snorted into his ale. *Only a baron*. Like any of them had ever even dreamt of holding such rank.

"That's right, that's right. Baron Medford. Died a few years' back, though."

"You think Lady Charity will stay, then?"

The woman called Bessie giggled. "If Lord Maxwell gets her in the family way, I 'magine she'll stay."

The voices dimmed as the ringing in Jasper's ears took over. *Medford*. No. *No bloody way*. The one time in recent years that his path had crossed with that of the nobility, it had led to the unfortunate kidnapping of one Charity Medford. The only unmarried daughter of the late Baron Medford.

Apparently, she was no longer unmarried.

Nor was she dead. He'd rather thought she was dead. Lucky little bitch.

Jasper pondered his mug of ale. Even with a new identity, Miss Medford—or rather, Lady Charity Maxwell—was now too close for comfort. As Willard Munro, he kept mostly to himself, but a man still had to work, still had to eat. There was no guarantee he could keep from crossing her path.

Bloody woman. He'd consigned himself to a life lived at the edge of civilization, and he still couldn't get away. If she saw him, it would take only one word to her husband or her ducal brother-in-law, and he was done for.

A fruit fly buzzed over and landed on the edge of his mug. He brushed it off, but the blasted thing flew right into the ale. If Jasper had been a superstitious man, he'd have taken that as a sign. Was he, like the fly, in over his head?

As it was, Jasper was not superstitious. Nor was he especially picky. He hefted the mug and took a long swallow. This was not the life he'd once dreamed of. He'd grown up among the dredges of society. Pickpockets, gamblers, light skirts…they were the fabric of his childhood neighborhood. But he'd always thought better luck was around the corner.

If he just lifted the right purse, or paid a favor for the right patron, he'd be done with all of this. He'd take his little windfall and move far away, to a house in a town somewhere where the townspeople saw loose floorboards as a problem to be fixed—not a convenient place to store coins so they wouldn't be stolen.

Only his luck never turned. And one job led to the next, until here he was. A wanted man.

Jasper cast a baleful eye at his mug. Seeing no sign of the

fruit fly, he tipped it up and downed the contents.

Chapter 14:

Blessed are they who yet find hope in the darkest of days...

Ismay Boyd got her first taste of Charity's "nightmares" at the end of her first week of employment, just two nights after the arrival of Nathan's new governess.

A bloodcurdling scream awakened Ismay. Always a light sleeper, she jumped from bed, throwing open the door that connected her room with Lady Charity's. Running footsteps sounded outside the door. She cracked it open and thrust out her head to see the white-faced governess, whose own arrival had been just two days before. She must have sprinted all the way from the other wing. "Go back to bed. 'Twas only a spider. A great, hairy one, to be sure, but 'tis quite dead now."

She slammed the door. She'd promised to protect her mistress's secret, and she would.

Moonlight flooded the chamber with a bright, otherworldly glow.

Lady Charity stood at the open window, her halo of blond

hair floating about her as she muttered about an escape plan. She was worried the window was too high to jump.

Calmly, Ismay approached her.

"No! No, don't come any closer!"

Ismay reached for the glass of water Lady Charity kept near her bed. She could fling it at her to startle her from her reverie...but that might make things worse. Slowly, never taking her eyes off her mistress, she took a sip. Then another.

The movement, so very normal, had the desired effect.

"Wait. What are you doing? That's my water. Why are you..."

Ismay saw the flare of recognition.

"Miss Boyd?" A shudder ran the length of the young noblewoman's body. She staggered toward the chaise and collapsed.

When the shaking subsided, Ismay sat down next to Charity, who was curled in a ball on the chaise.

Charity felt the other woman's hand resting lightly on her shoulder.

"I suppose now you understand why you were hired," she said tiredly. She'd been battling these demons so long, she was starting to wonder if she'd ever actually beat them.

"When that happens, do you know what causes it? Or what frightens you so? Or does it just...come upon you?" Ismay asked. There was no censure in her tone, only curiosity.

"I know." Oh, did she ever.

"Do ye want to tell me about it, my lady?" Ismay asked gently. "Sometimes it helps to talk to someone."

Charity tugged her hair. She was desperate to have someone finally understand. She'd wanted that someone to be Graeme. But she'd scared him off too soon. Then again, he was the one who'd sent the nurse to her, and Miss Boyd *did* have a way about her that made people naturally trust her. "The doctor says it would be better to forget. Speaking of it just means I'm dwelling on it."

Ismay nodded sagely. "Does he, now. I have no' the training of a doctor. Mayhap he knows best."

"But I can't forget," Charity blurted. "I've tried, and tried, and I always fail."

Ismay was quiet a moment. "Mmm. I can't tell you what to do, my lady. I can't even promise talking will help. But I have two good ears. If you decide you want to, I can promise I won't judge you."

The thick fear that had so long imprisoned her began to dissolve as Charity gave up fighting and took what the other woman offered. She spoke slowly, worrying the end of one ringlet between her fingers as she searched for the words she had to get out. "Something really bad happened. Afterward, everything in my life was…different. I tried to go on like things were the same, but it all fell apart. Things *were* the same. It was me that was different."

She knew Ismay Boyd had to be utterly confused, but to the woman's credit, she only waited as Charity worked up the courage to get more specific. These words could damn her. She had to get them out anyway. Bottled inside, they were already damning her. They were turning her into the creature of madness she was fighting so hard not to be.

"Last year, I did something foolish. Utterly stupid. My friend, Lady Beatrice Pullington, and I got caught up in an intrigue. A group of French informants had infiltrated London, trying to harness any knowledge that would keep General Bonaparte from his ultimate defeat."

"They did not succeed."

"No. They did not. But Bea and I overheard them making

plans. When we realized what we'd heard, we told the authorities. They were most impressed, especially with Bea, for she was the one who deciphered their code." She sighed, uncurling slowly from her ball. "She'd thought it a lover's note. A harmless mystery. We had no idea what we were getting into. After we told the authorities, I should have forgotten all about it, and gone on with enjoying my first Season." She smiled. "I had quite a few suitors."

"Of course you did, my lady. You are so lovely."

"You needn't flatter me, but thank you. My point is, I didn't stop there. I wanted to keep helping. I wanted people to think I was clever, too, like Bea. Those men were still on the loose, so I did some spying of my own. As I said, foolish. They caught me."

She hardly registered Ismay's soft gasp.

"They held me captive for, oh, I don't know. It wasn't very long, really, but it felt like an age." She gripped the chaise, her fingers digging into the cushioning. "I was so scared."

"They harmed you." Ismay took one of Charity's hands in her own.

Charity made a frustrated gesture with the other. "The doctor who examined me afterward proclaimed me unharmed." Sarcasm laced her tone. "What else would he say, with the Duke of Beaufort hovering anxiously in the next room?"

Ismay thought about that. Her expression said she didn't give much credence to the doctor's opinion, either.

"Did they...forgive me, my lady. Did they force themselves on you?"

Charity was quiet a long moment. "I don't know," she answered finally. "I was bound and gagged, and forced to drink something that knocked me unconscious. I don't know how long I was out, or what happened then. I—I don't think they raped me. My dress was torn, and I had many bruises, but…I don't think so. I awoke only shortly before the men were tipped off. They knew the authorities were after them. We'd been hiding in an old warehouse. They abandoned it like rats jumping from a sinking ship. But I was a problem. Their leader wasn't going to let anything slow him down. He directed the one of lowest rank to take care of it. Of me. The building had a cellar. Just a dirt hole. Very damp, being so near the docks. He dumped me there. Barred me in. And then he left me there, but not before he had his bit of fun." The vile words spilled out, picking up speed until they formed a torrent, washing over her, tearing at her with their power. Ismay Boyd kept hold of her hand, never letting go, providing an anchor to keep the torrent from sweeping her away.

"'Men like me, we don't often get the chance at a pretty set o' skirts like you,' he said," she repeated, the words burned into her memory like a scar.

"He touched me. Squeezed so hard it hurt. But he…" *Oh God, oh God, how do I say this.* Just the memories made her stomach churn. "It excited him too much, having this power over me. He hit me, forced me down. He tossed up my skirts, but before he could…complete the act, he, uh, finished." She ducked her head, expecting the piercing shame to choke off her words again. But, after a few shaky breaths, she kept going. "The last thing he did was leave me a parting gift. A tiny vial, marked with skull and crossbones. I saw the markings in the light of his lantern. Then he locked me in, taking the light with him."

Ismay's brows knitted. "Poison?"

"Yes. An insidious act of mercy. I could end my own life, if I chose, or wait for natural death in the deep darkness."

"Dear God," Ismay whispered.

"I was so angry, I flung it away. Not because I had faith I would survive. Just anger."

The nurse's expression, as promised, betrayed no judgment.

Relieved, Charity continued. "I thought I would die down there. It was so utterly black. No light penetrated at all. I screamed and screamed until I hadn't any voice left, but no one came. I felt the walls, the door, finding my way by touch, trying not to guess what little objects the toes of my slippers came into contact with. I felt for any means of escape. A loose board, another door. There was nothing but walls of clay and the single, barred door.

"I couldn't give up, not even then. I tried beating on the door, clawing at the walls. Nothing happened. The door was thick, but wood. I thought maybe, if I couldn't claw a tunnel through the walls, I could get past the door. I used my hairpins until they all bent and broke. Then my fingertips, until the nails and skin wore off and they bled. Still I kept at it, until the pain was too great.

"I knew that was the end. I had nothing left. No one would know where to find me. No one would hear me. I paced the length of that prison. Six in length, four across. Six, then four. Again, and again. I lost track of time. I might have slept—I don't know.

"At some point, I found myself just sitting on the dank ground. That's when I realized I'd been wrong. I did have one thing left—if I could find it."

"The poison," her nurse whispered.

Charity lowered her eyes, acknowledging the truth. "It shames me to know I sank so low. That I crept on hands and knees, searching for the hated thing I'd so casually thrown away."

"What happened?" Ismay held a hand to her heart.

"I found it, eventually. When I'd flung it and it landed, the stopper must have come loose. Most of the contents had leached into the ground." She paused. "To this day I don't know if, had that not happened, I might have taken the poison. As it was, my careless arrogance saved me. Because now I had another thought. If I *broke* the vial, the glass might succeed in carving through the door where my hairpins and fingernails had failed."

"Clever, and brave," Ismay murmured.

She laughed bitterly. "Do you know, that bloody vial was nearly shatterproof? I stomped on it, beat it against the wall, even bit it. Finally the curved lip at the top broke off, leaving a sharp edge. I took to the door again. It felt like I was making progress. I'm sure by then I was delusional, desperate. But I could feel a groove, feel it getting deeper. Of course, I was going to need far more than a groove to get free, but it was *something*. Until it shattered. I worked so hard to get one little piece to break off, and then it just fell apart, tiny slivers of glass penetrating my bloodied fingertips. It hurt so badly. I'm sure traces of the poison were still there…maybe that's why. I hadn't even realized that until now. I kept going, using the biggest slivers to do whatever I could, which amounted to nothing, until sheer exhaustion overtook me."

"My God," Ismay said, still in a whisper.

"I should have had more faith. Alex, that's my sister's husband, the Duke of Beaufort, and Lady Pullington's husband—though this was before they were married—found me after all. They brought me home, fetched the doctor, and hired guards to protect me until they caught all those men. And then we tried to put 'the incident' behind us."

"Oh, my lady, how could you?"

Charity gave a self-deprecating laugh. "Do you know, I thought at first that I could? That after a few days, my fingers would heal, the criminals would all have been caught, and I would go back to dance the waltz at Almack's and preen whenever I overheard someone refer to me as 'a diamond of the first water.'" She swallowed. "Things did not work out the way I had planned. Strange things would happen. Some days I was fine. Others, it all came rushing back to me, like I was in that dark hole again, with no way out. I began to have trouble sleeping. I began fearing crowds. Developing odd little habits, precautions that probably did nothing but somehow made me feel better. I would think I *was* getting better, and then some little thing—something others might not even notice—would set me off."

"Understandable."

Charity shook her head. "Not to everyone. And certainly not to people who didn't know what had happened. I told you before, that the doctor had prescribed laudanum because I had trouble sleeping. Now you know the real reason why."

"Oh, Lady Maxwell."

"Please, please do not pity me. I cannot bear it."

Ismay rubbed the back of her hand. The pity disappeared from her expression, but the understanding remained. She tapped a finger on her chin. "I think you must be very brave, to have lived through that and carried on, with most of London none the wiser. You must have felt so alone at times."

Charity blinked. No one had ever called her brave. Mischievous, and reckless, yes, but not brave. And there was no question that she'd felt alone. How was it that this one young nurse understood what no one else had?

"Ye know," Ismay added thoughtfully, "what you are describing sounds a lot like what happened to my brother."

"He was kidnapped?"

"Nay, nay. He was a soldier. Not one o' your fancy officers, mind, just a soldier. He fought on the Continent, against General Bonaparte's armies—the first time, before the general's exile. My point is, he saw some bad things. Soldiers who lost an arm, or a leg. Soldiers left to die on the battlefield because their wounds were too severe to allow for transport. Orphans going hungry in war-ravaged towns. I could go on, but ye have the idea. When he returned home, we were ever so happy to have our Joseph back. He hadn't a wife, so mum took him in, and gladly. But he weren't the same, my lady."

"How had he changed?" Charity was all ears.

"It was like ye jus' said. Couldn't sleep, and had terrible dreams when he did. His old friendships fell by the wayside. His new companions were mostly crusty old sailors—when Joseph tried to be social at all. Crowds made him skittish. Sometimes, he'd hoard food, or odd things like socks and string."

Oh, my. The young soldier's tale resonated with Charity. Though she hadn't made friends with any old sailors, she'd definitely forsaken her old set for a new, wilder group of friends. The rest was a pretty close match.

Still, she felt guilty for drawing the comparison. "He was a soldier, away at war for, what? A year? Longer? He must have faced troubles greater than I can comprehend."

"Two years, or two days…do ye really think it matters? Ye both looked death in the face, and ye both were affected by it. Do ye want to know the only real difference I see?"

She continued on, accepting Charity's silence as assent. "Begging your pardon, my lady, but my brother was never taken prisoner, never threatened with rape. When he came home, we praised his noble service, his contribution to our country's effort. But you? No one praised you. You put yourself at risk for Britain, too, but your efforts were hushed up, turned into something shameful. My brother *could* talk to people—when he was ready—and find acceptance among others who had suffered. I don't believe you have had that luxury, my lady."

Thick tears blurred her vision. "No. No, I haven't. I've talked to no one until now. I could have talked to Elizabeth, my sister. She would have listened. But she was so worried, and she wanted so badly for me to be happy and well again. I couldn't bear to tell her just how *un*happy and *un*well I really was."

"That must have been hard."

Charity read pity in Ismay's expression again, but the emotion was pure, without any calculation or condescension. For the first time, she didn't immediately want to claw back against it.

"I was told to tell no one," Charity went on. "If no one were the wiser, it would be as though it never happened. But if people found out…no man would ever take me for his wife. I would be ruined."

"That hardly seems fair."

A strangled laugh escaped her. "None of it is fair. But it is the hand I've been dealt. And since I am the one who shuffled the deck, so to speak, I've no one but myself to blame.

"No. That is *not* true! Not at all, my lady." Ismay caught up both Charity's hands in her own, gripping firmly, until Charity met her gaze dead on. "This is *not* your fault. Your attempt at heroics may have been foolish, but it did not give those men the right to do any of that to you. I might not have been raised by polite society, or among the wealthy of London, but I was raised to know right from wrong. What those men did was wrong."

Charity couldn't think, there was so much buzzing in her brain. Through the blur of her tears, the nurse's moonlit face took on an otherworldly appearance. Maybe she was an angel, sent from above. Or maybe she was just the one human in Charity's life who knew the words she'd so badly needed to hear.

Please, don't let go, she silently willed her companion. Ismay held tight. Charity began to tremble as the other woman's words sank in, took root. *Not her fault.* A great sob rose up and escaped, and before she knew it she was bent double, sobbing her heart out while Ismay Boyd, the nurse she hadn't even wanted, wrapped her arms around her and simply held tight.

The heaving sobs eventually subsided into a gentler flow of tears. Charity let them out, way past the point of caring what anyone thought. Ismay Boyd's arms never faltered.

When she was all cried out, emptiness overtook her. She raised her head, expecting to feel shame, or remorse, or *something* after all she'd just poured out. But there was nothing. And it was a good sort of nothing.

"Better?" the nurse asked.

Charity considered that. "Not good, but better."

Ismay gave a small shrug. "Sometimes it helps to talk."

"Miss Boyd?"

"Aye, my lady?"

"Did your brother ever overcome his…affliction?"

Ismay thought about that. "Sort of, over time. He's been home jus' over two year, now. He still prefers his new friends over the old, but he is sleeping better. A large crowd might still upset him, but a small gathering would be fine, if he knew the folks in attendance. I pray he will continue to improve."

Charity nodded. "And the…episodes?"

"Mum says they're very rare now."

Relief surged through her, bringing on a fresh spate of tears.

"There now, my lady."

"I'm not upset," Charity mumbled. "Miss Boyd, you are better than any doctor."

Ismay laughed. "Nay, my lady. I know that to be false."

"'Tis true," Charity insisted. "You have given me what all their potions and advice could not. You've given me hope."

Emotions spent, exhaustion took hold, and Charity felt her body drifting slowly back toward slumber. She cast a longing glance toward her bed.

"Miss Boyd, may I tell you one more thing?"

"Of course."

"It's been a long time, almost a year now, since the incident. For all I know, I am worrying over nothing—but not all of my dreams involve the past. Sometimes, the thought of the evil that still lurks, somewhere in this world, is what tips me over the edge. Two of those men were never caught."

This time, it was Ismay who looked like she would have trouble sleeping.

Chapter 15:

"The heart will break, but broken, live on."
— Lord Byron.

After sleeping the soundest, deepest sleep she'd slept in a year, Charity awoke full of restless energy.

The cavernous house would swallow her up if she stayed in it any longer.

She was tempted to track down her husband. Surely if she pressed his mother, or the various members of the staff, for information, *someone* would know where she'd be likely to find him.

But for once in her life, her conscience cautioned her, and she heeded it. She felt many, many times better this morning. She had hope, finally, that her demons would someday subside.

Still, her heart ached for Graeme. He'd walked into her life and, literally, swept her off her feet. She'd fallen so fast and hard, she'd ignored the warning signs. She'd known she wasn't ready, that marriage would expose her troubles. She'd just been too enamored of Graeme to give him up.

If she went to him now, with feelings still so raw, she could promise him nothing more than what he'd already had—and rejected. But if she remained here, where at least one person understood her and did not condemn her to a future of hidden lunacy, then maybe, just maybe, she could finally heal. She could become the woman Graeme loved and needed in a wife. It was what she'd meant to do anyway.

Not that she wouldn't have a few choice words for him when she *did* finally see him.

Since running after Graeme was not an option—at least not a *wise* option—and Nathan was tied up in lessons with the new governess, Charity was at loose ends. She even braved a visit to Graeme's mother, only to learn Lady Eleanor had a standing date with three ladies from church for luncheon and card-playing every Monday.

That revelation gave her pause. The elder Lady Maxwell was not the lonely recluse Charity had first thought. She had her problems, as well, but apparently her friends had not all abandoned her. In some ways, the Highlanders were turning out to be more civilized than their lofty London counterparts.

Maybe Graeme was right, and fate *had* brought her here. If that were true, then surely fate would also find a way to reunite her with him.

"Miss Boyd," Charity suggested brightly, as the two women walked back toward the manor from the dowager house, "Shall we go into town this afternoon instead?"

"If ye wish, my lady. Have ye something in mind?"

She shook her head. "I just need an outing. And that is precisely the sort of thing a lady's companion-in-training is meant to do."

"I should like that as well, my lady," Ismay responded, drawing herself up straighter as she often did when reminded of her "training." "Are you feeling up to it?"

"Yes. You needn't worry. The town is small. Nothing about it that would, uh, distress me. My troubles come mainly at night." In the days her nurse had been here, Charity had succumbed to the occasional bout of tears, but never during daylight hours had she shown so much as a hint of an "episode" that might be construed as madness.

Ismay's eyes softened. "I didn't mean it that way, my lady. I don't think ye're mad, not really. Just troubled, and there's no shortage of troubles in the world. I just thought ye might be tired after last night."

She doesn't think I'm mad. Another piece of the protective barrier she'd placed between herself and the world around her chipped and fell away.

When they reached the house, Charity rang for a footman and gave instructions to have a carriage and driver readied. It would mark the first time she'd left the estate since Graeme's departure. But after all, why not? Her husband might question her sanity, but he'd left no instruction that would force her to stay confined to Leventhal House. To be honest, she wasn't sure *what* he expected of her anymore. She squared her shoulders. She was Lady Charity Maxwell, the lady of the house. Cowering inside it was no way to live.

Grantown on Spey was but a tiny village compared to London, but it did boast a town square lined with shops. If there was one thing likely to cheer Charity up, it was an afternoon of shopping. Charity and Ismay exited the coach at the square, so they might explore at will.

The grassy block was filled with others of similar mind, enjoying the sunny afternoon while they ran errands, sold goods, and caught up on each other's news. The recent rains had left the streets washed clean, and budding blooms poked their heads up from many a flower pot and window box. The effect was charming, a far cry from the wilderness Charity had envisioned on the journey to the highlands.

Aside from the permanent stores, a number of outdoor vendors had set up booths. She stopped at each and every one to admire the townsfolk's wares. At one, she bought a lovely lavender candle, to the absolute delight of the vendor. She couldn't help but coo over a shop window filled with tiny knitted bonnets and blankets, though that was sure to set the gossip afire. Even Miss Boyd couldn't hide an amused smirk.

The enthusiasm of the people she encountered brought a real smile to her face. She hadn't quite gotten used to her new role as the earl's wife. In London, she hadn't been a nobody, but she also hadn't had shopkeepers falling over themselves to gain her patronage. *Especially* not shopkeepers—seeing as how most of London had known her father died in debt. Things had improved when Elizabeth married her duke, but Charity had always felt like, well, a charity case. Not so in Grantown. Some might call her shallow for soaking up the attention so happily, but she wasn't going to worry about that today. The boost to her confidence was greatly needed.

"Mac, no!"

Charity's musings were interrupted as a flash of brown and white fur sped across the grass and headed straight for her. She braced herself, but there was no impact. The puppy skidded to a stop right at her feet. It looked up at her with soulful eyes. His tail gave a little thump.

"Oh, Miss Boyd, just look at him!" Charity cried.

A young lad came running up. He looked between her and Miss Boyd, his mouth forming an O as he realized who they must be. He scooped up the puppy in one arm as he attempted an awkward bow. "I'm sorry, my lady. I hope 'e didn't frighten ye."

Charity smiled. "Not at all. May I hold him? You call him Mac?"

"Aye, my lady." He handed over the puppy. "Only, if ye please, I have a whole basketful of 'em what'll be getting loose if I don't get back there."

"You have a basketful of puppies?" Right then Charity knew, just *knew*, what her nephew Nathan needed more than anything else in the world. "Are they for sale?"

He laughed in disbelief. "Aye, that they are. Ye want a puppy, my lady?"

"Yes. Oh yes, I do. Very much."

"Munro!"

Jasper started. *Right.* That was him.

"Quit gawking at the ladyfolk and come help me wi' this wool."

He bobbed his head. "Aye, sir. Right away, sir." *That had been close. Too close. The blond chit, Charity Medford, had indeed come to Grantown. Only she was Lady Maxwell now.*

"No need to 'sir' me," his boss told him. "Just get on with it. There'll be fish comin' in after this, an' I don't fancy workin' after dark."

"Right ye are." He hefted his end of the pallet and loaded it on to the cart that would pull it down to the dock. The fine, thick wool of the local sheep was in high demand. The local weavers took what they could, and the rest was packed down, palletized, and loaded on to river barges that would carry it south toward the factories springing up in the larger towns.

Fish and other goods came and went from the docks as well. It was backbreaking, but there was plenty of work to be had.

Fortunately, the work required more muscle than thought. *Too close. If she had so much as caught a glimpse of him...* This would never work. He hadn't wanted to believe the rumors, but his own eyes had just confirmed them. Unfortunately, no amount of work on the docks was going to yield the kind of coin he'd need to start a new life far, far away.

The puppy was, as Charity had guessed he would be, a tremendous hit with Nathan.

She didn't dare bring him in the house, being uncertain whether he was housebroken. In her excitement over the idea, she'd forgotten to ask.

She brought him to the grounds behind the house, instead, where Nathan was engrossed in a nature lesson with the recently-arrived governess. Another of Lord Maxwell's hires. Charity ground her teeth. A nurse for her and a governess for his nephew. *Why, with both wards taken care of,* she could just imagine him thinking, *I can stay away indefinitely.*

No. She would not spoil this occasion with sour thinking. She straightened the bright red bow she'd attached to Mac's collar, then set the squirming bundle down.

Immediately he bounded over to sniff the two strangers. Nathan and the governess shot to their feet as Mac raced around them in happy circles.

Nathan sprang after the puppy, finally managing to tackle him in a bed of buttercups. The boy and puppy looked up at Charity, both panting, the red bow now crazily askew.

"Master Nathan, meet Mac. Mac, meet your new master." She made a grand flourish with her hand as she made the introductions.

"Master? Me? I'm to be...that is, he's *mine*?"

Charity's smile felt like it had stretched to engulf her whole face. "Unless you don't want him, of course," she teased.

"I want him! I want him! Oh, Aunt Charity!"

"I don't suppose you know anything about training him?" she asked hopefully.

He gave her a quizzical look. "Training him for what?"

Charity gave a half-laugh, half-sigh. "Training him *not* to do indoors, the sort of things puppies are supposed to do out of doors."

Fortunately, the governess came to her rescue. "The last family I worked for had a dog, my lady. I'm sure between myself and the rest of the staff, we'll get him sorted out."

"Lovely," Charity breathed. She wouldn't have had the faintest clue how to manage such a thing herself. Finishing school had included a variety of lessons, but none like that.

"Have you a moment, my lady? Master Nathan is quite proud of all he's learned this afternoon."

"Of course."

"Tell her, Nathan," she prompted.

"Hmm? About what?" Nathan's attentions were totally distracted by Mac. The two were looking for the perfect stick for playing fetch. Already, Mac seemed perfectly happy to trot along at the boy's heels.

"About your lessons."

"Oh, right." He frowned, thinking, then perked up. "Well, tomorrow, if the sky is clear, I get to stay up late so I can learn the names and positions of the stars."

Charity grinned, guessing the boy's excitement had more to do with staying up past bedtime than with the lesson plan.

"And today, Master Nathan?" the governess prompted.

"Today…" He thought for a moment, trying not to look at Mac, who was now nosing about a tree trunk. A birds' nest balanced on a branch well above his head. The nest's resident hopped along the branch, chattering down at him disapprovingly.

"Oh!" Nathan remembered. "We talked about the names of the flowers. And the heather, even though it isn't in bloom yet. Do you know the story about the heather, Aunt Charity?"

"No, I cannot say I do."

He puffed up at the idea he knew something she didn't. "Well, there's a story that when God was searching for a plant to cover the slopes of the Scottish mountains, he first asked the oak, the rose, and the honeysuckle. But they all said 'no.' The heather said yes, and so God gave the heather the strength of an oak, the…" he paused, trying to remember, "the sweetness of the rose, and the fragrance of the honeysuckle. And that's why it's so wonderful!"

Charity clapped her hands. "Well done, Nathan."

He grinned, then turned immediately to the governess. "May we be finished for today, please? Mac *needs* me!"

Charity stifled a giggle. "Please forgive me for interrupting your efforts. I can tell you are doing good work."

The governess waived off her apology. "Nay, my lady. We are just starting out, trying to whet his appetite for learning. There's nothing about today's lesson that cannot wait until tomorrow. A few hours with a new puppy will do more good for that boy than anything else I can think of. What a lovely idea to bring him such a gift. He'll have a playmate and companion for years to come."

Charity grew warm. "I thought Nathan and, well, the whole house, really, could use a bit of cheer."

"Aye, my lady. That they could." She looked up at the

manor home. "I haven't been here but a few days and—" She broke off, settling instead for a repeated, "That they could."

Chapter 16:

"Absence from those we love is self from self—a deadly banishment." —William Shakespeare

If she ever saw Graeme Ramsey Maxwell again, she'd kill him. She was getting stronger. Sleeping better. She could do it. Except that she wasn't given to acts of violence. But even on Charity's good days, Graeme's absence was a gaping wound that refused to heal.

After one week, she figured he'd had enough time to calm down, to think things over. He'd be back any day.

When a second week passed, her anger started to build. She was doing so much better, and Nathan had absolutely blossomed overnight. Between his lessons, the puppy, and the games she made sure to engage him in, he'd confided one afternoon that he was happy, truly happy, for the first time since his parents died. She'd had to turn away to hide her tears. Even the dowager countess had begun joining their outings and meals more often. And Graeme was missing it all.

When she'd finally caved and asked his mother if she knew

where he'd gone, she'd learned almost nothing, except that he had a number of friends with whom he enjoyed hunting. He hadn't even indicated to her whether he was leaving on business or pleasure. Knowing how Lady Eleanor's memory sometimes slipped, she'd asked the head groom as well. He hadn't known, either. Graeme could be nearly anywhere.

But why, oh why, would he stay away so long?

The answer hit her like a wave of icy water. *Another woman.* Did he have a mistress? Had he, upon realizing his wife was not all he'd hoped, simply abandoned her in favor of some woman he'd preferred all along but, for whatever reason, could not marry?

No. Her heart, wounded though it was, insisted this couldn't be true. She might not have known her husband for long, but she *knew* him. That wasn't his character. He'd planned for a life together with *her.*

The insidious thing about worries like that was, no matter how much her heart argued that Graeme was true, her mind could not shake free of the idea. Charity instinctively hated the woman she viewed as competition—never mind that the woman likely did not even exist.

But if she didn't, then why was her husband still gone? She couldn't think of another reason. Nor could she think of any way to bring him back.

Her menses arrived on day ten of what she'd begun to think of as "Life Without Graeme." Upon seeing the blood, she broke down crying once more. It was totally impractical, she knew, but she'd *so* hoped to be pregnant. After all, they'd made the most of their opportunities, up until his departure. Maybe it wasn't the best time to be pregnant, but that didn't stop her from wanting it. She'd be a better mother if she had more time to make peace with the past, and to learn to accept herself in the process. But Charity had always struggled with being practical. Now that she felt the improvement like a great weight lifting, she wanted everything all at once. Love, marriage, children... after all, weren't those the very things a young lady was *supposed* to want? The thought made her chuckle. For the first time in her life, she was being compliant, and yet the things she longed for hovered still just out of reach.

Well, fie upon him. At the very least, she could give her husband a taste of his own medicine when he finally did come back. Ignore him. Make him wonder if she'd even noticed his extended absence. Yes, she could do that. Maybe. If she could stay far enough away from him, physically, not to remember the smell of his skin, or the gentle roughness in his touch.

Charity grimaced. She was stronger than that, surely. Oh, who was she fooling? She'd fling herself into his arms the moment she saw him.

After one week, Graeme had had his fill of hunting. After two weeks, he was just plain bored.

At night, dreams of a blond temptress haunted his sleep. Quite a few of his waking hours, too. He hadn't thought of a solution, though. More doctors? Medicine? She'd had all that in London, he now realized. Had it been helping? Was *that* why she'd asked for a longer engagement? So she could continue treatment? Of course she wouldn't have told him, if that were true. She'd hoped never to need to. Had he, in whisking her away to Scotland, done her harm?

Guilt plagued him. Maybe he should offer to let her return to London. His chest felt hollow at the idea. Would they live separately? What if she couldn't be cured? What if he got her pregnant, and *then* found out she couldn't be cured? This was the fear that kept him from acting. He'd never before considered himself a coward. But he'd never before faced a problem that tore him apart like this. Even when his father had died, he'd known what needed to be done to carry on.

Thinking the races in Edinburgh would provide a better distraction, he traveled there next. The days on the road were a tortured reminder of the journey he and Charity had taken. But instead of the pleasurable distraction of her kisses, of her infectious laughter, and of the whimper of need she made just before he made her come, he bumped along the road alone, with only Tom Brevis, reticent even on his chatty days, for company.

Along the way he composed a letter to Miss Boyd, the nurse he'd hired for his estranged wife. Bloody hell. *Estranged. Wife.* The words were so wrong. But Miss Boyd had come highly recommended. Perhaps she could keep him apprised of Charity's condition. He kept his words simple, not knowing whether her skill at reading matched her skill at nursing. Then he crumpled the letter. Even if Miss Boyd received it and was able to write back, where would she send her response? He'd set no plans in stone. Besides, he was starting to think no amount of distraction was going to solve his problems. He knew his choices—either set her aside, seeing to it she had adequate medical care, of course, or take her as she was, and to hell with the consequences. Only one of those choices offered even a chance at happiness. Choosing recklessly had landed him here in the first place. This time, he was forcing himself to wait. Whatever his decision, he would make it with his eyes open, and he would live with it. He didn't need much longer. A few days more, and he'd be on his way.

The Edinburgh races were a great to-do, with noble and commoner alike in attendance. People traveled from far and wide to match their fastest thoroughbreds against one another, or, for proven but aging racehorses, to mate them. For two weeks at the end of spring each year, people in town could speak of little else.

The best vantage spots for the key races had been claimed long ago, but one benefit to being an earl was that when one wished to attend an event, seats usually opened up. Upon arriving at the grounds, Graeme was able to secure a good place with relative ease. He studied the board where the schedule of events was listed. Two hours, still, until the first heat of any interest. Time enough to wander the grounds. The bustle of activity—grooms, owners, water boys, regal animals, all on their way to somewhere important—kept his mind off his troubles far better than the solitude of hunting.

Turning a corner, he found himself face to face with a familiar figure. The Duke of Beaufort. Behind him stood Charity's sister, and next to her, a man Graeme did not recognize. *Bollocks.* Of course the duke would be here. Half of England's nobility probably was. It was just his luck to run into him.

His chest tightened. "Your Grace."

"Leventhal." The duke raised his brows. "May I safely assume you are now a married man?"

"I am." What else was there to say? Of all the barmy moves Graeme could recall making in his thirty-three years, his hasty marriage surely took the prize.

Elizabeth Bainbridge raised herself on tiptoe to look past Graeme's shoulder. "Oh! Is she here?" Her gaze flew to Graeme. "Is Charity here?"

Graeme briefly closed his eyes. "Nay, Your Grace."

"Where are you staying? Is she there? Can I see her?"

"I'm afraid not."

Her face fell. "But—where is she?"

"At Leventhal House. My family's seat. Near Grantown on Spey."

"You left her there, alone?" the duke asked. "Shouldn't the two of you be honeymooning?"

Graeme straightened his shoulders. How dare the duke try to turn this back on him, make *him* look like the one at fault. He didn't want to argue in front of Charity's sister. It took him several seconds to control his frustration. "Not alone. My mother is there, and my nephew, and the house is full of servants. With all the tumult of the past few weeks, I'm afraid she was not feeling up to another trip so soon." Harmless, as far as lies went.

The duke narrowed his eyes. "You were in a terrible hurry to marry her, to have turned around and left again so quickly. Are you in the business of horse racing?"

Now *that* would be a convenient excuse. But, unfortunately, not a sustainable lie. "Not exactly." He cast a meaningful glance at the duke's wife. "Perhaps we could discuss this later?"

Beaufort met his eye for a lengthy moment, his expression unreadable. "We will most definitely be discussing this later, Leventhal. Directly after this afternoon's race, I think." He gave Graeme the address of the location they were staying. He opened his mouth a second time, as though to issue some sort of warning, but shut it again without speaking. Giving Graeme a curt nod, he directed his party toward the racetrack.

Graeme spent the next few hours paying very little heed to the event he'd sought out as a distraction. He had half a mind to ignore the duke's summons, being fairly certain Beaufort intended to issue him the verbal equivalent of a good hiding. But Graeme was no school boy to be called to task. Especially not on personal matters. Then again, it was not generally advisable to ignore a duke, especially if you were related to him. Which he now was—a fact Beaufort had played a role in, albeit indirectly, by leading him to believe Charity was merely irresponsible and flighty, as opposed to truly troubled. A few honest words, spoken man-to-man, would have served them both better.

Well, he'd get those words in now. He might be outranked, but he would not go unheard.

Graeme was well-steamed by the time he arrived at the duke's lodging and was shown in to the salon. Decorated in rich wood and dark green velvet, he had the definite sense of stepping in to a man's abode. To his surprise, the fair-haired man from earlier in the afternoon lolled in a large chair across from the duke, though both men stood as he entered.

"Leventhal," the duke greeted him. "May I present Monsieur Philippe Durand, the artist."

The name sounded vaguely familiar, though art was not among his stronger subjects. "Paintings?"

"Yes," the Frenchman acknowledged, pleased by the recognition.

"Monsieur Durand," the duke continued the introductions, "this is Lord Maxwell, Earl of Leventhal, and my sister-in-law's newly wedded husband."

"A pleasure."

Graeme wasn't so sure. He'd assumed he and Beaufort would meet alone. He glanced meaningfully from the artist to the duke, eyebrows raised.

"Monsieur Durand is a most interesting man. You may find that he is quite pertinent to this discussion," Beaufort said. "Please, why don't we all sit down."

Uncertain now, Graeme selected a leather chair that would

allow him to see both men. Why would a French painter be relevant to the discussion of his sham of a marriage?

Unless…*nay*. Had this man been a beau of Charity's? Had she held some tendré for him? Had Charity held some misguided notion of winning him back? Graeme didn't attempt to hide his scowl.

"Let me get straight to the point. It disturbs me to know you left Charity alone so soon after your wedding," the duke said.

Again, Graeme wished Monsieur Durand would have the grace to leave. Unfortunately, the other man indicated no such intention.

Keeping his tone civil, he stated, "I think that ceased to be your concern when she became my wife."

"She is my sister in law. Of course I care for her well being. Your decision to elope made it difficult to ascertain her happiness."

"I assure you, she came willingly. And I would point out that no one, including yourself, attempted to stop us. You could have, you know. In fact, I gave you more than one opportunity to say what needed to be said. Your silence did me a disservice."

"Has your memory failed? I gave you far more leniency than her father would have, were the man alive. *You* were the one pressing for marriage."

"True enough. But as it turns out, I lacked a critical piece of information about my future wife—one you obviously were aware of, but chose not to share. Charity is at my home because it is the best place I could think to leave her in her state."

Monsieur Durand looked on with an expression of mild interest, while Beaufort's scowl was starting to match Graeme's own.

"Her state?"

"Aye, her state. Her…condition. I may be frustrated at having been hamstrung with an unsuitable wife, but I would not treat her with cruelty. She is safe at home. I even hired her a nurse."

"You did *what*?" the duke was half out of his seat, the Frenchman just behind him. "A nurse? As though she were a child or an invalid?"

Graeme sneered. "Isn't she?" He was tired of playing games.

"Bloody hell. Is she injured?"

"Injured? That's an interesting way of putting it."

"Why, exactly," the duke enunciated, "is your bride rusticating in the highlands while you are here?"

"I discovered her little secret. After which, I told her she was unfit to be either wife or mother. Don't worry, Your Grace, the nurse will ensure she comes to no harm. Nay, it is I who have been harmed, for now I am saddled with a wife who cannot fully fill that role."

The duke and the Frenchman frowned at one another, then at him. "Speak plainly, Leventhal. You said Charity was 'unfit.' Was she not a virgin? Or was she—" he wriggled a hand, "deformed in some way that makes the two of you unable to…"

"No, no." He swallowed, as images of Charity's lithe body beneath his sprang unbidden to her mind. Her body was perfect. Utterly perfect. *Damn.* "It's not her body that's the problem, it's her mind."

"Her mind."

"Aye." Graeme shoved his lustful thoughts away, re-warming to his anger. "How did you keep her secret for so long? Or did you simply hope that face of hers, combined with a dowry befitting a duchess, would be enough for most men to overlook her defect?"

"Defect? What in God's name is he raving about?" the Frenchman asked the duke.

"I assure you..."

But Graeme wasn't interested in hearing any more. "I wondered, I admit, why none of Charity's relatives rode after us, given our rather, ah, unconventional means of marriage. Hah. More the fool am I. No, instead of riding to her rescue, you were home, laughing and toasting to your good luck. Not only was she married off, but to a *Scot*—tucked conveniently away in the country where she would trouble you no longer." He stalked across the room to the table bearing the decanter and poured himself a brandy. Rude, but no more so than the duke failing to offer it to him in the first place. He lifted the glass toward the other men in a mock toast, and tossed it back.

"Leventhal, you begin to irritate me. Exactly what 'defect' do you find in my sister in law?"

The duke's tone was icy, but Graeme wasn't backing down. "She's *mad*, Your Grace. A lunatic. Raves incoherently. I'd have sworn she was awake, but she acted as though she didn't recognize me at all. Don't tell me you did not know."

The duke blew out a long breath. The Frenchman watched them both, now with concern in his eyes.

"Mad," Beaufort stated.

"Aye, mad."

"Tell me," asked the duke, "these ravings, as you call them. When do they occur? At night?"

"Aye, at night."

"Only then?"

Graeme shrugged. "That is when I have observed them. Of

course, I have not known her as long as you. But I assume, in order for her ailment to have remained hidden so long, it must not often affect her during the day."

The duke looked thoughtful. "And it is this condition of…madness, that has led you to abandon your wife?"

"It pains me to stay away," he admitted. "Much of the time she is simply the woman who so enraptured me as to inspire our elopement in the first place. But other times…one would believe the devil himself had hold of her."

Monsieur Durand looked agitated. "Beaufort, I made you an oath, that I would never again speak of certain events. I would ask that you release me from that oath now."

The duke scrubbed a hand across his forehead, then pinched the bridge of his nose. "She would have told him herself, if she wanted him to know."

"He is her husband. He has a right to know. Look at him. Think of her. They love each other, no? Yet they suffer. Also," the Frenchman added, leaning forward and carefully emphasizing his next words, "he can protect her better if he knows."

The duke nodded slowly. "True. All right. I release you." He turned to Graeme. "Were you in London last summer? Did you follow the news?"

"Nay," Graeme told him. "My sister and her husband had just been killed in a boating accident. Their young son came to live with me, and…suffice it to say, the news of the world at large was not my primary concern."

"Understandable. Bear with me, then, for my answer to you concerning Charity's condition will make more sense with a bit of explanation."

Monsieur Durand rose to pour them each another drink. Graeme watched him closely, noting that the Frenchman's own drink contained nearly a finger more of brandy than the others.

"Charity has a bright mind and a big heart, and until last summer, she never once experienced an episode of…what you call madness."

"Go on," Graeme said. He didn't want to get his hopes up, but if there was an explanation, or a cure… *I wasn't always this way.* Charity's truncated explanation echoed in his mind, the words repeating like an ominous drumbeat.

"Last summer, a small ring of French spies infiltrated London," the duke said. "They were attempting to help General Bonaparte in his quest to reclaim his empire."

"Lady Beatrice Pullington, whom I had only just begun to court, was unfortunate enough to intercept one of their communications."

"Lady Pullington is a good friend to both Elizabeth and Charity," said the duke. "Since Elizabeth was in delicate condition, what with expecting our son, Lady Pullington included Miss Medford in her adventure."

"Adventure?" Graeme asked, feeling stupidly lost. True, he hadn't followed the news, but this was quite a story the two men spun.

"She did not know, at first, that the note she'd received had come from the spies. She believed it a lovers' missive, and curiosity led her to seek its sender, so that the young man would know it had gone astray, rather than thinking it had been received and rejected. The note requested a secret rendezvous at Vauxhall Gardens. Lady Pullington and Miss Medford attended. Fortunately, they at least had the presence of mind to keep from being seen."

Vauxhall isn't safe. Charity's words from the picnic echoed in Graeme's mind. They were beginning to make sense.

"Ah, *l'amour.* My daring Beatrice. When she discovered the true nature of the note, she turned it over to the authorities," Monsieur Durand said. "I knew nothing of this at the time."

"Monsieur Durand knew nothing of it," the duke pointed out, "because *he* was among those suspected. A famous French painter, who'd never come to London before, suddenly choosing to spend several weeks there? The British Foreign Service knew Bea was sitting for a portrait. They asked her to observe him."

"Lucky for me." Monsieur Durand donned a lascivious expression.

Beaufort chuckled, then sobered. "We told Charity to have no more to do with the matter. She and Lady Pullington had started out thinking it a harmless adventure, but of course it was not. Charity never said it, but I think she felt we treated her like a child. She wanted to show she could be as helpful as Lady Pullington."

"In a matter concerning spies?"

"Yes. Don't get me wrong. Charity is not at all stupid, but she does act rashly. She was in over her head. Still, she gathered what she knew, and what she'd seen, and tried to piece it together. She believed one of the spies worked as a servant in the home of a family she knew. She started snooping around."

Graeme shook his head. "Dangerous." But it sounded exactly like Charity. From the first night they'd met, when she'd disguised herself to attend an illicit ball, he'd known she had a daring streak.

"*Oui*," Monsieur Durand agreed. "Unfortunately, she was caught in the act. The would-be servant did not know what to do with her. So he took her to the leader of his group. Kidnapped her."

"No." Graeme uttered a curse word he rarely gave voice to. He considered his drink, but found he didn't want it anymore.

Beaufort and the Frenchman looked at each other. "We found her," the duke said. "Two days later."

Graeme's throat felt thick. "Please tell me you killed each and every one of her captors."

"Given the chance, I would have," the duke growled. "They were gone. We found her, locked in a dank cellar on the riverfront." He closed his eyes briefly. "Lord Maxwell, they'd left her there to die."

Graeme leaned over, feeling dizzy and ill. "Was she...did they?" he rasped.

The other two men exchanged a long glance. "I don't know," the duke finally answered. "We had a physician examine her, after we got her home, and he said no. But of course, that is what physicians in the *ton* are paid to say, when a young lady's reputation is called into question."

"But this is different!"

Monsieur Durand threw back the remainder of his brandy and poured another. The duke reached for the decanter after him.

"Different, indeed. And yet not so different. If it were bandied about by the gossips that Charity had been held captive by a group of vulgar criminals, let alone raped by them, do you think it would have mattered that she'd been touched without her consent?"

Now Graeme closed his eyes. "Nay. The gossips would eat her alive. She'd be tarnished."

"Do *you* think her tarnished?" the duke asked sharply.

Graeme's eyes flew open. "Nay!" Then he realized that, only minutes ago, he'd thought exactly that—though he'd thought it was her mind, rather than her body, that was tarnished. "That is, not any longer."

The other man's shoulders relaxed. "Good. I'd prefer not to have to kill you."

"She could have told me."

The duke nodded. "I'd rather hoped she would. But Charity never spoke of what went on down there."

"When we found her," Monsieur Durand put in, wincing as he spoke, "her fingertips were reduced to bloody nubs. She...she'd tried to claw her way out," he finished in a whisper.

Graeme's mind rebelled from the image.

"For weeks afterward, she could not even leave her room without gloves. You understand, now, why we made an oath never to speak of this. We wanted to protect her from any further ugliness. We wanted her to go back to her normal life."

"Only she couldn't," the duke said. "She struggled. I know she did. The family...did what we could to help. As much as we wanted her to live normally, we also wanted to protect her."

"Of course you did." What dark hell had Charity lived through? Though his mind heard everything the two men said, he could not reconcile those images with the lovely, spirited woman he knew.

"Two of the spies were later caught," the duke went on. "The servant who first garnered Charity's suspicion, and a stage performer. The man they served, who'd sought the information they were trying to steal, was also caught." He looked at Monsieur Durand.

"My father," the Frenchman said softly. "The Brits were not so far off in suspecting me, as it turned out. They just had the wrong Durand." He knocked back the rest of his second brandy, and Graeme understood why he'd poured himself extra.

"But two were never caught. And Charity knows this."

"The nightmares…" Graeme mused, his mind shrinking in horror at what the content of Charity's dreams might be.

"Yes. The nightmares."

All three sat in silent reflection.

"It is not madness, then," Graeme said.

The duke sighed. "Not madness in the way of Bedlamites, no. But sometimes she *is* terrified out of her mind. It takes her a few minutes, upon awaking, to regain reason. We had to pay the servants extra to keep from gossiping."

Graeme scrubbed a hand over the stubble of his beard. "Your Grace, and Monsieur Durand, I cannot thank you enough for trusting me enough to share this with me. I know I have not earned that trust. I am horrified to think of what my wife has been through…let alone what I have unwittingly put her through, since. I am relieved as well, for the sort of madness you describe, if it can even be called madness, is unlikely to be the sort passed from mother to child."

"Ah." Understanding lightened the duke's features. "You feared having children together."

"Aye," Graeme said softly.

"Lord Maxwell, about the remaining spies—"

"Graeme," he supplied. "We seem to have moved well past the point of formality."

"Indeed. In fact, each and every one of our meetings thus far have proven quite…interesting," the duke chuckled. "Should we continue this acquaintance, I may never have need of my box at the theater again, for the drama at home quite surpasses the performances on stage. Graeme, then. As for the remaining culprits. The body of André Denis, the most skilled of the remaining informants, was found two weeks ago. Stabbed to death. No indication of the killer's identity. Denis had more enemies than friends."

"That's good, though, is it not? For Charity's sake?"

"I believe so. I'd prefer to know who killed him, and what information the killer may have extracted before committing the foul deed. But it is unlikely I shall ever gain those details. So yes, I believe this is good news for us."

"What of the other?"

"No sign of him."

The men were silent a minute, staring into their brandy as though it might offer up answers.

"My sister-in-law's description of the last spy matched that of a man with a surname of Morton. A small-time crook. His given name seems to change as often as his occupation. If he even is the same man, there is no indication he has had any other dealings in politics or espionage."

"Is he a threat?"

The duke glanced at Monsieur Durand, who shrugged. "I want to say no. If Morton has any wits at all, he sailed for the Americas months ago. Like as not, we will never hear of him again. But it is a loose end. My Beatrice never saw the man in question, but she too played a role in the downfall of the others. I do not like to think her safety is at risk."

The duke frowned. "Charity, to my knowledge, is the only person who can identify Morton by sight, and link him to the incident last summer."

"Then her life is in danger."

"That was my original concern in asking your wife's whereabouts earlier today. We do have men on retainer, who have been instructed to follow any leads that may reveal Morton's whereabouts—if he is even still alive."

"Men in London." His throat was dry. "Not men who could protect my wife this very moment."

"You know and trust your staff?"

"Of course." Most of them he'd known since boyhood. But how well did he know Miss Boyd, or the governess he'd just sent to Nathan? They were both women, so clearly they weren't the criminal in question, but what of their character? A letter of reference could be forged.

"She is likely as safe as can be," the duke asserted, alleviating Graeme's fears only slightly. "Though if I know my sister-in-law, she might be rather put out with you at the moment."

He almost chuckled. "I suppose I can see why."

"It may well be a fruitless effort, tracking Morton. But I will not stop looking until I know the last man is dead," Beaufort promised.

Graeme stood, feeling the effects of the brandy but forcing himself to push that aside. "Gentlemen, I must excuse myself. I am needed at home."

The duke smiled. "Indeed, you are. And, Leventhal, If I hadn't thought you a solid sort from the first night we met, know that I would never have allowed Charity to 'escape' to Scotland with you."

"You could travel together." Monsieur Durand suggested. "You share a destination."

"We do?"

"We had hoped to pay a surprise visit to you and your wife. Help celebrate the nuptials, since we could not be there for the actual wedding," Beaufort explained.

"I, on the other hand, am itching to return to London," Monsieur Durand said. "Horses are not my favorite subject matter."

"Your favorite subject matter is the woman who made you come here."

"True enough, the Frenchman chuckled, explaining to Graeme, "My lovely wife blessed me with a daughter six weeks ago. I am quite the proud papa. So much so that Bea and her mother became exasperated with my hovering and sent me off with Beaufort, here."

"He spent the entire trip here sketching the baby from memory. He's soft over her."

"As though you aren't soft over your son?" Monsieur Durand retorted. "The only difference is that I can draw. Besides, Bea won't say exasperated for long. She's probably missing me terribly not that she's had some room to breathe." He winked.

"Congratulations, Monsieur. It sounds as though you've found true happiness."

"*Oui.*"

"I hope to do the same. Given the circumstances, Beaufort, I would prefer to travel alone. I need to see my wife. I need to explain. And perhaps—forgive me—she does, too."

The duke gave him a long, measured look. "Agreed. Elizabeth and I had planned to stay through the races anyhow. I will grant you two weeks' head start. It took you less time than that to decide you wanted to marry Charity in the first place, so it ought to be plenty of time to sort out your misunderstandings."

He hoped so.

"After that, I doubt even I could stall my darling wife much longer. She is terribly anxious to hear all about the elopement. And I am certain Charity will be glad to have her sister present to help celebrate."

Or commiserate, should I fail. Graeme shoved the pessimistic thought back down to the dark place from which it had risen. He wasn't going to fail.

"Agreed. Two weeks." He was halfway out the door already as he spoke the words. His mind reeled. The spirited beauty he'd wed had endured more than enough horrors for one lifetime. Whether he'd known it or not, he'd added insult to injury by abandoning her. He prided himself on how well he cared for his people and his lands. Yet he'd endangered the very person most important in his life. He needed to get home. Fast.

Chapter 17:

"How poor are they that have not patience! What
wound did ever heal but by degrees?"
— William Shakespeare

As Jasper Morton saw it, he had two choices. Kill, or run. Killing the yellow-haired wench might or might not solve his problems, though. He'd still be a wanted man. The duke, and now Lord Maxwell, too, would triple their efforts to find him if he harmed her. Without Lady Charity to identify him, would the drawings she'd provided prove a close enough likeness?

His head hurt. It was too hard to think this through.

Much as he hated the idea of leaving the British Isles, a peaceful life here was looking less and less likely. America. Or maybe Barbados. Yes, Barbados didn't sound too bad. He'd heard a man could turn a quick fortune there—if he survived the trip there. He'd need blunt to book his passage, and even more to guarantee good treatment from the crew and captain. He'd heard the tales of food running scarce, ship captains who took bribes, and poor folk who scraped their life savings together to get on a boat, only to discover so many new expenses, that by the time they reached land, they'd indentured themselves as servants. Jasper, being an independent sort of man, did not think he'd take well to servitude.

He rubbed his ample nose. Spying hadn't made him wealthy. He hadn't even gotten the last two installments of pay he'd been promised, what with the whole operation going up in smoke. He could steal the money, but from whom? The only one in these parts likely to have that kind of coin on hand was the earl himself. He'd have to steal it out from under the nose of the lady whose living breath was his biggest threat.

Then he'd be free, once and for all. Surely they'd never chase him that far. He could forget all of it. He just had to do this one thing.

One last run. All or nothing. His fingers trembled and itched, fear and gleeful anticipation mixing in equal portions.

He had to plan this job. Planning was not his strong point. Jasper considered himself more of a creature of opportunity.

Where would the gold be kept? The earl wouldn't leave coin just lying about. He'd have some at Leventhal House, though. The banks were too far away for routine trips. Any valuable would do, as long as it wouldn't be traced right back to the earl. Good old-fashioned coins, even paper money, would make his life easiest, though. Save him the trouble of selling stolen goods, and of answering questions.

The best way to learn how to steal from a man was to work for him first. Learn his habits, and those of the household. *Bugger.* That was out of the question this time.

He could wait until the house was empty. Some kind of holiday, perhaps. Did they all attend church? Or he could plan on the next full moon…sneak in while the household slept. No. Too dangerous when he didn't know exactly where to find what he was looking for. An empty house was safer than a sleeping one.

First, he had to watch, and learn. He'd know when the time was right—as long as he didn't let Lady Charity catch sight of him first.

"He'll have to return sooner or later," Charity declared. Her husband had been gone three weeks. Nearly a month. Not that she'd counted the days. Or even the hours.

She told herself she'd stopped looking down the lane, stopped listening for the sound of hoof beats that would signal his return, but it wasn't true. No matter what else she turned her attention to, a part of her was always listening, always waiting. "Lord Maxwell is not the sort of man to ignore his estate."

"Nay, my lady," Ismay Boyd agreed, wisely keeping any private doubts to herself.

They'd just returned from a walk along the banks of the burn, and at the site of fresh carriage tracks, Charity had nearly started running in anticipation.

The tracks turned out to belong to a deliveryman bringing several of her trunks from London. And that just left her in a conundrum. Her delight at finally, finally having her things again, being able to change into a gown designed specifically to fit her, was tempered—if not actually eclipsed—by her dejection that the tracks had not belonged to one Graeme Ramsey Maxwell.

"He takes great pride in doing right by his people," Charity rationalized as the two women followed the footmen bearing the trunks upstairs. She kept her voice low, though her words gave nothing away that the servants wouldn't already have speculated upon. "And there is Nathan. And his mother."

"Aye, my lady."

The footmen set down the trunks near the foot of Charity's bed. "Shall I send a maid upstairs to unpack, milady?" one of them asked.

"Not now. I should like to do it myself. I'll signal later, should I require assistance." Charity nodded to the footmen, dismissing them, and closed the door.

Miss Boyd waited expectantly.

"So he'll have to come back."

The nurse-turned-companion cocked her head. "An' what then, my lady? I see ye have something in mind."

Charity wet her lips. As desperately as she longed for Graeme's return, the idea she flirted with now made her nervous. How would things be, between them? What would he say? What would she say? Could she convince him to hear her out, to give their marriage another chance? She'd never expected him to stay gone so long. What if he came back determined to cast her aside? Even the idea crushed the breath from her body.

"Tell me, Miss Boyd. Did your brother, the one who went to war, ever find love? Has he married?"

If her companion was confused by the seeming change in topic, she didn't show it. "Nay, my lady, but that doesn't mean he isna' deserving of love."

Charity felt deflated. "But his troubles..."

"Nay," Ismay hurried to explain. "My brother's story is different. 'Twas not his return from war that left him lonely, but going off to battle in the first place. After he left for war, the lass he was enamored of married another. By the time he returned, she had one baby and another on the way.

"He didn't blame her, really. Two years is a long time, an'

without any promise he'd even live to return. My brother just hasn't met another since then to turn his eye. But I 'ave hope for him yet. With so many crofter families moving to the port towns, there are a good many unmarried lasses in Inverness now. When the time is right, he'll find the one that warms his blood." She paused. "When you asked about my brother, 'tis because you want to know if there is hope for yourself?"

Charity nodded. "That sounds selfish, doesn't it?"

"Nay, my lady. It sounds normal."

Normal. What a lovely sounding word. "I think I'd like to meet your brother someday. I hope he does meet a lass who warms his blood. When I met Lord Maxwell...well, he certainly warms mine."

Ismay giggled. "A good thing, since you've married him."

"A good thing, if he'd stayed. Not so good with him gone. I know I have...problems," Charity admitted. "But I don't want my husband to look at me as a woman who needs a nurse. As an invalid. That's not the whole of me, not at all. I want him to remember the rest. I want him to look at me the way he did on the night we met."

"Oh? An' how was that, my lady?"

Charity lowered her gaze, fidgeting with the latch on the first trunk containing her belongings from London. She pressed on. Modesty wasn't going to help her now. "Like he wanted to ravish me." She snuck a glance at her companion.

A wide smile spread across Ismay Boyd's careworn face. "Like that, eh?"

"Like that," she confirmed, smiling back. The latch released, and she pushed up the trunk lid to see a colorful array of fabric. Her dresses. The smile grew wider. "And also," Charity added, "I think, he looked like he wanted to protect me—so that no one else could do the ravishing."

"An' that be the perfect way for a man to look at the lass he plans to marry."

Charity lifted out a day dress of daffodil yellow, which she laid on the bed. "So how do I get that look back?" She returned to the trunk. The next gown she reached for had been designed for her first official ball last summer, when she'd made her bow to Society. Made of delicate ivory silk, it was modest yet deceivingly alluring. Cut in a long column, the dress clung to every curve. The low cut of the bosom was modified by an inset of gold ribbon. Matching gold accents set into the tiny cap sleeves and along the single flounce at the bottom gave the gown a certain symmetry that made it hard to look away.

She heard Ismay's soft gasp. "Oh, my lady, how lovely. 'Tis fit for royalty."

"From my first ball," she said. "I only wore it the one time."

"Oh, but why?"

Charity shrugged. Unmarried young ladies were expected to wear pale colors representative of their virginal state. She'd always pushed the edge of that, however, preferring cheerier shades like the yellow dress. This particular gown *was* lovely, though. Fit for a wedding gown—if she'd had a more traditional wedding.

Her companion was eyeing it thoughtfully. "If you moved that gold ribbon to beneath your bust, my lady, would the gown stay in place?"

Charity considered. She'd had lower-cut gowns and, as long as the fit was proper, her breasts had never come popping out. The placement of the gold ribbon on this particular gown had been a nod to her status as an innocent. As a married woman, there were fewer restrictions on the cut and color of what she could wear. "Yes, I think so."

"Have you others like that?"

Charity continued pulling out clothing. Whoever had packed her trunks had included mostly her day gowns and warmer items, perhaps thinking them more practical for her new home. There were a few evening pieces, though, appropriate for theater, balls, and what she was starting to think of as "city venues." She set those aside. To that pile, she added the lacy night shift the innkeeper's wife at The Dog and Anvil had thought to purchase on her wedding day.

Ismay Boyd fingered the pieces reverently. "If I may speak boldly, my lady, I think you and your fine lord will have a better time of it if you tell him the things you told me."

"I know," Charity agreed softly. "At first, I was too afraid. I couldn't bear the thought he might reject me. Of course he found out anyway—and then he was too upset for me to say much of anything."

"What's done is done. You canna' change that. You can only be honest with him when he returns."

"I will," she vowed.

Ismay held up the lacy night shift. "Aside from that, if it's a good ravishing you're after, I believe you will have little trouble holding your husband's eye."

She knew she was blushing. "The night we met, we were both attending a very…decadent…event. My costume covered my face, which allowed me to bare other areas without fear of judgment. I want to remind my husband of the sensual, mysterious woman he saw in me that night." Graeme had pursued her relentlessly. Deep down, she knew this wasn't a case of the old proverb about the hottest flames burning out the fastest. She just had to make him forget the image of a madwoman tucked away in the countryside, and remind him that, in spite of her troubles, she was the passionate creature he could not resist.

"Perhaps if we summoned a seamstress for a few modifications…"

Charity smiled. "Yes, let's do that." Clearly, Miss Boyd was not in a position to offer specific advice about seducing one's husband. The wild abandon and hedonistic pleasures Charity had witnessed the night she'd met Graeme were far, far outside the other woman's experiences. The harem dancers, the shadow play… If the seamstress in question had any skill, Charity imagined she could take care of the rest.

Chapter 18

Graeme left his coach and driver behind in Edinburgh. He could travel faster alone. He rode like the hounds of hell were after him, spurred on by the anger he directed at himself. After the first few hours, though, common sense sank in. The number of inns where he could change horses between Edinburgh and Leventhal House was limited, and a worn-down mount would leave them both stranded.

Still, he kept the pace as brisk as he dared. His wife was more than beautiful. She was spirited and strong-willed. She'd lived through something no woman, no *human*, should ever experience. What was the chance she'd take being discarded by her husband lying down? What if she'd decided to take herself right back to London, where she'd come from? Where her family might smother her, but at least they hadn't *abandoned* her? Would his staff have written to him, or even known how to reach him, if she had?

Damn. Now he knew why she'd been so desperate to explain—and so afraid. He'd been too stubborn to listen. Too convinced that what he'd seen would damn their fledgling marriage. He'd sworn to love and protect, then failed at both. His nights on the road were wasted. He stopped at inns for the purpose of safety—hazards on the road were hard to see at night. As a lone rider, one misstep of his horse could be a disaster. Not to mention making himself an easy target for those who traveled outside the law. But the hours of darkness were wasted. Sleep refused to come.

By the third day, he had a good idea how Charity must feel sometimes. He rode up to Leventhal feeling haggard and spent. Looking it, too, if the expressions on his normally-stoic staff were any indication.

He handed the reins of his weary mount to the head groom, a man everyone called "Red" after his bright, bushy beard. "Give this one some extra oats and a good rubdown, would you?"

"Sure thing, milord."

"Everything secure on the homefront?" he asked casually. Red was an observant man. If aught was amiss, he'd be among the first to know.

"All is well. Something worryin' ye, milord?"

He thought fast. "The last inn I stayed at mentioned there'd been a couple undesirable sorts on the road in recent weeks. Just wanted to make sure no one had been bothered here."

The groom shook his head. "Nay, milord. Saw the remains of a campfire down by the burn a week or so ago, but whoever it was never came up to the house. Probably one of the crofters out looking for a new fishing hole."

"Probably. Just keep an eye on things."

"Aye, milord."

He turned toward the house. He'd had a rather silly fantasy that Charity would see him and come running to greet him, but that didn't happen.

"Lord Maxwell. Welcome home." Mr. and Mrs. Saxonberry greeted him next. A raised brow from the butler sent the remainder of the staff scurrying back to their work. "You must be exhausted. Is aught amiss with the carriage?"

He shook his head. "Nay. It should be along in a day or so. Where is she?" *Please don't let her be gone.*

"My lord?"

"My wife. Lady Charity." Wasn't it obvious? "Where is she?"

"I believe she went out walking, my lord," the housekeeper replied. "Shall I have a meal made up for you? Or a bath?"

At least she wasn't back in London. Thank God. "Walking?"

"She does so, my lord, quite often."

"Where? Is anyone with her?" His voice came out sharper than he'd intended.

"I couldn't say, my lord. Perhaps Miss Boyd."

He closed his eyes. There was no reason to worry. Grantown on Spey, after all, was hardly a hotbed of criminal activity. Nothing of interest ever happened on Maxwell lands, unless it be a too-adventurous lad getting himself stuck in the quarry.

Still. What if she got lost, or turned an ankle? She shouldn't be alone. What if *she* explored the quarry? Knowing Charity's sense of adventure, he wouldn't put it past her.

"Is she usually gone long?" He could go after her. Run about, searching wildly. He'd look as mad as he'd accused her of being. The irony did not escape him.

The butler made a gesture that, were it anyone else, would have meant "how am I supposed to know?"

"She did not ask for a picnic basket, so I would think not

terribly long, my lord."

"If you see her return, please send her to me."

"Aye, my lord."

"And Nathan? Where is he?"

The housekeeper bobbed, pleased with a question she could answer to his satisfaction. "Upstairs in the nursery, my lord. The new governess ye sent seems to be working out right nicely, my lord. Well educated, she is. Been teaching him reading, numbers, and nature. You should hear him rattle on about his lessons."

At least he'd gotten one thing right.

Graeme went up to greet his nephew, who did indeed regale him with tales. That is, after throwing himself into Graeme's arms for a good, long hug. Guilt pinched him again. Charity wasn't the only one he'd treated poorly. It was time he stopped trying to perfect everything, and everyone around him, and just became the father and husband they needed.

Nathan's enthusiasm almost took his mind off the woman he'd missed like the very breathe that fed his lungs. *Almost.*

When he heard her footsteps outside the nursery—he recognized her *footsteps* for God's sake—he quickly stood, eager as a schoolboy. He dimly registered the disappointment on Nathan's face. "I'm home to stay, now, lad," he promised. "You wouldn't want me to ignore your Aunt Charity, would you?"

Nathan shook his head. "I like her. She brought me Mac."

He ruffled the boy's hair, and slipped out the door just as Charity was about to knock.

He closed the door softly behind him. Suddenly, he didn't know what to do.

Lady Charity Maxwell, his wife of a few short weeks but the woman he would surely love forever, stood before him. He stopped, as did she, her lips slightly parted. The two of them stood in the corridor, unmoving. He just stared at her. She stared back.

Myriad expressions flickered across her face. He couldn't read them. Couldn't even begin to guess. Maybe if he'd been here, where he belonged, instead of traversing the countryside while jumping to his own damned conclusions, he'd know her better. He'd understand what she would think at a time like this. Of course, if he hadn't done those things, there wouldn't *be* a time like this.

If he'd thought this would be easy, he'd been mistaken. Charity did not rush to his arms, proclaiming how terribly she'd missed him. Of course she didn't. Instead, she eyed him warily.

He cleared his throat. "You've been out walking?"

She nodded slowly. "Most every day. I've begun to understand the appeal of Scotland."

"You like it here?" he asked, unable to suppress the eagerness in his tone. The fact that she'd not only stayed, but found his homeland appealing...he wasn't sure what it said, but it said *something*. Didn't it?

"I do. I like the freedom of it, the chance to explore."

The very thing he'd been about to take from her. His first instinct had been to make her promise never to go out again without either himself or a guard present. Did she have no regard for her own safety? He bit his tongue, literally, knowing she would not appreciate the protective gesture no matter how heartfelt it was.

Unaware of the direction his thoughts were going, Charity went on. "I never had that in London. Not really. Sometimes we would visit relatives in the country, when I was a child, and we would run off to play for hours on end. But the older we got, it was important to my mother that we stay in London, so my sister and I could see and be seen."

"Not an uncommon preoccupation for a mother." This was not at all the conversation he'd expected.

"Perhaps," she allowed. "Everything was properly scheduled, and I was never without a proper escort." A hint of amusement crinkled her eyes. "Well, except the one night I dressed in the costume of an Indian princess and snuck out the side door."

"A fortuitous move, as it turned out." That was better. He could hear her flirtatious spirit coming back to her.

"Was it?" she asked, the teasing gone.

He hated that she had to ask. He closed the distance between them, his hands coming to rest on her upper arms, just above her elbows, as he willed her to meet his gaze. "Of course it was."

Instead of looking up, she lowered her gaze as she nodded, a tiny frown marring her perfect features. "But Scotland, your home, is different."

What was going on? He wanted to crush her against him, but he could feel that, no matter how close he held her, a vast gulf of emotional difference separated them. She should be crying, or shouting, accusing him of all his transgressions against her and against their marriage. Instead, she spoke in a detached, carefully modulated tone, about the differences between here and London. He would have rather she yelled at him.

Then it struck him. She probably thought *he* still thought she was mad. If she yelled, she'd only be proving it. Bloody hell, what a mess. He could just tell her what he knew. But that seemed disrespectful, especially when she was trying so hard to prove she was normal. An invisible fist clenched his heart. He wasn't good at this, guessing at her emotions.

A scuffle behind the nursery door alerted them to Nate's continued presence.

Graeme hid his smile. "Perhaps you would walk with me, now?" He didn't need his nephew overhearing their conversation, even if it was, so far, eerily mundane.

She flicked a glance toward the crack at the bottom of the nursery door. "Certainly, my lord."

He took one of her arms and tucked it firmly at his side, then led her downstairs and toward the door to the gardens. "You were saying…you like it here?"

It was a weighted question. He could see that she chose her words carefully in answering. "Yes, there is a certain charm to the land. Only…I do miss my sister."

"Of course you do. Perhaps we could ask her to visit." *Since she'd be here in two weeks anyway, invited or not.*

Her eyes lit. "I'd like that, very much."

They passed into the kitchen garden and down the path, the herbs giving way to nonedible plants and flowers.

If she knew Elizabeth was coming, would she present everything was fine just to put on a good face? He wanted to reconnect for real, first.

Not that he'd managed to do that just yet. They were still dancing around more important things. But she was here, and at least she was talking to him. It was a start. "We'll write to her, straight away. Tell me what else you've learned about Scotland."

"The people are different."

"We are?"

She nodded. They'd stopped at the edge of the cultivated garden. She stared out at the grassy hills beyond. "The people here are just…people. Less worried about putting on airs."

He had to smile at that. "Just wait until you get to know them better. They may not place as much importance on formalities as the *ton*, but I'll warrant the villagers can rival any London miss for gossip."

She looked dismayed. "But they've been quite welcoming."

"Ach, lass, don't get me wrong. Of course they welcome you. They want you to be happy here. They want you to stay. But don't think for a minute that your arrival here wasn't whispered about, speculated upon, and analyzed up, down, and sideways."

"Most likely the same could be said of your absence, so soon after my arrival," she retorted, the veneer of civility finally cracking. She turned slightly away, pulling her arm from his as she folded both of hers across her body. "I suppose you think that, since you chose to abandon me here, rather than packing me off to Bedlam, I should be grateful?" The lightness of her tone could not hide the snarl beneath.

Ouch. Her words cut deep. More so because she was right. At least they were finally getting to the heart of things. "A grave misunderstanding on my part—one for which I owe you my deepest apology. You needn't worry overmuch about the gossips, though. They would have had nothing but empty speculation to go on. I told no one of my reasons for going, save Miss Boyd."

He ached to reach for her, to just erase the past weeks. Physical passion had come so easily to them right from the start. Maybe if he rekindled that connection, the others would follow? But, no. The protective stance of her body, her arms folded as though to hug herself, to keep herself upright, told him he would need to do more to earn back her trust.

"Miss Boyd has kept our secret," she whispered.

He did reach for her then, reservations cast aside. He

wrapped his arms around her own, encasing her in a double embrace. Nothing more. Not yet. He just needed her to know he was there for her now, even if he hadn't been before.

She didn't push him away. He even thought he felt her relax, just a bit, into his body. He breathed deeply. How had their marriage gotten this far off course in so short a time?

He rested his chin on her head and stared off towards the hills as she had moments ago, hesitating. "It didn't turn out to be that difficult to keep, did it?" He wasn't really asking as much as acknowledging.

She gave a tiny shrug within his arms. He didn't let go. To his surprise, she answered. "Miss Boyd has actually been quite helpful. Her presence is a comfort. I wanted to hate her, you know, when she first arrived."

He stifled a laugh. "I thought you might hate her still."

"No. She's very good."

He wasn't sure what she meant by that. Was it her nursing skills that were good? Had Charity actually needed those...had his absence worsened her condition? Or did she just mean Miss Boyd was good, as in a nice person to be around?

"I'm glad, then. Was she out walking with you just now?"

"No, not this time."

He hated to spoil the moment, but his protective instincts wouldn't let him do otherwise. "It makes me happy to know you have grown fond of my homeland. But, dearest, I really would prefer you not go walking alone."

Lady Charity Maxwell—who hadn't even owned that title long enough to become accustomed to it before her husband left her—felt her ire rising. She shrugged off his embrace and turned to face him.

He looked like he'd aged ten years in the short weeks he'd been away, yet somehow he was as handsome as ever. How could she love him so much and be so mad at him at the same time?

She'd plotted for hours about how to seduce her husband when he finally returned. Now that he was here, it was much more complicated. Oh, she still wanted to wind up naked in his arms, but she couldn't do it while she was so upset with him. He wanted to waltz back into her life and tell her how to behave? Pretend like nothing had happened? She hadn't realized until now that her feelings went way beyond heartbreak. She was just so *angry*.

Heaven above. The man hadn't been home an hour and her emotions were all in a windstorm. "Why shouldn't I walk alone? What's it to you if the madwoman gets lost in the woods? I should think you'd be relieved. It would free you to go find the 'suitable' wife and mother you wanted in the first place."

"I don't believe you a madwoman, lass," he said quietly. "You are eminently suitable. You may very well be the only woman on earth who will ever suit me."

His gentleness, his protectiveness, only increased her frustration. He could say he needed her, that he cared for her. But his actions had proven otherwise. "Your opinion seems to have changed quite suddenly."

Even if he was a man prone to jumping to conclusions, she knew him well enough to know he *wasn't* prone to drastically changing his mind after reaching said conclusion. "What made you change your mind?"

Graeme cleared his throat. "Walk with me again."

He took her arm once more, and they circled the garden, coming to stop at a stone bench, while he explained. "I had a lot of time to think. Spent two weeks at the hunting box of an acquaintance of mine, surrounded by nothing but wood and brush. By the end of those weeks, I could think of little else but you. But I still didn't know what to do. It is one of my fondest wishes, you know, to give Nathan a passel of younger siblings. I truly feared, with madness running on both sides of the family, we might doom any children we had to an unbearable life." He stopped suddenly. "Of course, I realized those worries could already be too late. Were they?"

"My lord?"

"Are you with child, beautiful wife?"

"Nooo…" she said slowly, trying to follow his thoughts. Oddly, his look of disappointment pleased her.

"So I stayed away a while longer," he continued. "Maybe I'm just slow. My father always used to say it took a long time for a thought to penetrate my thick skull, but once it did, it never slipped back out." He gave a self-deprecating laugh. "I suppose he was right. And then…well, then I ran into Beaufort at the races in Edinburgh. He was with a certain Monsieur Durand. The three of us had a rather long conversation."

The anger left her like a sailboat in a sudden absence of wind, leaving only a drifting weariness. She sank down on the garden bench. "Oh. So you know."

She'd almost thought, for a moment while he spoke, that he'd come to this decision alone. That he loved her unconditionally, even if he still thought her mad. Knowing that he'd spoken to Alex Bainbridge and Philippe Durand…they wouldn't have been able to relay all of the things she'd revealed to Ismay Boyd, for she'd never spoken of them before. But her two rescuers had certainly known enough to paint a picture for her husband. So where did that leave her?

"All right," she said dully. She gave a little wave of her

hand. "You asked me once, why the duke sent men to shadow me. The answer I gave that night at Vauxhall was true, but only a small piece of the truth. I won't walk alone anymore. You can walk with me, or send a guard, or whatever."

Graeme frowned. This wasn't what he'd wanted. A submissive Charity was no Charity at all. Worse, it was he who'd repressed her. He sat beside her. "We'll figure something out, sweet. I want this to be your home, not a prison."

Tears welled in her eyes. "Everywhere is a prison. Even inside my head."

"Oh, my love." He swallowed, hard. "I wish you had told me."

"You never gave me a chance to explain. You just left."

Graeme ran his tongue over his teeth. She was right. He hated that she was right, but she was. He took a deep breath. He came from a long line of Scottish warriors and clan chiefs who understood the art of battle far better than the art of apology. He was enlightened enough to know when one was called for, dammit, but could not for the life of him come up with words that would set everything to rights.

He started simple. "I'm sorry, love."

He saw a flicker of surprise in her eyes. But she didn't say anything back.

"I am ready to listen now, love. To anything you need to tell me."

"How could I tell you? Everyone warned me, *tell no one. No man will want you if they know*. I thought I could hide it. I might lose you otherwise. You would no longer desire me."

"I don't know who these men are, that would blame a woman for crimes committed against her, but I am not one of them." His eyes softened. "And as for desire…"

She moistened her lips, her gaze caught with his. "Yes?"

"I will desire you until the day I draw my last breath."

"Are you sure? Even knowing…what you know?"

"Let me prove it to you."

Chapter 19

His mouth came down to capture hers. Gently at first, almost tentative. She didn't want tentative. A needy sound escaped her throat. She'd tossed and turned so many lonely nights, dreaming of this. Afraid he would never come back. She kissed him in return, pliant and willing.

He groaned as uncertainty gave way to absolute possession.

Her head fell back, baring her throat and thrusting the tops of her breasts toward him. His tongue met hers, stroking and thrusting as he clutched her closer.

She gave herself over to his touch, needing to forget, even for a moment, the pain of the past weeks. He cupped her breast, dragging his mouth from hers to kiss her throat, causing her pulse to leap.

"I could never stop desiring you," he murmured against her throat. He bent his head lower, to the top of her breast, while his thumb grazed her nipple.

"More," she whispered.

"Come upstairs with me."

She nodded, and they beat a hasty retreat to the master suite, away from the eyes of any curious servants.

The moment the door closed behind them, his fingers worked the laces and hooks of her gown. She shrugged off the garment, and her chemise, as soon as they came loose. His shirt and trousers followed quickly after, and he tugged her toward the bed. She couldn't stop touching him. A flurry of stroking tongues, urgent fingers.

They hit the bed and she collapsed on top of him, reveling in the feel of his skin, the hard planes of his body pressing into hers. He looked up, noticing the colorful silks she'd draped from the bedposts. She'd almost forgotten them—a part of her plan to make him desire her.

"Very exotic," he murmured.

"I thought they might remind you of a certain Indian princess."

"*You* remind me of a certain Indian princess."

His thumb found her nipple again, and the only response she managed was, "Mmmm."

"Shall I show you the things I wanted to do to you that night, my princess?"

"Oh, yes."

His mouth took the place of his thumb, and Charity forgot everything else. Need spiked through her, sharp and pleasurable at the same time. He drew on her nipple until she cried out, grinding her hips against his hardness, desperate for him to fill her.

He lifted her hips and shifted beneath her. She settled back down, sheathing his cock, throwing her head back as she rocked back and forth. She'd needed this for too long. They both had. She could feel him already, thickening, pulsing hard inside her. He wouldn't last long. Neither would she.

She came with another cry, shudders racking her body as she fell against him. He held her to him, rolling them both over until he was on top. He thrust again, and again, and found his own release, spurting into her as a long groan of satisfaction escaped him.

He gathered her close, holding her tight. Neither of them tried to speak. It felt so good to be in his arms again. After a time, though, his arms grew heavy. The haggard lines marring his features smoothed out. Eventually, Charity realized her husband had fallen asleep.

When Graeme awoke, Charity was no longer beside him. Disappointment filled him, though since he had fallen asleep midday, he couldn't really have expected her to stay. He pushed himself up from the mattress and strode to the window. Judging by the sun hanging low in the west, he'd slept a solid couple hours. After the unrelenting journey home, he'd needed the rest.

His protective instincts urged him to check on his wife. Was she still all right?

One look in a mirror, and he forced himself not to. After all, that sort of hovering was exactly what had spurred her rebellion back in London. Instead he called for a bath and a shave, both desperately needed. Charity must have missed him nearly as much as he'd missed her, if she'd allowed him to make love to her in the condition he'd arrived in. Did their lovemaking mean everything was settled? He considered himself a lucky man, but not *that* lucky.

Once he felt human again, he went downstairs. He listened for Charity's lilting voice, but heard nothing. *Stop worrying. Give it time.* Following his own advice was not easy.

Moving through the house, Graeme noticed other changes. Aside from the addition of the governess, none were his work. The windows of the front room had been washed until they sparkled, the curtains thrown back so sunlight could stream in. A pile of nature drawings, detailed studies of leaves, bark, and a birds nest done in a childish hand, lay atop a side table in the hall. His nephew had a good eye. Graeme hadn't known that.

Nathan himself was now happily chasing a spotted puppy over the back fields, the grin splitting his face an expression Graeme hadn't seen since the lad came to live with him.

He passed by the library, where Miss Boyd was chatting with his mother. Both of them clicked away with knitting needles and balls of yarn. He hadn't seen his mother so comfortable and engaged in years. A basket sat between the two women. Socks, his housekeeper informed him, for the Wounded Soldiers Society. The local weavers had donated yarn scraps leftover from larger projects. Not only that, but the dowager countess had begun taking her meals at the main house again. Interesting.

Although Charity was nowhere to be seen, Graeme had a pretty good idea who was responsible for the changes. For all her faults, Lady Medford *had,* apparently, raised her daughter to know how to preside over a large household. Add that to Charity's natural charm, and the residents of Leventhal House were becoming exactly the sort of close-knit household he had hoped for. Only they'd been doing it without him.

Charity's sparkle naturally breathed life into her surroundings. Not only was she *not* insane, she was amazingly capable. The transition from London life to running an estate in the Highlands would be a challenge for anyone. Yet she'd done it, and without the reassurance of a husband by her side. She'd done it while fighting back the demons of the past, determined to live life on her own terms. To go through the ordeal she'd endured, and emerge with such unbroken spirit.... Regret flooded him.

She lived every day knowing there were men out there who'd tried to kill her, and who might try again. Who wouldn't have nightmares, or occasionally crawl under the bed? As tempting as it was to lock her in a tower for her own protection, he couldn't do that. She'd never fully trust him again if he barged back into her life acting as though he had all the answers—no matter how galling it was to admit that he didn't. He was going to have to learn to live with his own fear—the fear that someday, someone might lurch up from Charity's past to try to rob him of the most wonderful woman in the world.

Charity dressed carefully for dinner. She hadn't needed her elaborate seduction plan, but she still didn't quite understand where things stood between she and her husband. She wasn't one to hold a grudge. She just didn't *know*. He was back, and he'd made love to her. So at least she knew he still desired her. Did that erase her own hurt feelings? Maybe. She could understand why he might have felt betrayed, or his fears about the effect on their future children. But did he think less of her now, knowing how foolish she'd been? Knowing she'd been exposed to cruel and base men?

Her silk gown, the intricate styling of her tresses, and the delicate pearls at her throat all formed a sort of armor, shielding her from the ugliness of that past.

Perhaps he didn't hold it against her. He had, after all, returned in great haste. He'd called her his love, his sweet. Lord Maxwell wasn't the sort of man to fling such terms around lightly. Hope burned like a flame in her chest, stronger and steadier than before.

When she reached the dining room, the dowager countess, Miss Boyd, and Nathan were already there. "Come, Master Graeme," Lady Eleanor teased her grandson, "you must leave your puppy with the servants. He won't wish to sit through a long dinner."

"But neither do I," Nathan whined, not bothering to correct her on his name.

"But you must learn, if you're to be master of the house one day."

"What, am I already being usurped?"

Charity started, not having heard Graeme's approach. He was clean-shaven, smelling of sandalwood and soap. She breathed him in, little flames of desire already licking along the edges of her consciousness. His fine white shirt and dark jacket stretched across broad shoulders. He came to stop beside her, his hand resting lightly at the small of her back.

"Uncle Graeme!"

The elder Lady Maxwell looked confused for a moment. Then her eyes cleared and she lowered her head. "I've done it again, haven't I?"

Graeme opened his mouth to reassure her, hating that his arrival had caused her embarrassment, but Nathan jumped in first. "'Tis no matter, Nana. Aunt Charity found a portrait of Uncle Graeme as a child, and even I think we look the same. But now that he's back, I can't sit in his chair anymore and pretend."

Graeme raised a brow. "Pretending to be master, eh?"

Nate shrugged sheepishly, and Graeme reached forward to tickle him. The boy dodged. Graeme gave a half-hearted chase, making all of them break into laughter. A footman quietly removed Mac, so the puppy could have his own dinner at the back of the kitchen. The awkward moment forgotten, they took their seats.

Miss Boyd flicked a nervous glance at him from her place far down the table. What had he done to set the members of his household on edge whenever he was near? True, he knew Miss Boyd's real occupation might not merit a place at the dinner table, but he'd essentially authorized it when he'd notified the staff that she was training to be a companion.

He wasn't certain how, but somewhere along the way, the people most fundamental to his life had stopped treating him as an approachable man and started acting as though he were a distant lord. A certain amount of deference came with his title. He knew that. The rest was too much. He couldn't just *order* them to relax, though. He obviously needed to show them he would welcome it if they did.

Through the open window, the beat of a snare drum broke the evening stillness. A burst of piping followed.

"What is that?" Charity asked.

"Ach. That'll be Red an' his band practicing for Pipers' Fest," he answered, letting his brogue shine through in deference to the Scottish festival.

"Pipers' Fest?"

"Aye." Being new, Charity wouldn't know about the annual musical festival. "Every June, Grantown hosts a competition for pipe and drum groups. Over the years, it's become quite an event. Our own Mr. Red is one o' the top competitors. He's still sore about coming in second last year to the Bog Country Beaters. I imagine they're bound and determined to take first this year. Like as not we'll be hearing quite a lot of them in the next fortnight."

"What else is at the festival?" Nathan asked.

"Goodness, you haven't been either?" the dowager countess asked.

"I don't think so," her grandson said, frowning as he tried to remember.

"Well, there are all the performances, of course," Graeme answered, "and a craft fair, a children's parade, usually some dancing, and of course all the local establishments turn out to sell food and drink."

Nathan keyed in on one phrase. "A children's parade?"

How thoughtless of him to have forgotten. Maybe he really had become a distant, standoffish lord. "Aye. How would you and Mac like to march in the parade?"

The boy nodded eagerly.

"Shall we all go?" Charity asked.

"That sounds lovely," his mother agreed. Even Miss Boyd was smiling.

His head groom's timing for this evening's practice could not have been better, Graeme realized. "I'll ask Red what time The Lost Pipers are set to perform. I'm sure it would give them great pleasure to have the whole of Leventhal House turn out in support."

"The whole house?"

"Why not? The staff would welcome a surprise holiday, don't ye think? It will be fun."

The wariness melted away and, around the table, faces smiled at him.

"Uncle Graeme, if we all go cheer for Mr. Red, he'll be certain to win, won't he?"

He chuckled. "I don't get to be the judge, Nathan, but I daresay we'll make it hard for him to lose."

Graeme left the dinner table that night with a spring in his step. He hadn't managed to get Charity alone since making love to her, but all things considered, he'd made more progress today than he could have dared hope. If he continued in this way, it would, just as he'd told his nephew about Red's pipe and drum band, be hard for him to lose.

Red and The Lost Pipers were not the only ones practicing for Pipers' Fest. Jasper Morton was practicing, too, at least as hard as the pipers. After all, he had a lot more at stake.

After scouting out the local inn and taverns, he'd determined exactly what he'd suspected. None kept enough gold on hand to furnish the voyage he had planned. Unless he stole from all of them, which didn't seem a very bright plan, his options were limited. Leventhal House never seemed to empty out. He'd almost made up his mind to travel to the port city of Inverness and try his luck there, when he overheard two of Lord Maxwell's servants singing his praises for offering them an extra afternoon off if they came out to support the Pipers' Fest next Sunday.

Even Jasper could appreciate the irony of the opportunity *that* presented.

As soon as his shift at the docks ended, he eased through the woods at the edge of the burn. This was his third visit. The first had been weeks ago. Then, he'd gotten discouraged, since Leventhal House's bustling, ever-present staff guaranteed someone was always about. But since Lord Maxwell himself had provided the solution to that problem by offering them all a holiday, he'd returned. He counted the servants and studied the entrances and exits of the manor, always lurking out of sight. He needed to know how many there were, so that he could count on the day of the festival. He would know when it was safe to go in, and if anyone had stayed behind.

"Mac!"

The boy's spotted mutt raced toward him, followed at a distance by the young master.

Bugger. Jasper turned and ran—directly into a tree. Reeling, he kept going until he reached the burn. He jumped in and crossed, hissing in shock as the icy water soaked through his boots and trousers up to his knees. On the far side, he ducked behind a large outcropping of rock.

The pup stopped at the bank, sniffing all along the waters' edge, then giving a plaintive whine.

"Mac!" the boy called again, his form barely visible through the trees.

The dog looked exactly at the spot where Jasper stood, then turned around and trotted back to his boy.

Jasper rubbed his chest, where his heart had near jumped out a minute back. *Blimey.* He was getting too old for such stunts. He gazed sorrowfully at the sodden state of his only pair of boots. Living outside the law used to make him feel smart, like he'd gotten away with something. He hadn't felt that way in a long time.

He'd had enough for today. No need to lurk further—he knew all he needed to know.

Graeme's two-week "head start" before the Duke and Duchess of Beaufort arrived was nearly up. Fortunately, he believed they would find Charity happy and content.

This morning, she'd been combing her hair when he walked into the bedroom carrying a rope ladder, which he proceeded to stash in a decorative box beneath the windowsill.

At her wide-eyed stare, he shrugged. "Sometimes the line between genius and lunatic is a blurry one. You told me you did this back in London, and I realized the idea has merit."

"You did?" she asked dubiously.

"Aye. Not just in the event of an attack—though I am not discounting the possibility—but what if there were a fire? We are both safer with a second means of escape. I put one in the nursery, too." It was true. At first he'd done it merely to put her at ease, but the more he'd thought about it, the more the generations of warrior-protector blood flowing through his veins told him there was solid logic in being prepared.

She dropped her hair comb and flung herself into his arms. Tears spilled down her cheeks as she kissed him fiercely.

He kissed back. "I'll put one in every room of the house if it makes you this happy."

"I love you," she responded.

He kissed the tear tracks at the corners of her beautiful eyes. "I love you, too."

Scooping her up and carrying her to the bed, he proceeded to show her how much.

Only afterward did he remember the other purpose he'd had in coming up to their room. Lying back in bed, his wife's head tucked against his shoulder and her hair spilling across his chest, it came back to him. "Remember how you said you missed your sister, and would like to invite her for a visit?" Graeme asked.

"Yes!" Charity lifted her head. "Have you heard from her?"

"In a way. If my guess is right, she will be arriving tomorrow."

"Truly? How do you know?" Charity hopped up, half-sitting now, her blond locks tumbling over her breasts like some erotic mermaid. He struggled to focus.

"She was with her husband in Edinborough. They were planning to pay you a surprise visit after the races ended." He gave her a sheepish grin. "Given the rather unconventional nature of our marriage, at least by London's standards, I think they wanted to see for themselves whether you were happy.

"Of course, at the time the duke and I spoke, things were, well, awkward, due to my misunderstanding. So I asked him to give me time to sort out the knowledge he'd just imparted, and to make amends. He consented to two weeks."

As of today, his official reprieve was over. Given the hurried nature of his trip home, though, Graeme had tacked on an extra travel day to his estimate of the duke and duchess's arrival.

"I hope I did the right thing in asking them to wait. Will they find you happy, my sweet?"

Charity paused. The tiny furrow between her brows told him she was giving the question serious consideration. "I am happy," she finally said. "Not in the blissful, carefree way of Nathan playing with Mac, but happy nonetheless. I have a husband who cares for me and who cares enough to ask about my happiness. I have a lovely home, and am learning to know the land and the people."

Graeme smiled. It wasn't exactly the answer he would have hoped for, but it was an honest one. She was still lonely for the familiar activity of London life, he surmised, and possibly still wary of doing anything that might scare him off again. Well, he'd promised to love and protect her, and he wasn't going to break either of those promises a second time. As for London, a taste of it should be arriving soon.

True to Graeme's prediction, the duke's coach pulled up shortly after noon the following day, spilling out Alex and Elizabeth Bainbridge.

Charity greeted them happily, having spent the morning buzzing about the house, directing the servants in an effort to have everything fresh and clean.

Elizabeth hugged her, then held her at arm's length, giving her a critical eye. "You look...flushed," she announced.

Charity laughed and led her sister by the hand into her new home.

"Your trunks arrived?"

"Yes." Charity twirled, showing off the daffodil gown of which she was so fond. "Can't you tell?"

They passed most of the afternoon in chatting in the way that sisters do—seemingly of inconsequential matters, but intimate in their knowledge of one another and how those little matters make up the fabric of life. They accompanied Graeme and the duke on a horseback tour of the grounds, but, after dinner, declined to join the men at the card table, preferring to simply relax in one another's company.

"I've missed you," Charity admitted. "Even before coming here, I think."

Elizabeth inclined her head. "There has been a great deal of change, for all of us, in the last year." She lowered her voice. "Are you happy here? I know when we last spoke in London, you were growing enamored of Lord Maxwell, and I thought you had begun to give his suit serious consideration...but then you eloped, just like that, and I wondered..."

Charity knew what she was asking. "The elopement was not a matter of *necessity*. To be honest, I had no idea of the plan until the night we left, when Graeme sprung it on me."

"Wait. Are you telling me he abducted you?"

"Not abducted. Just...surprised. I went willingly enough." She couldn't help but smile at the memory. "You know me. When have I ever been able to say 'no' to an impractical but dashingly romantic idea?"

Elizabeth's lips quirked. "Never."

"Exactly. Besides, Graeme promised me that such elopements practically are the tradition in Scotland."

"But are you happy *now*?" her sister pressed. "If not, I'm sure there's a way…"

Charity gazed at the silhouette of their two husbands seated in the far corner of the room, at the warm luxury of her surroundings, and lifted her hands. There was too much to put into words. "Yes," she finally managed through the thickness in her throat.

"Sometimes the first few months of a marriage are the rockiest," Elizabeth observed.

She would know. Charity remembered, belatedly, that her sister's blissful state hadn't been the immediate result of her wedding day. She and the duke had experienced their own trials, and come through stronger as a result. It was a good reminder, one that lent strength to her own hopes.

"Marrying Graeme was the right choice. He's a good man, Elizabeth. It was me that…I didn't tell him everything, and then…"

"I know."

"It's much better, now. I was so angry when he hired Miss Boyd, but then she turned out to be immensely helpful."

"Your companion?"

"She's actually a trained nurse," Charity whispered. "He thought…"

"Oh. Oh, no."

"He doesn't think that anymore."

"Good."

"When he was…travelling, I felt so alone. I ended up confiding in Miss Boyd. I told her everything. Things I'd never told anyone—not even you, E. I'm sorry."

"I understand. You weren't ready then."

"Exactly. I thought Miss Boyd would—I don't know, judge me—but she didn't. The more I talked, the farther the fears seemed to shrink into the past. When Graeme came back, he didn't condemn me either. He was just relieved to know it wasn't a hereditary madness. He tries too hard to protect me now, but that is his nature. The nightmares are coming less often. E., I think I'm actually, finally, returning to normal."

Elizabeth reached over and gave one of Charity's curls a big-sisterly tug. "Who would have thought a second kidnapping would cure the ills of the first?" she quipped.

The next day, the whole household buzzed with excitement at the prospect of the holiday afternoon. The maids wove ribbons into Elizabeth and Charity's hair. Nathan, so proud to be marching in a parade later in the day, hardly dared go outside to play that morning for fear of mussing his clean shirt. Charity tweaked his ear and whispered "Go ahead. You've clean shirts to spare. I'll call you in with plenty of time to change if you must."

"He looks up to you," her sister observed.

Charity just smiled.

Before long, everyone was ready and turned out in their Sunday best, the picnic baskets were packed, and those with coins to spare had counted them carefully for what they might desire at the festival.

Leventhal House lay just under three miles from the town center. Certainly the distance could be walked, but with everyone in their finery, only a few of the staff chose to travel by foot. The nobles and Miss Boyd divided into two carriages, while the rest of the household members piled onto carts or rode horses behind them.

"We are like our very own parade," Nathan observed.

"Indeed we are. How lovely. I haven't been in a parade in years," his grandmother indulged him, as they and Miss Boyd climbed into the second carriage.

"But we don't get to march in this one." Obviously, in Nathan's opinion, marching was superior to riding.

Charity rode in the lead coach with her husband, Elizabeth, and the duke. Elizabeth kept furtively glancing between she and Graeme. Charity knew she was trying to assess for herself whether they were happy.

Charity pinned on a serene smile, but as they drew closer to the town square and the noise of the festival penetrated the walls of the carriage, her stomach knotted.

They had to stop several blocks away from the square due to the crowds. Alighting, Charity saw that her husband hadn't been exaggerating when he'd said people came from all over for Pipers Fest. The square was packed, the noise cacophonous as various bands warmed up or gave impromptu performances. Where had they all come from? The crowds roaming the streets must have sprung from the very hills of the Highlands.

Elizabeth realized the problem only seconds after Charity. She leaned over. "Are you going to be all right here?" she murmured, so only Charity could hear.

"I think so." When Graeme asked the same question moments later, she repeated her answer, hoping it would prove true. The festival was far bigger and more chaotic than she'd imagined. She took a breath to steady herself. She could do this. At the top center of the square, the townspeople had set up a makeshift stage, from which the audience and other activities fanned out. The tantalizing smell of grilled meats and roasted nuts wafted through the air. Bright vendor displays showcased inexpensive but decorative fans and parasols that had many a lass stopping to part with a coin. Traditional woolens abounded, as well as toy pipes for children to learn to play.

Charity melded into the center of her own cluster of family. The servants, free for the afternoon, drifted off to explore. The duke lead their group, with Elizabeth by his side. Charity focused on his shoulder blades, steady and reassuring, and on the feel of her arm tucked in the crook of Graeme's at her side. They paused at the edge of the grassy space before the stage.

Along the street to the north, Charity could see the children lining up. So could Nate. Composure forgotten, he leaped up and down. "May we join them? Is it time? We mustn't be late! Mac and I have been waiting *forever.*"

The duke quirked and amused brow, and Elizabeth held up a hand to cover her smile.

Graeme opened his mouth with what Charity thought would be an admonition to the boy to be patient, but then he shrugged. Giving Charity's hand a squeeze, he let her go. "I'll be back shortly," he murmured, before turning to his nephew. "Aye, Nate. 'Tis always better to be early than late. Come along, then."

They strolled off together, leaving the adults chuckling as they heard Graeme ask, "Shall we endeavor to be early to your grammar lesson tomorrow morn, as well? What say ye?"

Near the stage, two giant drums were set up. A pair of bearded men walked over and, using large padded drumsticks, began beating a pattern that resonated over the noise of the crowd. People looked up and began moving toward the center of the square, heeding the signal that indicated the beginning of an event. Others simply kept doing what they wished.

The dowager countess and Miss Boyd had their heads bent together. After a moment, Ismay led the elder Lady Maxwell toward a display of fans. Charity smiled to herself. Graeme's mother surely had any number of exquisite fans, or the means to buy them if she wished, but even she wasn't immune to the spirit of the festival. Or perhaps she'd reached a point in life where impressions didn't matter, and a pretty fan was pretty no matter its maker. Hmm. Charity rather liked that idea. Perhaps she'd buy one as well.

An earsplitting blast of bagpipes broke through the noise. Charity covered her ears and ducked, but the rest of the crowd surged toward the street, lining up along the sides to watch the parade. In the sweep of moving bodies, Charity looked up and realized she'd broken away from her group.

Her breath started coming faster. Shallow. She couldn't *get* a full breath.

She called for Elizabeth, but the bagpipes were playing in earnest now. Being petite, she had no hope of seeing over the heads of those standing between them. Graeme, off with Nathan, was too far to hear her. The duke. He was tall. She strained to look for him. Apparently the Highlands bred tall men. The crowd was filled with them. She looked for dark, well-cut hair. *Was that him?* A group of laughing pipers passed between them before she could lock in on the man in question. The swirl of bright colors and noise assaulted her senses. Too many unfamiliar faces. The crowd seethed and eddied around her like a stormy ocean, with Charity a single, solitary island. Why had she ever thought she could do this?

Too much. It was too much.

She wanted to see little Nathan march about, wanted to cheer on Leventhal House's head groom and his band…but the urge to flee was even stronger.

She needed Graeme. Or Miss Boyd. There was no hope of finding either of them at the moment. No way could she do this alone—but she wouldn't cause a scene. She didn't want it bandied about for weeks to come that the countess had run screaming like a madwoman the moment a few bagpipes began to play.

Calmly, fighting for a full breath while her heart banged around in her chest like the beat of the signal drummers, Charity turned and walked away.

She thought to walk down to the line of carriages, to seek a few moments of solitude while she gathered herself. But the sound of the pipers and drummers reverberated through the streets, through her very flesh. The horses stamped, and even blocks away from the square, people milled about. People with strange faces who turned to stare at the young countess.

Charity passed their carriage kept walking. Tears of embarrassment streaked down her cheeks. Just when she'd thought she was pulling her life together. She couldn't let the townspeople see her like this. What would Graeme think? Would he worry? Would he know where to find her? She should have left a note. Where? On the carriage?

She willed herself to turn around, but she couldn't face going back there. Her feet kept planting themselves, one in front of another, seeking the place she'd begun to recognize as a haven. Slowly, the cacophony of music and people faded.

When Leventhal House came into sight, she drew the first full breath she'd managed since arriving at Pipers' Fest.

She closed her eyes briefly as a shudder ran through her. She'd have to apologize to Nathan for missing the parade. Elizabeth would understand. So would Miss Boyd. And Graeme...she prayed Graeme would understand. In the two weeks since his return, he'd professed to understand, to empathize. She knew he no longer worried that her affliction could be passed on to their children. But she hadn't actually done anything "mad" in that time, either. At least today she'd resisted the urge to run, or to hide, hands pressed over her ears. She didn't want to embarrass him in front of the townspeople who so looked up to him. If anyone in the boisterous crowd even thought to question her departure—if they'd even noticed, she could simply say she'd felt unwell and walked home. The "alone" part of the walking might set some tongues wagging, but after all, she was a married woman now. And a countess. Surely that should give her some freedom.

Weary now, she climbed the steps before the entrance and pushed the door open, breathing in the now-familiar scent of home. She rolled her shoulders, feeling the tension give way. *It will be all right*, she told herself. *So I don't like crowds. That doesn't strip me of my sanity. It only means I should avoid crowds. Some people avoid spiders. No different.* Pleased with her reasoning, she headed past the library and up the stairs. A bath with lavender would be the ideal balm to her frayed nerves, but she'd have to wait until the staff returned for that.

Clunk.

Muttered curses spilled from the library door.

Charity jumped, whipping around.

They'd left the house empty. Or had one of the servants stayed behind?

One of double doors separating the library from the hall stood open.

Ice flooded her veins and she stopped in her tracks. Frozen.

Standing before her was the embodiment of her nightmares, rummaging in the drawer of her husband's desk.

Chapter 20:

"The fact that you are willing to say 'I do not understand, and it is fine,' is the greatest understanding you could exhibit." —*Wayne Dyer*

Charity couldn't breathe. Again.

Her mind said to back away, but her blood had turned to ice, her limbs to wood. Before she could convince her unresponsive body to obey the command, Jasper Morton looked up.

"Bloody hell!" He fumbled, reaching for a pistol lying several feet away.

Too late, her mind grasped the significance of the item he sought. He leveled the weapon at her. "Now ye're here, ye may as well come all the way in."

She couldn't budge. This was worse than her nightmares.

"Now, wench!"

Her feet moved of their own accord, stepping forward as commanded. *Traitors.* Why did they obey his command and not hers?

Morton circled around her, keeping the gun trained in her direction, and shut the door. "Stay right there."

She nodded, her lungs screaming for air as she struggled to draw breath. She had to get out of here. Had to. This could *not* happen again. Not here. Not now. Not when she'd finally, almost, had it all.

Morton set the pistol down, needing both hands as he maneuvered some of the smaller furniture in the room up against the door.

The window caught Charity's eye. The glass was thick, and the latch often stuck, but if she could get before he realized—

"I said don't move!"

She stopped, realizing her feet had given away her plan even before she'd decided on it as a course of action. *Damn.* Her feet seemed bent on betraying her. The rest of her body was in on the plan, too. Her heart beat so loudly they could probably her it back at Piper's Fest. She couldn't let him see her fear.

He glanced at the end tables stacked against the door, then looked wildly around the room as though he'd forgotten something. His glance fell on one more small but solid table. He moved toward it.

Desperate, Charity leapt for the gun. She snatched it as he lurched forward, nearly dropping it before getting both hands around it and raising it toward him, hands trembling.

"You don't know how to fire that thing."

She eyed the pistol, hefted its weight in her hand. He spoke true. She'd never even held one before. But he didn't have to know that. "It doesn't look too complicated. You threatened me with it. So it must be loaded. You seem like a smart man. Too smart to threaten a woman with an unloaded pistol." Her voice came out remarkably steady.

She knew from the curl of his lip she'd guessed right. Privately, she had significant reservations as to his intelligence, but intuition told her flattery would gain her far more than ridicule with this man.

"You won't know how to aim."

She shrugged. "True. I might miss. But I might not. Do you think luck is with you today, Mr. Morton?"

He scowled. "Never had a lucky day in me life."

"In that case, I would think very, very carefully if I were you. I am tired. And when I get tired, I tend to lose my patience. I have rarely had a restful night's sleep since last summer. And do you know why?" Ire gave force to her words. "Why, yes, I believe you do."

He stared at her for a full minute. "I'm tired, too."

"You cannot possibly expect me to feel sorry for you."

"Naw. Not asking ye to. I done some bad things. Don' expect pity from no one."

"Good." The pistol felt heavy. She contemplated her choices. To get past the door, she'd have to move the furniture. To go out the window, she only had to manage the latch and crank it open. The one to the right was smoother than the left. Keeping the pistol pointed in his general direction, she moved to the window. She felt for the handle. It turned, but barely. She risked a good look at it and pulled harder.

With a garbled cry, he tackled her. "Not this time, bitch."

Charity's head smacked against the windowsill as she went down, making the room spin. The pistol went flying. Both of them went after it. Morton was faster.

"Now, if ye know what's good for ye, you'll do as I said the first time. Don't move."

She nodded, her head sore. "This won't work." She

gestured to the stacked up furniture. "He'll get past those. Lord Maxwell is on his way back this very moment."

He shot her a scornful look. "Of course he will. But not without makin' some noise. An' by the time the door is open, I'll have me pistol pointed at yer pretty head, an' I daresay he won't come no further when 'e sees that." He went back to the desk he'd been searching when she first interrupted him.

Damn. It was true. Graeme would never knowingly endanger her. Maybe the windows could work in her favor after all. When Graeme found her, he'd have no choice but to back away. But he could come around outside…

As though reading her thoughts, Morton looked at her, scowled, and drew the drapes.

Feeling beleaguered, Charity asked, "What are you looking for? Whatever it is, just take it and go."

"Bit late for that, now. Why couldn't *you* just stay away?"

She frowned. Why did that question seem so hard? "Why would I? This is my home."

"Well, all I'm looking for is a way out of it. Out of this whole bloody country. Ye may not believe me, but I did no' come here today to kill ye."

"Then don't."

He shook his head. "Ye're leavin' me no choice."

"Even if you kill me, you'll never make your own escape. The others will be here any moment."

"Charity?" Her sister's voice echoed outside.

Morton frowned. "Who's that?"

"My sister. She is with my husband, and hers."

He swore. He had more creativity than she would have given him credit for, Charity thought detachedly.

"Charity?" Graeme this time.

"Don' say nothin.'"

She kept her mouth shut. The lever turned on the library door, and the door ran into the resistance her captor had contrived.

"What the..."

"Don't come any farther. I've got yer wife in here, and there's a pistol pointin' at her. I see so much as a hair on your head, an' I shoot."

The oath she heard from outside the door rivaled that of her captor. Then there was silence.

She stared at the man she'd hoped never to see again. He stared back. *Now what?* She wanted to ask, but had the wisdom not to.

It looked as though the past months had not treated him kindly. His clothing was rough and patched, his fingernails ragged and dirty. His words filtered through her overwrought brain. *Don' expect pity from no one... All I want is a way out of it. Out of this whole bloody country... Ye may not believe me, but I did no' come here today to kill ye.*

He could be lying. Probably was. But if he spoke the truth, maybe she could rescue herself.

"Why are you so tired, Mr. Morton?"

He didn't reply. She watched as he eyed the fine furnishings of the library, then reached out to stroke the spine of a leather-bound book with one dirty finger.

"I never growed up in a place like this," he answered, if it could be called an answer. "Didn't even know such places existed. Ma died when I was six. From then on, I only ate what I could steal."

"No one would take you in? Or give you work?" She really, really did not want to feel sympathy for this man.

"Not likely. Not on account o' Pa. When your Pa 'as swindled most everyone in the neighborhood, folks get to feelin' less charitable toward ye."

Charity's own father had left a few creditors feeling swindled in his day. "But you were just a child."

He shrugged. "Not all that uncommon, boys on the streets. Only orphanage for boys was always full, 'specially in winter. In summer the older ones would run away, thinkin' they could fend for themselves. And ye could, if ye was willin' to take whatever work came along, honest or no.'"

Charity didn't know what to say. But she wanted to keep him talking. "That must have been hard."

"Didn't occur to me to think whether it was hard or not. Wasn't raised with folks who knew any kind of life besides hard."

She scuffed the toe of her slipper along the edge of the rug.

"But like I said. I done some bad things. I know it. Things what canna' be undone, either. That's wha' makes me tired. These things I've done, they walk around wi' me. I been doin' honest work in Grantown. But there's no amount o' honest work that'll stop me from bein' a hunted man. Not now. I know it."

She waited, eyes narrowed.

He rubbed at his bulbous nose with the back of his hand. "I came looking for coin. I know, I know. Still a crime. But I wasn't meaning to hurt no one. I thought if I could get enough for passage to the Americas, or maybe Barbados…"

"You should turn yourself in."

"Ye're mad."

"So I've been told," she acknowledged wryly.

"They'll condemn me to death."

"You're going to die anyway. There is no escape, Mr. Morton. Even if you somehow slip away today, my husband and my brother-in-law will not rest until they find you again.

The duke's men won't chance losing you a second time. They will kill you first. If you turn yourself over now, though, you'll stand trial."

"If I turn myself in now," he countered, "your husband will shoot me on sight."

It was a possibility, but Charity didn't want to dwell on that. She sensed Morton was starting to weaken. If he grew desperate, he might act suddenly. Rashly. Which would not be good for her.

"Lord Maxwell is a just man. I believe he'd allow you to go to trial—especially if you let me be the one to ask him. Perhaps you have valuable information that would aid your case," she suggested. If he'd been hiding here the whole time, he might not know the others were dead. Charity wasn't going to be the one to tell him. If he thought he could bargain for his life, he might let her go.

She continued on, keeping her tone as polite and rational as she could. "Besides, even if you were condemned at trial, there's an awfully good chance you'd get a reprieve. You weren't the leader of that group. The authorities know it, too. Likely you'd be transported instead. Surely that's better than certain death."

He shrugged. "Mebbe. Mebbe not."

"It's more of a chance than you'll have today."

"You could make 'em promise to let me go."

"You know they won't."

Jasper's lip curled. He punched the solid desk in frustration, then yanked his hand back, wincing at the pain. "Yeah. I know."

"Let me go first," she cajoled. "I will explain to the duke and to Lord Maxwell that you wish to turn yourself in. They will see you have not harmed me, and that will give credence to your claim."

He heaved a sigh. Seconds ticked by.

Charity softened her voice nearly to a whisper. "There is no other way out, Mr. Morton."

His lips twitched, his jaw worked, but no sound came out. Finally, he grunted and jerked his head to the door. "Go."

Charity backed slowly toward the door. The end tables had been knocked askew by Graeme's earlier attempt to enter, but it still took her putting her full weight into her hip to nudge them out of the way. She felt for the latch behind her, not trusting her former captor enough to turn her back on him. She found the latch and the door gave way, sending her tumbling through.

Elizabeth was the first to see her. She ran forward, throwing her arms around her sister.

"Where are the men?" Charity asked, breathless.

"Outside. Trying to—wait." She stopped, eyeing the door. "Is he still in there?"

Charity nodded. "Get Graeme."

Elizabeth was back with the two lords in seconds. Both bore weapons. Seeing Charity safe, they hesitated barely a fraction of a second.

"Don't shoot him!" Charity shouted, realizing their intent.

That stopped them. "What?" Graeme, halfway into the library already, kept his weapon trained on Morton so he couldn't escape out the window. How ironic would it be, Charity thought wildly, if *he* made it out the window when she hadn't?

"He surrenders. He wants to stand trial," she explained.

"You want me to cart this no-good miscreant all the way back to London so he can stand trial?" the duke asked incredulously.

"He did spare my life."

That registered with her husband. "True."

"He shouldn't have been here in the first place!" Beaufort burst out.

Charity shrugged, still not knowing how much of Jasper Morton's story could be trusted. "He said he needed money for passage on a ship."

"I'll bet," Graeme growled.

"If the courts decide he is to hang, so be it," she quietly continued. "But I don't want his blood on my hands."

The two lords looked at one another. Graeme blew out a breath. "All right, Morton. If ye meant what ye said, walk over here—slowly. Hands in sight."

There was a shuffle of footsteps on the other side of the door. The duke reached through, grabbing Morton by his upper arm while Graeme kept the gun steadily aimed.

Morton didn't put up a fight. Graeme and Alex led him outside, turning him over to Tom Brevis, Graeme's driver, who made quick work of binding his wrists and setting up a watch.

Charity observed the whole thing. None of the men suggested she do otherwise. Strangely, the hatred and malice she expected to feel never materialized. Jasper Morton had done terrible things. She probably didn't know most of them. But in the end he'd had a choice. Letting her go meant accepting the possibility of his own death. One sacrifice would not erase the past—but it did deserve her acknowledgement. Finally, when her enemy was bound and slumped against the outer wall of the stables, she cleared her throat.

He looked up, glanced at the rope around his wrists, and met her eye.

"Good luck at trial, Mr. Morton."

His head jerked in something like a nod. "Live well, Lady Maxwell."

She nodded in return, then turned and, feeling strangely light, walked away.

When they were all back in the house, Elizabeth asked the question on everyone's mind. "How on earth did you talk him into letting you go?"

Charity's lips quirked. "I daresay he found me more frightening than I found him."

"Ye can't be serious."

"Not possible," the duke agreed.

"Oh, it's definitely possible. I'm crazy, remember?" She pointed to her head and rolled her eyes.

Graeme tried really hard not to laugh.

"Seriously, I think he was just worn down, tired of running, and smart enough to know he'd never make it off Maxwell grounds alive if he harmed me."

"Very true," Graeme confirmed.

"I'm just glad you're safe. Now, would you please, please stop scaring me half to death?" Elizabeth begged.

"I'll try." She gave an impish smile. "I'll probably even succeed, because I've decided on a new purpose in life."

"You have?"

"Oh, yes. I'm going to make it my highest priority to provide both Nathan and little Noah with a whole passel of cousins."

"Finally, a mission where my support will be welcomed," Graeme quipped.

The duchess's mouth fell open.

For several minutes, none of them could stop laughing.

Finally, when the commotion of the day had died down, Charity sought the sanctuary of the bedroom. Graeme entered just behind her. He approached, reaching out a hand to stroke her hair. "You are the bravest woman I know."

Thank you, would have been an appropriate response. But Charity was still flying too high. "I know." She'd thought the rest of her life would be lived with a measure of uncertainty. With André Denis dead and Jasper Morton in custody, that fog of uncertainty had lifted, leaving only rays of sunshine.

He laughed at her immodesty. "Let me tell you something you don't know, then. I decided something on the way to Edinburgh. On the way *there*, not on the way back," he emphasized.

"You did?" She didn't know where he was going with this.

"I did. And do you know what I decided?"

"Nooooo." She clasped her hands behind her back, waiting.

He drew them out from behind her and held them in his own. "Charity, I decided that, even if you *were* mad as a hatter, you are still the only woman for me. The only woman I love, and will ever love." He frowned. "I hadn't yet figured out what to do with that decision, which is why I didn't rush back right then. But I knew that there was just no way I would ever stop loving you."

"Well," she said softly, "you must be relieved, nonetheless, to know my sanity is intact. For the most part." She lowered her gaze. "I do have some problems. Today at the festival…"

"I know—and it doesn't matter. Loving you has taught me so much already. I went to London to try to find a wife that would fit into this perfect mold I had imagined. Lass, God love ye, but you'll never fit anyone's mold. You are your own creature, and all the more wonderful for it. But ye didn't stop with teaching me to love only you. I see how Leventhal House is changing all around you. My own mother has some, as you call them, problems. You and Miss Boyd accepted her into your lives, made her feel a welcome part of the family again. And Nathan is often far too worried and serious for a boy his age, but you accepted him, too, and he is coming out of his shell. He's smiling again."

"That he is," she said softly.

"I had to learn those things. I am so accustomed to shouldering responsibility, that as soon as I saw a hint of weakness in someone, I naturally added them to my list of things I needed to protect, to take care of. I was trying to do right, but in focusing on the weaknesses, I lost sight of the many wonderful traits they brought to my life. I pushed them away."

Graeme exhaled, long and slowly, feeling the tension melt. It felt so good to get it off his chest, to finally put words to the ache that had gnawed at him for so long. Even better was the understanding that it didn't have to stay this way. It *wouldn't* stay this way. Because Charity had brought change to them all.

"I don't think your mother or Nathan thought you did such a thing."

He wasn't going to let her absolve him of guilt. "They might not have thought it, but it was the result nonetheless. And I tried to do the same to you."

The corners of her mouth quirked up. "I wouldn't have let you, you know. Not forever."

"No?"

"No. But you see, I didn't know I could do all those things either. When you left I was..." She shuddered, then drew a deep breath before going on. "Crushed. I thought everything was over. Our marriage, the wonderful life we had in store. Maybe I really was crazy and a burden. I couldn't live up to your expectations, couldn't be the wife you wanted and needed. I thought about leaving. But if I left, I would just go back to my family in London, and I was a burden to them, too."

"They care for you greatly. Your sister, especially." He gave a wry laugh. "I get that now. When I first met them, I admit I found them somewhat overbearing. I was missing a piece of the picture then."

"I know. I love Elizabeth, too. My mother, well, she tries. But an unwed daughter is always a burden. And a daughter who is wed but has run from her husband, even more so."

"Ach." There was an undeniable element of truth to that.

"So I had some things to learn, too. Miss Boyd helped. I had to learn to live with myself, and focus on what I could bring to Leventhal House, instead of the things holding me back. How could I fault your mother or Nate when they were doing the same?"

"Ye did more than not fault them. Ye love them."

"Yes." She gave him a sheepish smile. "I seem to love people—at least people related to you—rather easily. I thought if I could grow stronger, and make this into a household you could be proud of, then perhaps you might look at me once more like you did before." She threaded her fingers together anxiously. "It isn't there, just yet. But—"

"Aye, it is." He stepped closer, pulling her hands from behind her waist and wrapping them around him.

"It is?" She gazed up through her lashes.

"Aye."

"Oh." Her tongue darted out to moisten her lips. "Maybe you're right. You...you're looking at me that way again."

"What way, love?"
"Like you want to kiss me."
He did.

Epilogue

Three years later

"Son, I hope you don't take offense when I say that today is tied with the day of your birth for the position of 'proudest day of my life,'" the Dowager Countess of Leventhal said as she stood alongside her son, his wife, and their young family and watched as the final nail was hammered into place. A freshly-painted sign now hung over the door of what had, for a number of years, been her house.

"None at all," Graeme replied, giving Charity's hand a squeeze, then joined the rest of the family and staff in a round of applause. "All the ladies here have good reason to be proud."

The sign read "Lady Maxwell's Home," which left a lot to be said, especially as the dowager countess had moved back into the main house, meaning neither the elder nor younger Lady Maxwell actually lived there. But it was the only name they'd all been able to agree on, since the idea had germinated with both women. The home was not a hospital, or an asylum. It was just a residence for a few new members of the Leventhal staff whose eccentricities made it difficult for them to live and work in a society that didn't always understand them.

Not long after the birth of Charity's baby girl, Ismay Boyd had approached her about leaving. "My lady, I don't believe you really need me here anymore. You and his lordship are obviously doing well, the baby will have its own nurse, and Lady Eleanor will be all right as well if I go."

There was truth in her words. Time had worked its magic in healing Charity's wounds, and while the dowager still had her moments, they'd all learned to be at ease with that. The trouble was, as Charity protested, "You've become like family."

Ismay had blushed. "Thank ye for saying so, my lady, but I'd feel better working somewhere I was truly needed. Thanks to your training, I could find a position as a companion, perhaps, or as a nurse again."

When Charity had relayed Miss Boyd's decision to Graeme's mother, her face had fallen, then suddenly perked up. "What if she could do both? What if, instead of her leaving to find people who need her, we bring those people here?"

Thus was born the idea for Lady Maxwell's Home.

Miss Boyd had indeed left, but only to recruit her brother and acquire the supplies she deemed necessary for this new venture.

Joseph Boyd, Ismay's brother, and his wife of one year would function as caretaker and cook. Ismay would provide nursing skills and, perhaps more importantly, an open mind and listening ear.

So far, they had two residents. The first was an acquaintance of Joseph's, a battle surgeon who'd retired after the Battle of Waterloo. In retirement he'd discovered a love for growing things, the scent and sight of new life a balm to the death and destruction of his previous career. He had a habit, though, of muttering to himself about disturbing thing like festering wounds and dull blades—topics that had cost him more than one job, given their tendency to make others uncomfortable. The gardener at Leventhal House, though, was near deaf. His daughter, who, at twenty nine years of age had been thought firmly on the shelf, had surprised everyone by accepting an offer of marriage from a butcher in a neighboring parish, leaving the position of gardener's assistant open. The solution had been an obvious one.

The second resident would move in tomorrow, now that the renovations to the house were finished, ensuring safe and separate quarters for females and males. Callie was a timid woman who scarcely spoke. Lady Eleanor had been the one to invite her, having learned her story through the ladies with whom she attended church. She could knit and weave brilliantly, replicating any pattern shown to her—though her extreme shyness meant people often left a sample at her doorstep, and returned a few days or weeks later to find she'd copied it exactly, or even improved upon it. Sometimes they left a few coins, or a basket of food, as payment. When her family had moved to the coast a few years earlier, they'd washed their hands of their savant daughter, and her cottage had slowly crumbled around her. Lady Eleanor and Ismay both believed Callie had a gift that far outweighed her oddities, even if helping her adjust to her new home might take a while.

There was room for one or two more, though no particular hurry to fill the rooms. For now, Ismay was happy to feel needed, and the Maxwell ladies were happy to share the acceptance they'd so long craved and finally found.

Besides, Graeme and Charity were busy filling other rooms.

Charity had only been half-joking when she'd proclaimed that she planned to make it her highest priority to provide both Nathan and little Noah with a whole passel of cousins.

With the short christening ceremony of Lady Maxwell's Home complete, the family walked back to the main house. Baby Annalise, who would turn two years old in the fall, perched happily on her father's hip. Baby number two, Charity suspected, would arrive shortly after the birthday of her firstborn. Nathan was desperately hoping this one would be a boy, having not quite reconciled with the gender of his first cousin. Fortunately he had Mac as his stalwart sidekick, and often he had playmates from amongst the crofters or the staff's children, now that Leventhal House had transformed from a lonely manor to a bustling, welcoming estate.

Charity tipped her head back toward the old dowager house. "This is not quite what you imagined, when you set off to London in search of a wife, is it?"

Graeme, careful not to dislodge his daughter from her perch, leaned over and kissed the top of his wife's nose. "Nay," he agreed. "'Tis much, much better."

ABOUT THE AUTHOR

Allegra Gray grew up with her nose in a book and her head in the clouds—that is, when she wasn't focused on more practical things like, say, learning calculus. Perhaps all those books inspired a spirit of adventure, because at the age of seventeen she embarked on a career journey that has (so far) included serving as an officer in the U.S. Air Force, grad school at Virginia Tech, teaching English, and managing defense contracts in the Middle East. The best thing about this breadth of experience? When she tried her hand at writing novels like the ones she'd always loved, she recognized at once that she'd found a *true* passion. Allegra is the author of four historical romances, including the "Daring Damsels" trilogy of *Nothing But Scandal, Nothing But Deception, and Nothing But Trouble*. She lives in Colorado, where hiking and skiing in the mountains vie for time in front of the computer. She is currently at work on a mainstream series inspired by her long-held desire to unveil stories obscured by the mists of time.

ALSO BY ALLEGRA GRAY

In this series...
Nothing But Scandal
Nothing But Deception

Other books...
The Devil's Bargain